"Carefully crafted and plotted." —*Publishers Weekly*

From the beginning of a lawyer's investigation to the tense moments before a jury's verdict, the women in this compelling collection are dedicated to the law—and will do whatever it takes to see that justice is served . . .

Defense attorney Mairead O'Clare wonders if divorce may have been a motive for murder in **Terry Devane**'s provocative tale of sex, greed, and sin.

In **Jonnie Jacobs**'s story, a rich widow's stepdaughter is willing to devise any scheme to gain control of the family fortune—legal or otherwise.

Nora DeLoach spins a yarn about a man arrested for the murder of his wife and the paralegal sent out to get "his side of the story."

And other stories by

**Taffy Cannon, Michael A. Khan,
Claire Youmans, Rochelle Krich, Carroll Lachnit,
Sarah Caudwell, Carolyn Wheat**

and other . . .

WOMEN BEFORE THE BENCH

D1238716

WOMEN BEFORE THE BENCH

EDITED BY
Carolyn Wheat

INTRODUCTION BY
Linda Fairstein

BERKLEY PRIME CRIME, NEW YORK

This is a work of fiction. Names, characters, places, and incidents either are the product of the author's imagination or are used fictitiously, and any resemblance to actual persons, living or dead, business establishments, events, or locales is entirely coincidental.

WOMEN BEFORE THE BENCH

A Berkley Prime Crime Book / published by arrangement with Curtis Brown, Ltd.

PRINTING HISTORY
Berkley Prime Crime hardcover edition / March 2001
Berkley Prime Crime mass-market edition / February 2002

Visit our website at
www.penguinputnam.com

ISBN 0-425-18387-4

Berkley Prime Crime Books are published by The Berkley Publishing Group, a division of Penguin Putnam Inc.,
375 Hudson Street, New York, New York 10014.
The name BERKLEY PRIME CRIME and the BERKLEY PRIME CRIME design are trademarks belonging to Penguin Putnam Inc.

PRINTED IN THE UNITED STATES OF AMERICA

10 9 8 7 6 5 4 3 2 1

Contents

CRIMINAL DOCKET: THE PROSECUTORS

CRIMINAL DOCKET: THE DEFENDERS

THE VIEW FROM THE BENCH

Introduction

The peculiar qualities of womanhood, its gentle graces, its quick sensibility, its tender susceptibility, its purity, its delicacy, its emotional impulses, its subordination of hard reason to sympathetic feeling, are surely not qualifications for forensic strife. Nature has tempered women as little for the judicial conflicts of the courtroom as for the physical conflicts of the battlefield. Womanhood is modeled for gentler and better things . . . than the profession of law.

Justice Edward Ryan, Wisconsin Supreme Court, 1875

THE first woman to practice law in the colonies arrived here from England in 1638. Margaret Brent, who settled in Maryland, became not only the governor's appointed counsel but also a renowned litigator and brilliant strategist. Her unique presence so confounded the Americans that most court records refer to her as "Gentleman Margaret Brent."

While a handful of women pleaded their own cases in local courts throughout the states and territories from that date forward—most frequently in regard to family estates and property disputes—there is no record of a woman being formally admitted to the practice until 1869. Arabella Mansfield, a twenty-three-year-old college graduate who had apprenticed at her brother's law firm, was the first to apply to the Iowa bar, despite its specific provision that entrance was limited to "white male persons . . . who possess the requisite learning."

Just a few years thereafter, when Lavinia Goodell attempted to gain admission to the Wisconsin bar, Judge Ryan's 1875 decision, excerpted previously, reflected the views of many within the legal profession and most of the public. In the late nineteenth century, at a time when women could not vote, serve as jurors, or hold elective office, it hardly seems surprising that they were not welcome in the well of the courtroom. As recently as 1964, an article in *Time* magazine summarized the legal profession's view of lady lawyers as "unfitted for trial work, suited for only matrimonial cases or such backroom fields as estates and trusts."

In 1969, exactly one hundred years after Mansfield's historic achievement, I graduated from college and entered law school, with only a dozen other women in my class of more than three hundred students. When I expressed my interest in public service and my plan to join the best prosecutor's office in the country—an unparalleled training ground for a career as a litigator—I met serious resistance from the man who was responsible for the outstanding reputation of that agency.

In my first interview with New York County District Attorney Frank Hogan, who had already served for more than a quarter of a century, he questioned my reasons for wanting the job, as well as what made me think I was capable of doing the work. After all, with close to two hundred lawyers on his staff, only seven others were women, and most of them were delegated to assignments that never brought them before a jury, or had them dealing with the graphic language or physical evidence in violent felonies and murder cases. "Young lady," Mr. Hogan said sternly, "this job is much too tawdry for someone like you."

Thirty years later, I am still a prosecutor in that great office—where half the staff of six hundred lawyers are women—so obviously I have thrived on tawdriness. Now I also have the delightful company of colleagues for whom the law, and literature, are much richer. Krich's

Jane Palmer and Caudwell's Eve Lampeter could not have pleaded their causes just a few decades ago. Jacobs's Hannah Trilling would not have dreamed of calling herself "a rainmaker," and the O'Shaughnessys' Nina Reilly need not have bothered to hang out a shingle. Esther McQuigg Morris, who became the first woman judge in America in 1870, noted for her calico dresses with matching hair ribbons and neckties, must have longed for the partnership of Wheat's "Dragon Lady" or Maron's Deborah Knott.

Reading this fascinating collection of stories about civil suits and criminal cases, I was reassured with every page I turned that if a woman is judged by the company she keeps, it is a pleasure to be before the bench with this flourishing, entertaining, and vibrant cast of characters.

Linda Fairstein

CIVIL WARS

Juggernaut

Perri O'Shaughnessy

Pamela and Mary O'Shaughnessy are sisters who write under the pen name Perri. Their series of legal thrillers features sole practitioner Nina Reilly, a single mom with a law office in Lake Tahoe. Pamela is a former criminal lawyer, while Mary worked as a writer and editor on multimedia projects. In addition to their successful collaboration on the Nina Reilly books, they publish eclectic short stories on the World Wide Web.

From the Hindi jagannath. *A large, overpowering, destructive force or object—an idol of Krishna that is drawn on a huge cart during an annual parade, under whose wheels devotees throw themselves to be crushed...*

THE first accident gave Neal the idea for the second accident.

He had spent the evening of the first crash pouring coins down the throat of the silver beast . . . his name for his favorite slot machine at Harrah's Tahoe. As usual, when he was about to give up, eager, in fact, to watch the cherries, plums, and jackpot signs line up, signifying nothing, three bars *kachunged* into place and seventy-five dollars in tokens pinged into the bin. It was not a big win, considering his investment that evening, but it was enough to keep him going until his eyes were bloodshot and the free drinks from earlier in the evening had invaded his bloodstream and slithered over his brain stem. Now he felt tired. Exhausted. Oh, how he could not wait for bed.

His car was hard to find because he had not parked in the usual spot, so he floundered around the lot looking for it under stars bright as burning spear points, shivering. Up here in the Sierra, November always came as a rude shock. October blew through like fire, all reds and oranges and gusting wind. Winter chased right behind it like a hound from some bone-biting, cold hell.

Finally, he found the Toyota crouched in the far end of the lot, almost touching the dark forest beyond. He wished he were drunk, but no such luck. The abysmal state of his stomach had kept him prudent, along with the hot cups of coffee there toward the end of the session.

Too bad, because a clear head brought him around to thoughts of Juliette, who would be waiting at home, mad because once again—*once again*, she would say, in that new and strident tone he hated—she had to spend the evening alone. Of course, she wouldn't say that at first; she would stand at the kitchen counter watching him with her mouth sullen, refusing to talk, refusing to respond.

As he started the engine, he drifted into a pleasant fantasy. She would decide for once to treat him right. He would come through the door and find her sleeping in a pretty pink negligée like the one she wore when they were first married. He would crawl into bed. Her fragrant arms would rise to pull him down beneath the cool white sheets. Not a word would be spoken; no guilt would be heaped on him.

Checking his rearview mirror for oblivious drunks, he backed out slowly, drove through the valet parking area and out toward the street, where he stopped to wait for a break in traffic before entering. It was while he was there, mentally with Juliette, imagining what they would do in bed, that a stretch limo roared up behind him, screeched its brakes, skated into a skid, and slammed into him with the force of a locomotive.

* * *

THE next day he awoke in the hospital, loaded up on Darvon. He had been thrown forward, almost through the windshield, he was told. Luckily, car traffic along the highway had been light, so no other car had been involved. Aside from a moment of paralyzing fear as he saw the car sliding along the ice toward him in his rear-view mirror, he remembered almost nothing of the accident.

He was shook up, that was all. The doctor and the chiropractor he found later legitimized the exaggerated backache and the TMJ. His lawyer settled for twenty-five thousand from the limo company, and with another twenty-five hundred thrown in by the casino for nuisance value, he had enough for bills and gambling money until February.

To add to his good fortune, there had been that moment when Juliette arrived at the hospital, gorgeous and young, her blond hair shimmering down her shoulders like the falls near Emerald Bay. He basked in the envy of his fellow patients and for just a few moments there at the beginning when she thought he was really badly hurt, he basked in the glow of her concern.

"Your hands?" she had asked first thing and for a second, he couldn't think why she would care. Then he remembered. He played the piano in the bar at the casino, didn't he? When he had a job, which she thought he did.

"The doctor says no permanent damage," he told her.

She pulled his hands to her chest and left them there to feel the pulsing beat underneath her sweater. Five years of her, and he would never get enough.

The windfall caused problems. Soon after he got home from the hospital the fights with Juliette resumed. She wanted the money, wanted to put him on an allowance,

wanted his paychecks, wanted to save for a future, and
yammer yammer yammer. He never could hold his own
in an argument with her. Her words pounded on him like
a club, so he hurt her back the only way he knew how,
with the back of his hand and sometimes when she just
would not shut up, with his fists. He always regretted it,
always begged for her forgiveness, and she always came
through after a day or two.

If she ever left him . . . but he would not allow her to
leave. She knew that. He would hunt her down and bring
her back. He had done it before, and she knew he would
do it again. Marriage made two people one. He would no
more let her go than he would let his left leg walk off
without him.

Nothing meant more to him than Juliette. She was his
biggest score, the one he would hold on to.

One day, a few months after the first accident, Neal
went shopping at the jewelry store at the outlet center for
a little present for her. He wanted something that would
tell her exactly how bad he felt about a minor fracas of
the night before. The saleslady pulled out a display of
glamorous-looking gold necklaces. All the glitter in one
place made him nervous—he turned his back briefly to
count his money.

He had spent most of the insurance settlement, so he
counted out his singles. When he was satisfied he could
just swing the thinnest gold chain and was about to say
so, the saleslady said, "Let me show you some other necklaces I think you'll love!" Sweeping the expensive chains
back underneath the counter, she came up with another
display that looked identical to him. Leaning in conspiratorially, she had said, "Vermeil. All precious metal, of
course."

"Gold?" he had asked.

"Sterling silver with a fine layer of gold on top. Better
because it's just as beautiful and has the same intrinsic
worth, but is more reasonably priced."

"I'll take it," he said, selecting a thick, flashy one he knew Juliette would love. He would tell her it was solid gold. She would never know the difference.

While the woman stooped under the counter finding paper to wrap it up, he happened to look out the store window. Out on the highway, a Caddy was hanging a left in front of a beat-up white Pontiac coming down the opposite side of the highway.

Only the Pontiac couldn't stop, not with the icy sleet coating the road. There was that same eerie moment of screeching brakes and watching a quarter-ton of metal sliding forward on pure inertia. Then *crrrunch!*

The Pontiac driver got out, rubbing his neck. Lucky break for him.

That moment, an idea that he had nursed like a seed since November sprouted into full foliage. Here was real money, ready for the taking. Risky, but a much better bet than the slots. A way to bring peace back home, enough to please Juliette, enough to get him out of hock, enough for a few more games, any one of them a potential big winner.

All he had to do was make sure whoever hit him next time was massively insured. And make sure he didn't get killed.

And he knew just the man to help him out.

The saleslady handed him a small package wrapped in metallic paper. "She's going to love it."

"She will," he said. "You are so right."

*   *   *

THAT afternoon, after he gave Juliette the necklace and collected his thanks from her, he said casually, "Why not call Leo and Carol? Invite them for dinner tonight. They haven't been by in quite a while."

They were sitting together on the couch in the living room. A rare fire burned, and Juliette's cheeks glowed orange as persimmons in the light. She had been studying for a test at the kitchen table. A sophomore at the community college, she wanted to better herself, she always said. Still holding the chain, she turned to look at him. "But you hate Leo."

"Correction," he said. "Your big brother hates me. Always getting on me about the way I treat you." He had a lock of her hair between his thumb and forefinger. His hand slipped along like it used to slide over the ivory keys a long time ago when music seemed to have a direct line from his imagination to his fingers. He laughed, although he didn't feel funny. "He had you all lined up to marry some straight little civil engineer, some meatloaf who would agree with everything he said, yessir, that's right, Leo, uh-huh, you are so smart . . ."

He waited for her to say she was glad she'd married him but she was silent, looking into the fire.

"Old Leo doesn't get it," he went on, annoyed, but aware this was not a good time to pick a fight. "How close we are. How well we fit."

"No, he's never understood it," she agreed, and her hand tugged on the new necklace.

The words grated, and the feeling behind the words grated more. Was there the tiniest suggestion that she, too, didn't understand it? He made his voice calm. "But hey, he's family. We should see them more."

She had turned back to him. He put a lot into the smile he gave her. She smiled back tentatively, then jumped up to make the call. She thought this was a peace offering like the necklace, another part of the "I'm sorry" game. Fine. Whatever it took.

He hoped she would cook something tasty, something to take his mind off those dark, glowering eyes of Leo's, and Carol's jittery chat.

They arrived about seven, stomping the snow off their shoes in the entryway on a thick rug Juliette put there for that purpose.

"Sonofabitchin' cold night," Neal said, holding the door, giving them a big smile.

As usual, the wrong thing to say. A thought policeman, Leo was already glaring at Neal. Leo thought he was better than Neal, better educated, more intelligent, classier . . . Just thinking about it made Neal angry, but he kept his smile locked in place.

Fortunately, Carol and Juliette smoothed things over, making those female sounds that reminded Neal of spicy smells, permeating the air with promise but ultimately just amounting to a lot of warm air breezing through the room. They made it through dinner with just one really bad moment, when Leo mentioned that he had spent some time down at Harrah's one night with some out-of-town associates . . . only reason he'd ever go into one of those nasty places . . . and was so disappointed that Neal was not, as advertised within the family, playing in the piano bar. "Asked the bartender," Leo had said, shoveling in a mouthful of cacciatore. "Told me they hadn't seen you in months."

That made Juliette send Neal a visual promise that said *Later, honey, you will make me believe he is mistaken or this lovely evening that started out so well will be spoiled.* "That guy must be new, Leo," was all she said. "Neal's been working steady, haven't you Neal?"

"You betcha." Below the table, he had her hand in his and had to repress a sudden desire to crush her knuckles until they cracked. She had married a musician, an artist, for Chrissake, not some poor slob with a routine job. She needed reminding. His fingers were strong. No doubt one hard squeeze would take care of anything further she might care to remark if he wanted to stop her.

But Carol interrupted his thoughts with a surprisingly welcome suggestion. "How about a movie? There's one at the Y I'd love to see."

Juliette brightened, withdrew her hand from his, and ran for the newspaper to check for times. Leo continued to separate items on his plate, prissy and offended-looking at the green spreading of the spinach. "I'll pass," he said when Carol returned.

"Aw, Leo," Carol said. "Live a little."

"Go without me. I have some paperwork."

Leo worked for an insurance company, strictly a nine-to-five job that involved no late nights and no overtime. He just said things like this to make himself sound like a mover and shaker to others, the phony ass.

"Nothing that won't wait," Carol said to her husband.

See, now, this was exactly the kind of thing a man could not let pass. This was direct confrontation. Leo was pussywhipped, the dry little shit, and he didn't even know it.

"You girls will have a better time without us," Neal said. "Go salivate over Brad Pitt. I'll give Leo a lift home. Then I'll put in some practice time."

Token protests, but eventually the girls drove off in Leo's car. Leo finished his dessert and coffee, eating methodically, not saying a word, then got up. "Gotta go," he said.

"Stay for a drink," Neal said, pouring Leo's favorite poison into two small glasses. "Cheers."

"Yeah," Leo said, lifting his glass and draining it.

"Another?"

"You're driving," he said.

"Oh, thanks for reminding me," Neal said. "But don't let that stop you. Have a drink for both of us."

Neal managed to get three more stiff ones down Leo and got him talking about his work. And over the course of the next hour, by prodding and pushing, he extracted the names of several prominent Tahoe people who carried especially good policies, Leo's best clients.

"See, here's the thing," Neal told him then. Leo's normal reticence had relaxed as he related exciting tales of his exploits in the insurance business. He was stretched out on the couch, glazed and receptive, just like Neal needed him to be. "Here's the thing, Leo. I'm really glad you stayed tonight, because I've got some bad news and I didn't want to talk about it in front of the girls."

"I knew it," Leo said. "You had to be up to something. Well, I don't have any money to lend you right now. You can forget it. I'm scraping by myself, if you want to know."

"Oh, Leo. Man, I don't want your money. No. It's— it's a medical thing." Neal explained about the carpal tunnel syndrome the doctors had diagnosed in the hospital that would make it impossible for him to use his hands in the future, and watched Leo's mediocre mind attempt to take it in. That's right, Leo, put it together, he thought. Musician, hands, carpal tunnel. Ah!

"But this is terrible," Leo said, the light finally penetrating his thick skull. "You won't be able to support Juliette."

Well, he didn't really anyway, hadn't for a long time, but Leo didn't need to know about that. He didn't need to know how the music left Neal one day, never to return, and somehow even the most lowdown drunk at the bar noticed when he played now. The music had gone. He couldn't even hold his own in a lobby at a Nordstrom's these days. His reputation in this little town was right down there with the dirtiest rat in a Dumpster.

Leo didn't need to know that Juliette was clerking in a real estate office part-time mornings to pay their rent. Juliette wouldn't tell him.

Neal laid it on thick, so thick, he had his wife and himself living out on the streets within the next month.

"Then you'll live with us," Leo said, horrified. "I'm not going to let my sister go down, Neal. Never. If you can't be a man and take care of her . . ."

"That's a very kind offer, Leo," Neal had said hurriedly, striving for a whipped-puppy effect in his voice. "But you know how proud Juliette is."

Leo knew. How Juliette bragged about her husband the

artist. She lorded it over her brother in this one regard, and it was the one thing that Neal felt kept her by his side and protected from criticism sometimes, his mystique as an artist. She really respected Neal's talent. And now that talent would be gone, laid waste by a devilish medical fluke! Leo was eating it up.

"This will kill her," Leo said, sounding truly miserable. "She'll have to quit school. Neal, I don't have to tell you how disappointed I am. You promised our mother and father, bless them both, that . . . You must have some fall-back!"

"I have thought of something. It's—an unusual opportunity. Only it involves you. You've got a lot of guts, Leo, and I know you're going to pitch in to help us so we don't lose our home."

"Anything for Juliette. Count me in," Leo said, relieved. To seal the deal, he offered his glass up for an unheard-of fifth snort.

But the details of Neal's plan shocked him. It took the rest of the evening and some careful manipulations before Neal eventually wore down his resistance. At first, Leo agreed only to help with research. He refused to play an active role in the accident. He would help Neal with the setup because his sister needed help so desperately, but he did so only under the most indignant moral protest. There, his involvement must end. They went back and forth. Neal needed him to get in the game. Otherwise, the authorities might suspect. Leo couldn't see why Neal wouldn't simply apply his brakes, get rear-ended, and collect without Leo's involvement.

"Got to make it look good, Leo. Gotta make 'em believe."

"You're good at that," Leo said then.

"What do you mean by that?"

"You got my sister, didn't you?"

Neal laughed, even though inside he was fuming. He hadn't acted to get Juliette. She loved him for who he

was, not who he pretended to be. All the smoldering
fireworks between the two men flared up at that point,
and it took Neal's return to a cold, logical analysis to
convince Leo that, in fact, his way was the only way.

"It's dangerous, Neal. You realize you could be badly
hurt."

"I won't let that happen."

"You won't be able to control it!" Leo yelled.

"Quit worrying. That's my problem. And whatever
happens, Juliette will be set for life."

Those words worked like magic. Leo didn't give a
damn what happened to Neal except as it related to Juliette.

Still, Leo didn't give in easily, although after that
point, he had most definitely stepped on board the bus.
Before he settled down he asked a million questions:
Couldn't Neal just slam on his brakes in front of someone
and leave it at that? Why did Leo have to cut him off?
Wouldn't it look suspicious? Would Neal wear a seatbelt?
Did it matter if the accident happened in California or
should they go over the state line and into Nevada to
maximize how well they would do in a settlement?

"Leo, take it easy. I'm the one going to get hurt, not
you and not Juliette, remember?"

Leo broke out in a cold sweat at that, so Neal had to
soothe him yet again, patiently breaking through his objections, pouring the liquor, painting comforting word pictures for Leo, keeping things at his level. "Two things are
absolutely all you have to do, Leo. Cut me off, so people
see I stopped for a reason. And find me a juicy mark. Has
to be a drinker," Neal said. "I talked with my lawyer this
morning and asked him a few things . . ."

"You didn't tell him!"

"No, no. Just got him talking generally about my old
case. He said if the limo driver had been drinking, well
that would have opened up a whole new pocketbook."

"Gross negligence?"

"Punitive damages, my man."

Three weeks later, they were set. Leo had chosen a client with two DUI arrests in her background, who had just bought a big, heavy Mercedes and played roulette at Caesars every Friday night with two of her lady friends, but always drove home alone.

They had worked out every detail. Once in, Leo was a meticulous planner. He drew up careful diagrams on paper they burned in the fireplace afterward, listed time frames, pulled out charts that gave some information on what speeds were most likely to cause lethal collisions, and bogged them both down in trivial issues until Neal was bored silly.

"We'll have your car serviced the day before," Leo had said, "so there's no confusion about some mechanical failure."

"Sure, Leo."

"I've got a great mechanic. Let me make sure it gets done."

"Fine, Leo." Anything to shut him up.

They waited on the highway side of the club in the whizzing traffic. The mark, who Leo said was a widow, always used valet parking and always made a left out of the lot, then drove two miles before turning off the highway. That gave them plenty of time to get the game in place.

Neal had parked two blocks up, Leo three. When Neal saw the bronze Mercedes pulling out of the lot, he swung out ahead of the mark, motioning to Leo as he passed.

Traffic was perfect, busy but moving well, and there were nice long stretches on the road where you could get going pretty fast. Leo would have no trouble moving into position when the time came. Neal felt like his nerves had moved to the surface of his skin, he felt so electric, so alive. To keep his mind off the pain to follow, he flashed to the penthouse suite at Harrah's he and Juliette would rent for a month or two, about the new car he would buy, about all the hands of poker he could play without gut-tearing fear . . . He'd never humiliate himself at a piano again, never put up with some slobbering lonely heart who wanted to hear him play the same old song again and again until he thought his fingers would crack into pieces . . . Who knew crashing could be such a high?

She was weaving, he noted with satisfaction, glancing into his rearview mirror. She had the visor down, so he couldn't make out the face, but her arms were slim. She looked young. For a moment he wondered about her, about what he'd be doing to her. He slowed, and behind him she slowed. He sped up and she sped up. They were dancing together, and she never even noticed the chore-ography. Like an automaton, she followed his lead until he knew he had her. All so smooth, so perfect . . . and then suddenly, bursting ahead like a true maniac, all his timidity apparently left behind when he got behind the wheel, good old Leo blew out in front to cut him off. As planned.

And Neal jammed his foot on the brake.

* * *

EMILY Chuvarsky could not tell the story without cry-ing. She sat in an orange client chair across from Nina Reilly, petite and perfect in her jeans and turtleneck sweater, shaking her head and interrupting herself. She tried several times to come out with it, but broke down every time. Outside, snow blew at an angle away from the lake. The drifts along the road were five feet high and Nina was thinking about closing up early to be sure she made it home to the cabin on Kulow.

"This car cut him off. He just . . . he came to a dead stop, right there in the middle of the road. I barely had time to brake. And so I hit him! His c-car burst into flames!" she cried. "I got out and ran up to see if I could do anything but the flames had reached the front . . . someone pulled me away. I heard him screaming. I dream about it. I heard him . . . and then the car exploded."

Nina looked down at her desk. "The police report says he had a five-gallon can of gasoline stored in the trunk of his Toyota. His wife said she didn't know he kept gasoline in the trunk, and if she'd known, would have asked him to remove it."

"What a horrible way to die." Letting her head fall back, Emily screwed her eyes shut and covered her face, her shoulders clenching tightly. "My insurance company is negotiating with his widow. But my policy only covers two hundred fifty thousand, and she feels she should get much more because . . ." She stopped, and her arms fell down into her lap. "She lost her husband. I do understand. But I don't have that kind of money."

Nina said, "You were drinking that night?"

"Wine with dinner," Emily said. "Three miles home on a road I've driven a million times. Maybe I had one glass too many but I wasn't falling-down drunk. I went to a seminar on living trusts once and the lawyer mentioned that if you're ever picked up for drunk driving to refuse the Breathalyzer test, so I refused when they asked me. They took a urine test a couple of hours later."

"The results on that won't be in for a few more days," Nina said. "Refusing the Breathalyzer won't make any difference. They'll just extrapolate back to the time of the accident, using your weight and the elapsed time."

Emily said, "I ought to just take my medicine, you know? Go to jail for reckless driving, file for bankruptcy. The guilt is horrible. I don't sleep. There can't be anything worse in this world than killing a person, an utterly innocent person who never dreamed his life would be cut short like that—it's a nightmare! It's over for me, I'm going to hate myself for the rest of my life. But . . ."

Nina listened. After two years of solo practice in her little Tahoe office, it was something she was finally learning to do. She didn't offer words of comfort or false assurances. She waited to hear it all first. Emily opened her purse and her wallet and pulled out a small photo. Nina took it.

A little girl, Eurasian, bright-eyed and still in baby teeth. "She's deaf. What money I have from my husband's life insurance, I need for her education. I want her to have the best. Right now, she's in a wonderful school. They do whole-language training, a mixture of signing, lipreading, and speaking. She's thriving there. I can't take her out. I can't!"

"What's her name?" Nina asked.

"Caitlin." Emily returned the photo to her wallet.

"You saw the man—Neal Meurer—get cut off?"

"Another car cut right in front of him. I don't think the driver even knew what he did. He was long gone."

"Do you remember anything about the car?"

"A sedan with ski racks," she said promptly. "Wait a minute. I remember the license plate had three eights. I noticed that because my late husband was from Hong Kong. He told me how lucky the number eight is considered to be in China and I just had time to think, what a lucky license plate . . ."

"That's great." Nina wrote that down and thought, *Amazing*. Nobody ever noticed license plates.

"I just thought of it."

"Be sure to go to the police station on Johnson Boulevard tomorrow and tell them you want to add that to your statement."

"I'm not positive. I'll think about it a little more."

"What about the man in that car? You're sure it was a man?"

"Oh, yes. He had a mustache. They're out of fashion now, so I noticed."

Nina wrote that down, too. After a few more minutes and the business of the retainer agreement, she followed Emily out to the parking lot of the Starlake Building. Then, buffeted by the storm, she fought her way down Pioneer Trail in the Bronco. At the corner of Golden Bear a pickup suddenly spun out in front of her. Pulling sharply to the right, she hit the snowbank. Behind her, brakes squealed.

But the car behind her didn't hit her, just honked savagely and continued on its way. Very cautiously she backed into the darkening street and drove home, teeth gritted, furious because sudden chance events that ruined lives weren't acceptable to her. She didn't believe in accidents.

*　　*　　*

A few days later, with light snow still falling, the lights were on in the middle of the day at Lake Tahoe Community College. Nina caught Juliette Meurer coming out of her Poli Sci class with a tall, bespectacled young man who had his arm around her and was kneading her shoulder.

"Oh," she said when Nina introduced herself. "Am I allowed to talk to you?" Standing near Nina, who was on the small side, she towered. She was almost as tall as the man standing with her.

"It's not a lawsuit yet," Nina said. "It might help."

"This is Don."

Don shook hands, saying, "Juli's been through a lot." He seemed cool and kept his distance. Without asking, he tagged along to the Bronco, climbing into the backseat behind Juliette. Nina drove them to the Pizza Hut near Ski Run, and the three of them sat down in a booth and ordered coffee.

Nina started slow and easy, letting Juliette Meurer relive the moments after the Tahoe police called her, listening to her talk tearfully about Neal's incredible talent, his charm, how she missed him so much . . . In spite of the reports of frequent brawls at the house, a few of which resulted in calls from the neighbors to the police, she sounded very much in love with her husband. Don glowered next to her, saying nothing. The two of them went very well together, Nina couldn't help noticing, both handsome, athletic, blond and long-haired.

"The gas can in the back," Nina said. "It bothers me."

"Neal was stupid about cars. The weather has been so bad, if you ran out of gas in the mountains you might freeze. Maybe that's what he was thinking. Poor Neal. But he would have been fine, except the woman—your client—she had been drinking, hadn't she?"

"Mmm," Nina said. "But the thing about the gas can, you know, is that it had prints on it that weren't Neal's."

"What?" Juliette looked stunned. "Why would the police take fingerprints?"

"Oh, to be thorough. What's amazing is that there were prints left to take. Luckily, they found an intact piece ten feet away in a drift."

"Those prints probably came from the guy who sold Neal the gas," said Don. "Where's a big mystery in that?"

"Well, at first I thought that too, and it was hard to check because the can didn't have the store sticker on it or anything. But this is a small town. My investigator managed to locate the fellow who sold that gas can. He remembered selling one three days before Mr. Meurer's death, at the Chevron at the Y, and he recognized it by the bits of paint color left on the metal piece the police found. That can was the only one he could spare that day, a really old one."

"So?" Juliette said.

"Well, the thing is, I showed him a picture of your husband just to confirm everything. And this fellow who pumps the gas says it wasn't Neal Meurer who bought it."

"He's just making a mistake!"

"Said the man was short, with blue eyes. Wore a parka, muffler, ski hat. But Mr. Meurer had brown eyes, didn't he?"

Juliette nodded.

"Strange, don't you think?"

Don's blue eyes stared at her. "You can see what she's doing, can't you, Juli? She's weaseling her client out of trouble. She sees disaster heading straight their way. It's her job to do anything to head it off." He half-rose. "Let's get out of here."

Nina shrugged. "The gas attendant could be wrong but the expert fingerprint expert isn't. Your husband never touched that can."

"Then—the rescue workers!"

"They had a fire and your husband to deal with."

"Oh," Juliette said, "this is too much. You're trying to tell me somebody else put the gas can in the back? That Neal was murdered? Well, who—who would have put the can there except your client, then? Nobody forced her to run into Neal that night."

"Who would want to kill Neal, Juliette?" Nina asked the woman. "My client says she never even met your husband. And I hear there were a few domestic problems between the two of you."

"Your client is responsible! She ran into my husband and killed him!" Juliette wailed. "She was drunk! God, are you serious about all this?" Don yanked her to her feet.

"Come on," he said urgently. He looked down at Nina, who was calmly sipping her coffee. "I detest you shysters," he said in a thick voice. Then he was pulling Juliette away toward the exit. Juliette looked back once, her face a mask of anguish, blue eyes filled with tears.

* * *

NINA'S investigator, Tony Ramirez, spent a week working on the three eights.

Tony, who was on the shady side of sixty and had the relaxed attitude to prove it, hailed from the low-tech school of investigation. He could have worked with the police to obtain a list of hundreds of people in California and Nevada with triple-eight license plates, and things could have gone on for months, but he liked to use his noggin to save himself work, as he put it.

"Neal's sister lives in Illinois with her husband and five kids and hadn't talked to Neal for years. She's off the hook. There's no other family. So I looked to the workplace. Turns out Neal didn't have no workplace. I checked the license on his last supervisor at the casino—no eights on his plates. I checked Neal's gambling buddies and his bookie. No triple eights. Then I looked for Neal's women, only there weren't any recent ones I could find. He had stuck to his wife like a leech for the past five years."

Nina read through the police report again while Tony stood at the window, flipping through his notes.

"So maybe he just pulled a Pinto," she said. "Emily gets a personal judgment for wrongful death against her for about a million dollars and goes to jail for reckless driving, and her daughter leaves school."

"When you put it that way I feel like I better hustle back out on the street and do better," Tony said.

"At least her blood alcohol analyzed down to point five," Nina said. "She wasn't impaired as a matter of law, not this time anyway."

"The fingerprints came back from NCIC. Whoever bought that gas can has never had trouble with the law and ain't in the system."

"Juliette gets the money. So we check out Juliette. We look at her friends and family."

* * *

SOUTH Lake Tahoe is a small town, and Nina knew Leo Dole, who was her brother Matt's auto insurance agent, as well as Juliette Meurer's brother. Leo's office was at Round Hill Mall, around the lake on the Nevada side. He was waiting for her, and he was terrified; she could see that.

Short, not much taller than she was, and according to Tony he had triple-eight license plates on his sedan. That

plus his obvious terror excited her. She couldn't believe
he had agreed to see her without consulting his own lawyer first, and she wanted to be very careful.

No need. Leo proceeded to spill his guts, and it wasn't
a pretty sight.

"When I told Neal I'd do it, I was drunk," he said.
"The next morning I called his house and left a message.
'No way,' I said. Neal would understand what I was talk-
ing about."

"But he talked you back into it?"

"No! That's what I'm saying! I refused! Absolutely!"

"But it was your car," Nina said. "A witness saw the
license number. 6KLS888," which was a slight bending
of the truth, since Emily had remembered only part of the
license, but he didn't need to know that.

"It wasn't me. Somebody must have taken my car. I
park it out front all night—it was snowing . . ."

"You left the keys in it?"

"Those Cutlasses, you can hot-wire them in three seconds . . ."

"So you're claiming someone tried to frame you? Who
else did you tell about Neal's plan?"

He gaped. "Nobody!"

"You didn't tell Juliette? Or your wife?"

"I . . ." He shook his head weakly.

Nina took out a portable fingerprint kit. "Leo," she
said, "if you're innocent, you'll do this."

Looking guilty as hell, he shuffled up close. When he
looked up she saw brown eyes and thought, *Phooey.*

*   *   *

THE snowchains requirement had snarled traffic into a
pile of stationary ski racks, but somehow Tony Ramirez made it up the hill from Reno to bring the print
comparison back to Nina's office a day later. This latest
Sierra storm had dumped two more feet and South Lake
Tahoe looked quaint as Santa's village.

The expert had found no fingerprint match. Leo Dole hadn't handled the gas can. Nina had also obtained prints on coffee cups from Don and Juliette, and those results were in, too. No match, no clue. Nina studied the whorls and notches and lines on the blowups as if they were hieroglyphics that might reveal a hidden story. "Tony," she said. "I just can't put this together."

Tony pried off his hiking boots and sticky, wet red socks. "Can I?" he said. She nodded and he laid them across the heater. The musky smell of wet wool swarmed through the hot office.

"We're making progress," Tony said, drying his toes with a tissue from her desk. "There was a conspiracy, whether Leo stayed in or not. Emily was set up, no doubt about it. Leo or somebody cut Neal off deliberately per the plan and Emily was the fall guy."

"But nobody would be stupid enough to arrange a rear-end collision with five gallons of gas in his trunk," Nina said.

"A double cross," Tony said. "Neal's partner decided to make it permanent."

"Juliette would get the money," Nina said. "She's at the center of it. But whose prints are these? Who bought that can of gas? Some short, blue-eyed ghost. None of these people is short and blue-eyed. Juliette must be nearly six feet tall. Who drove the Olds Cutlass that cut off Neal Meurer? A man with a mustache, Emily said. Nobody I know in this case has or had a mustache."

"A buck sixty-nine at the joke shop," Tony said. "Cheap whiskers for kids four and up." He rattled the keys in his pocket and looked worried. "Nina, don't drive yourself too nuts with this stuff. Our job is to do our best, then let the chips fall."

"I can't do that. I feel responsible for Emily. I feel if I push harder, work smarter and go that extra step, I'll arrive at the heart of the matter. That's the only way to a just outcome. Then there's nothing to regret."

"Just don't expect thanks when you've killed yourself for months and you hand over the bill for your outstanding service."

Nina sighed.

"C'mon," Tony said. "Let's continue this conversation over at Paolina's. A glass of red wine and something smothered in olive oil and fresh pesto will put things back into perspective. What do you say? You drive."

"What about your socks?"

He pulled the boots on over bare feet and stood up. "Keep 'em for a souvenir."

*   *   *

NINA got home about seven-thirty. Hitchcock and Bob were out front under the floodlight and Bob was making a snowman, a very peculiar snowman with a rubber dog ring on top like a halo. Hitchcock ran to the truck and gamboled around it while she swung down and shut the door. "You know he's going to jump on it and destroy all your work," she called to her son. "He loves that ring."

As if taking note of her words, Hitchcock turned abruptly and made a beeline for the snowman. Bob grabbed for the ring, snatching it off the snowman's head just before the dog made contact. "What's this, boy? C'mon, what's this?" He waved it at Hitchcock, who jumped vainly, tongue lolling, for his toy, until finally Bob put it back on top of the hillock of snow that made up the snowman's head. In one final heave, Hitchcock leaped valiantly into the air, landing with an audible *oof* near the top. His jaws closed around the ring. Bob jumped on, too. For an instant he clung to the hard-packed snow, arms circling the head as if to protect it. Then the whole thing—snowman, dog, and boy—toppled into a cloud of snow.

Hitchcock chewed vigorously on his ring, feeling zero guilt about destroying an hour of hard work. Lying in the white powder, Bob laughed helplessly. Destruction was far more gratifying to a boy his age than building.

Nina went into the cabin. Bob had made himself frozen burritos as she had instructed, but appeared to have had a run-in with the microwave in the process. She found that mess easier to clear away than Emily's. Removing the cracked glass tray, Nina swabbed down the insides of the microwave almost gratefully.

By ten o'clock, Bob had been nagged through his shower and into bed. Nina sat on the rug in front of the fire with her glass of sauvignon blanc, comfortable in her silk kimono. She was trying to think, but the thinking kept turning into a kind of dozing, a hypnogogic dreaming. She kept thinking about the rubber ring and Hitchcock, such a patsy, going for it, doing his dogged doggy number, until he actually got what he wanted . . .

So easy to know what he wanted. In the end, so simple to get it.

*   *   *

"I'M sorry to disturb you," Nina told Carol Dole the next morning. Carol was in a plaid wool robe and glasses. Nina had watched from the Bronco while Leo drove off to work.

A small woman, Carol had blue eyes behind the specs that were blinking against some strong emotion right now. She tried to close the door, but Nina's two-hundred-dollar Manolo Blahnik high heel was wedged between the door and its sill.

"Ah ah ah," Nina said. "It's me or the cops. You'll do better with me."

"Go away."

"It's cold out here. Twenty degrees and dropping, I'd say. We can talk with the door open and run up your heating bill or you can let me inside and we'll both be better off."

Carol looked once more at the shoe in the door and

gave up. "Come in," she said ungraciously, opening the door and turning her back to Nina.

The house showed a lot of pride around its shined surfaces. On the walls, signed lithographs hung: a gaudy Peter Max, an English cottage scene by the guy who billed himself as the Painter of Light in his TV ads. A Picasso print of a scribbled hand holding a flower. Showy knick-knacks decorated the bookshelf.

"Leo says he told you about Neal's plan," Carol said. She was sitting on the white leather couch, bare legs crossed. Her robe gaped a little, exposing an angular bosom.

"How did you get involved?" Nina said.

"He was too worried to keep his mouth shut about this."

"Leo saw an opportunity in Neal's plan, didn't he? He could set his sister up for life and get rid of her troublesome husband, all in one stroke. Did he ask you for help, or was it your idea to buy the gas can and put it into the trunk? Neal had no idea it was there, did he? But you and Leo had easy access to Neal's car, and you fit the description . . ."

"You're barking up the wrong tree. Leo and I had nothing to do with it."

"Short and blue-eyed. That's how the person who bought the gas can was described," Nina said.

Carol Dole shook her head. "Have you taken a good look at your client lately?" she asked with a smile wide as a half moon. She tipped her head back so that Nina could follow the long line of her throat. It reminded her of Emily screwing up her eyes, closing them, leaning her head back . . .

Emily, petite, blue-eyed.

"Emmy was my best friend in high school," Carol said. "That's where she and Neal met. Then just a couple months ago, after her husband died, she came across him again."

Carol's meaning hit Nina hard. Emily had lied to her. Well, clients lied. She knew that. "So you know Caitlin," she said.

"Who?" Carol said, and Nina felt like she was drifting off into some kind of space, only it wasn't calm and peaceful there. Supernovas were going off all around her.

Through the distant chaos she heard her voice saying quite normally and correctly, "Emily Chuvarsky's little girl?"

Carol's laughter brought her back to earth.

"Emmy a mom?" Carol said. "You have to be kidding. She hates kids. It was Neal she loved after her husband died. Neal knew it, and he played her for a lot of money before she realized he'd never leave Juliette. She used to go listen to him when he was playing piano, before he got fired. Music is the way to so many women, have you noticed? Neal sure used it that way, when it suited him."

"If it was Emily, then she was working with you or your husband," Nina said. "Triple eights."

"So she was the one who made up the story about our license plate? You really scared Leo with that one. I thought it must be her. I remember one time she said we were lucky with the eights."

"You're saying—do you realize . . ."

"All I'm saying is, I didn't do a thing to anybody."

"Did you tell her about Neal's plan?"

"Just to show her she was better off forgetting about him."

* * *

"EMILY?" Nina's client looked flushed and pretty, as if she'd walked all the way to the office.

"Yes?"

"I talked to Carol Dole about you."

"Oh," she said, all her prettiness falling behind a frown.

"You lied to me about Caitlin."

"I always loved that name," she said after a pause.

"She's cute, too, isn't she? I found the photo stuck inside a book I bought at the Salvation Army."

"You lied about knowing Neal, too."

She tapped her foot, examined her fingernails, and didn't say anything for a long time.

"Maybe you need to find another lawyer, one you feel comfortable telling the truth."

"I just—everything I say to you is confidential, right?"

"That's right."

"I guess you already figured out most of the story. Might as well know the rest. I did know Neal. He was a liar and a cheat. He gambled away a lot of my money. He hurt me . . . drew me in and made a fool of me."

"You hated him."

"No." She breathed in short breaths, impatient to be understood. "I never hated him."

"Carol told you that Neal had come up with a plan."

Emily Chuvarsky studied Nina for a while, then seemed to come to a decision. "When I heard about his idea for a crash scam, it set off something in me, something I didn't even know was there. I started thinking, wouldn't it be perfect if he should get his while trying to screw yet another unsuspecting victim? Almost a biblical justice."

"You put the gas in his tank."

She shifted her body in her chair, looking uncomfortable. "I was over at Carol's when Leo drove up in Neal's car. He had just had it in for servicing and was about to take it back to Neal, but we were all hungry, so he left the keys on the counter in the kitchen while they went out in Leo's car to get us some food.

"It was fate, you see? I saw those keys lying there . . . I thought about Neal, how horrible he was to me. I felt such pain . . . and I picked them up. I didn't even think. I just took Neal's car and ran over to Chevron for the gas. I hid the can under a blanket in the trunk before Carol and Leo got back. I didn't worry about prints. If I thought at all, I guess I thought the car would be destroyed in a crash."

"You wanted to kill him."

"I loved him," she said simply, as if even a child could see that explained everything. "But he hurt me so much. So I . . . engineered a little divine intervention. God rode beside him that day. If he had done nothing wrong, he would have lived, you see?"

"But you hit him, not someone else."

"My rotten luck," Emily said with a bitter laugh. "After that last DUI, I needed new insurance. Carol talked me into buying from Leo, and he sold me a big fat new policy! So here I am driving home one night and suddenly Neal's in front of me. It happened so fast! I didn't realize it was him right away. I mean, I sure didn't expect it. Next thing I know, I'm stepping on the brakes, but the road's so slippery, I slide right into him! God—what a riot—isn't it funny? I can't stop laughing—the bad luck part—but you know, it's a small town—the bad luck part is, Leo, who had me fresh in his mind and never liked me, must have picked me to be the mark!"

"The triple eights . . ."

"Oh, Leo was there that night, whatever he and Carol say. He's the one who cut in front of Neal, wearing a mustache that hung crooked, just like everybody in that whole damn family, including my so-called friend, who never could keep a secret, even when we were thirteen. Oh, God. They'll never be able to keep quiet about this."

"You realize you're in terrible trouble now, Emily. The system doesn't forgive murder."

"Yes, thanks for nothing! You could have just helped me, forced Juliette to settle within the policy limits instead of dragging up all this old business!"

She didn't really appreciate the extent of the calamity she had set off, yet, did she? Her first mistake had been a headlong, thoughtless rush into the fray, but her biggest mistake had been involving Nina.

Clasping her bag, Emily stood up. "I suppose I will get that new lawyer."

"Good idea." Nina also stood.

"Carol and Leo have figured everything out by now, thanks to you. They'll hurry to protect themselves. No doubt the cops will follow close behind."

They would, and they would get her, too. She should have forced her insurance company to settle with Juliette. She should never have put herself in front of the legal machine because now Nina had turned on the ignition and the wheels had started up. They would roll inexorably from here on out until they crushed her beneath them.

"Here's a check," Nina said, scribbling one out and handing it to her. "The retainer, less my expenses."

Emily took the check, studied it, and frowned.

She went out the door. "Shyster," she said, pulling it shut behind her.

* * *

WHEN Nina got home Hitchcock made a rush for her and began licking her stockings. "Get off me, you damn hound," she said, making for the upstairs bedroom.

She lay down, imagining what the courts had in store for the impetuous Emily. She wondered if she'd ever feel the desire to get up again. She wondered if there was still a Peace Corps and if they had any openings in Gabon. Maybe the villagers there would thank her for doing a good job. Maybe there, passionate women did not make lamentable mistakes.

"Mom," Bob said through the door, "I made a tuna casserole."

"You're kidding!"

"In the microwave. It's steamin', Mom. Plus I poured you a glass of wine out of the bottle in the fridge. It's on the kitchen table. And the news is on."

Nina opened one eye. White fell through the twilight outside the window.

"Mom?" At the same moment, Hitchcock barked. He wanted to come in, and he wouldn't take no for an answer.

"I'm coming," Nina said. Feeling older and not a bit wiser, she got up and opened the door.

Built upon the Sand

Jonnie Jacobs

*Recovering San Francisco lawyer Jonnie Jacobs is the au-
thor of a mystery series featuring amateur sleuth, artist, and
single mom Kate Austen in addition to her legal thrillers star-
ring attorney Kali O'Brien. Her latest title in the well-reviewed
series is* Witness for the Defense.

THE room is warm, the air thick with a cloying mix of
aftershave and cinnamon danish. The other associates
at the table are busily scribbling notes. I can hear the
scratching of pens above the drone of Aaron's husky
voice. I draw an ornate R on my legal pad, circle it with
stars, then quickly cross it out before anyone catches a
glimpse.

Rainmaker. I roll the word around silently like the first
sip of fine wine. It's a term you won't find on the bar
exam or in any law school syllabus, but it can make or
break your career.

Me rainmaker, I say to myself, sounding like an Indian
from an old-time television show. I know I'll never play
with the big guys, but I'm feeling pretty heady nonetheless. I, Hannah Trilling, have brought in my very first
client.

I watch the other faces as Aaron explains that Alicia
Goodhue has sought the firm's services on my account. I

can hear the unspoken thoughts as clearly as if they'd been uttered in unison, though only Drew gives actual voice to his amazement.

"*The* Alicia Goodhue?" he asks. "How did you manage that?"

They don't mean to be disdainful, but they are all under thirty, full of their own importance and never quite sure what to make of a fellow associate who is the widowed forty-two-year-old mother of adolescent twins.

I give a blasé shrug, seeing no need to explain that Alicia Goodhue latched on to me only because my landlady's cousin happens to be her hairdresser. After all, contacts are contacts, and not all of us can play handball with corporate CEOs or golf with former linebackers.

Aaron Stern, who in fact knows about the hairdresser connection, merely confirms Alicia Goodhue's identity. "I'm sure none of you need to be reminded that we respect the privacy of *all* our clients."

"Even when they do little of that for themselves," Drew adds with a droll roll of the eyes.

Alicia Goodhue is the only child of the late Walter Goodhue, local real estate tycoon. Twenty-eight and twice divorced, she seems to favor men with little regard for the work ethic—or for women. Her name and photograph appear regularly in the social columns, although not always in the most favorable light. There are, in fact, many who regard her as selfish, shallow, and spoiled.

There is a murmur of congratulations as the meeting adjourns. "*Good luck,*" Drew adds under his breath.

"What do you mean?"

He grins. "The way I hear it, the woman is used to getting what she wants. Rules be damned."

*   *   *

Two days later, Alicia Goodhue is sitting my office, tapping her heel against the polished mahogany of the office chair.

"But there *must* be a way," she insists. "That's what attorneys *do*, they find loopholes."

I bite my tongue, silencing the defensive and not particularly professional responses that come to mind.

Despite the designer clothes and abundant jewelry, Alicia Goodhue in the flesh is neither as elegant nor as attractive as she appears in photos. Her build is heavier, her skin rougher, and her nose more prominent. I can't help thinking she looks something like the Disney rendition of Cinderella's elder stepsister.

Alicia leans forward and looks me in the eye. "Daddy would have wanted her to take care of me." The *her* in this remark is Lillian Goodhue, Walter Goodhue's widow and Alicia's stepmother. "I don't see why she won't help out."

I start to explain. "You say your father left her the money outright . . ."

"It's going to be mine someday."

"But until then—"

"I will not sit idly by," Alicia says, sounding as though she's stumping for political office, "while Lillian fritters away money that is rightfully mine."

"Surely you have money of your own?" The question comes out sounding like an accusation, which isn't what I intend, although it's not far from what I'm thinking. Like most San Franciscans, I've read about Alicia's lavish parties and caught snippets of her travel itineraries in the lifestyle section of the paper. I doubt seriously that Walter Goodhue failed to provide for his daughter.

Alicia appears not to take offense, or maybe the innuendo simply slides over her head. "Not much," she says in answer to my question. "I mean, uh, Daddy was quite generous when he died . . ." She lifts her chin and adds, ". . . but money doesn't last forever, you know."

Unfortunately, I know all too well, though I suspect that we're talking about vastly different kinds of money. When Bob died, I had to sell the house so that the kids and I could afford to eat. It's only now, in my third year of practicing law, that we've begun to think about anything but the necessities.

Alicia pulls out a cigarette and quickly lights it, then looks around for a non-existent ashtray.

I remind her of the San Francisco ordinance prohibiting smoking in the workplace.

"Then let's pretend we're not at work." She smiles and drops the match casually onto the carpet. "Anyway, Lillian is being unreasonable. That's nothing new, of course, but now she's really gone over the edge."

I decide to ignore the cigarette. "What do you mean, over the edge?"

Alicia eyes me appraisingly, taking a moment before she answers. When she does, it's with studied precision. "I worry that Lillian is growing senile. Maybe it's Alzheimer's or something."

"Have you spoken with her doctor?"

Alicia brushes the air with her hand. "He's useless. He's an old crony of hers anyway."

"What makes you think Lillian is getting senile?"

"She wears colors that don't match, hasn't had her hair or nails done in months."

"That's hardly senility."

"She repeats herself, too. Forgets words, goes on and on about trivial stuff no one is interested in." Alicia sucks on her cheek, thinking. "She's gotten rid of my father's investment counselor and has decided instead to handle the finances herself. That's a recipe for disaster right there."

Closer maybe, but not necessarily a mark of senility either.

"She's got a soft heart for every charity in the city, too. She even hands out money on the street."

My mind flashes on the image of an elderly woman tossing hundred-dollar bills into the air like confetti. "Large sums?" I ask.

"I don't know," Alicia says impatiently. "More than I'd ever give away for sure. She's squandering money Daddy intended for me. And when I ask for a little, she starts quoting Dr. Laura."

"I see." And what I see does not warm me to Alicia's cause.

"Daddy intended for me to be taken care of. And I would be, if Lillian wasn't so . . . if she wasn't losing her mind. I think she needs one of those, what do you call them, conservatorships."

Alicia takes another drag on her cigarette, then grinds it out in the soil of a nearby philodendron. She stares into space for a moment, then looks at me, suddenly animated. "That's exactly what she needs. She's incapable of managing her finances on her own."

"There are—"

"I'd like you to draw up the paperwork as soon as possible."

"It's not quite that simple," I explain. "You'll have to file a petition with the court outlining the need for a conservator. There will be an investigation, and I would assume she'll argue—"

"Just do it," Alicia snaps. "And quickly."

AARON Stern pops into my office not long after. "So?" he says, curiosity tweaking the corners of his normally sad eyes. "What did our newest client want? A high-profile lawsuit? A million-dollar business venture?"

"A conservatorship." While I explain Alicia's mission, I open a window to air the office of cigarette smoke. "I'm uncomfortable with this whole thing. With Alicia, really. It sounds to me like she's simply after Lillian's money."

Aaron leans against the credenza and scratches his cheek. The senior of the three partners in the firm, he is also my mentor and friend. Having each lost a spouse to cancer, we formed an early bond of friendship. But where

I'm determined to move on with my life, for my children's sake if not for my own, Aaron cannot let go of the past. At sixty-one, he still appears youthful, with a lean frame and a full head of silver hair. But inside, he's an old man.

"Our role is that of advocate, not judge," he reminds me.

I nod.

Aaron's shoulders hunch forward. "It's your call," he says at last. "Whatever you decide, we'll stand behind you."

*   *   *

PUBLIC sentiment to the contrary, not all lawyers swim with sharks. Before I try to convince a judge that Lillian Goodhue is unable to manage her own finances, I want to convince myself of that fact.

I glance at the passing addresses, which more often than not are located on discreetly placed but hard-to-read brass plaques. Lillian Goodhue lives in Pacific Heights, an area of the city renowned for its stately mansions and expansive, not to mention expensive, bay views.

I find the correct number and ring the bell, wondering if I'll be able to talk my way past whatever maid or butler opens the door.

To my surprise, Lillian Goodhue herself answers my ring. I recognize her immediately from her pictures, then remark silently that she has aged considerably since the photos were taken. Not her skin, which is remarkably unlined, but in most other respects. There is a lackluster quality to her appearance that I associate with the down-and-out elderly. Her hair, which is a dull gray, lies flat against her head and her dingy white blouse is stained in front.

Maybe, I decide, Alicia is on to something after all.

And then Lillian smiles. It is a smile that transforms her face. I can see what a beauty she must have been.

"Come in, dear, I've brewed a pot of tea, but I can make coffee in no time. There's sherry, too, if you'd prefer."

I'd been intentionally vague when I'd called to arrange the meeting, and now hoped I hadn't misled her. I opt for tea, which she serves in dainty, gold-trimmed china cups. We sit in a large, high-ceiling room, which is cluttered and dusty though just short of being dirty.

"So you're a lawyer," she says, settling on the edge of her seat. "So many women are these days. When I was young it was teaching or nursing." She sips her tea. "I was a nurse. Until I married Walter, that is."

"Nursing is a good career."

She sighs. "Yes, it is. I wish that I'd continued working instead of building my life around Walter. Now that he's gone, I have nothing."

I merely nod. Death and loss are not subjects I discuss easily.

"I miss him so. I have no reason to get up, no reason to get dressed and go out. Everything seems so, I don't know . . ." She stares blankly at the opposite wall. "It's like I'm watching it all on a black-and-white screen."

I think back to my own dark hours and wonder if depression might not be closer to the mark than senility.

"There's still Alicia, of course," Lillian continues. "But now that Walter's gone, we don't seem to have much in common."

"Actually, it's because of Alicia that I'm here."

Lillian has the teacup almost to her lips, but she replaces it on the table without taking a sip. "What's she done now?"

"She's worried about you."

"That'll be the day." Lillian laughs without humor. "More like she's trying to get her hands on my money."

It's an assessment I can't deny, so I say nothing.

"That girl doesn't have a responsible bone in her body. She's selfish and careless, and it seems to me, increasingly mean-spirited. Devious, too. I'm not going to bail her out of whatever trouble she's in. Not this time. I won't do it."

"She's not in any trouble that I'm aware of."

"Why did she hire you, then?"

I skirt the question. "Do you have a financial advisor, Mrs. Goodhue?"

She lifts her chin. "I did, but I fired him."

So Alicia was right about that.

"He was always talking yields and percentage returns and tax deductions. I'm not interested in squeezing the last drop out of every dollar. I invest in government bonds and corporations that do good for people. I'm more than willing to pay taxes and help out those in need."

"How about a lawyer?" I ask.

"Fired him, too."

Though I am loath to admit it, I am beginning to understand Alicia's concerns.

"He was just as bad," Lillian continues. "Always wanting to tinker with things, make them more complicated than they needed to be. Besides, he was a most unpleasant man. Not like you, dear. He was the kind of lawyer who gives the profession its tarnished reputation. Here, have some more tea."

Lillian is eager to talk, clearly pleased to have a companion for however brief an interlude. We discuss gardens and Italy and the dismal state of politics. I find myself drawn to Lillian Goodhue. She is a woman of wit, warmth, and the clarity of vision that's born of experience. While she is clearly one to speak her mind, I don't see anything that would convince me she is senile.

"Do you know Millay?" she asks out of nowhere.

I have no idea what she's talking about. A dance? A foreign language? Another attorney?

"I'm sorry, what was that?"

"The poet. Edna St. Vincent Millay. Are you familiar with her work?"

"Some of it."

" 'Safe upon the solid rock,' " Lillian begins. "Do you know that one?"

" 'Safe upon the solid rock, the ugly houses stand. Come see my shining palace, built upon the sand.' "

She laughs. "A kindred soul." Then she turns serious. "Such wise counsel. If only it weren't too late for me to find a stretch of sand."

*   *   *

THE following day, for good measure, I talk to Lillian Goodhue's former financial advisor and her doctor. The advisor, a man younger than I, dismisses Lillian as a nut case. When pressed, however, he is unwilling to use the word *senile*.

"She won't listen to reason," he says, "but I know plenty of younger people who are the same."

Her physician chuckles when I explain the reason for my call. "Dementia, no. At least not in the medical sense."

"But using the term more generally?"

He hesitates. "We're all our own people, Lillian more so than some. Age has a way of accentuating our eccentricities."

*   *   *

THAT night, as usual, my children treat dinner as an unnecessary inconvenience. Jeremey nibbles on left-over pizza; Samantha wants only salad. Neither seems inclined to eat the baked chicken and string beans I've prepared. When I start to protest, their expressions go flat.

"Lecture 103A," Jeremey says to his sister.

"Save your breath," Samantha advises me. "You tell us the same thing over and over. Must be Alzheimer's or something."

They both laugh. Adolescent humor leaves much to be desired. But I am struck, too, by how much they sound like Alicia.

I am washing the orange Pyrex baking dish I got for

a wedding present when the phone rings. I wait for the kids to pick it up, knowing the odds are that it will be for one of them. On the fifth ring, before the answering machine can kick in, I reach a soapy hand for the phone.

"Have you got the conservatorship papers drawn up yet?" Alicia asks.

I explain that her petition hasn't a prayer in court. "Even if Lillian doesn't contest it, which I'm betting she will, no judge is going to find her in need of a conservator. The law is intended to address extreme situations . . ."

"This *is* extreme."

"The petition won't hold up."

"It has to," Alicia insists. "Nobody knows her better than I do. She's incompetent. I'm willing to testify to that."

"It takes more than your say-so."

"I can find people who will back me up. How many do we need?"

"I spoke with her doctor and stockbroker today."

Alicia scoffs. "They wouldn't dare go against her wishes. I'm talking about people who owe me, who won't be afraid to say what needs to be said."

I am growing increasingly uncomfortable with the direction of our conversation, and tell her so.

"I won't let her fritter away my money," Alicia insists.

"It's hers. She can do with it what she wants."

"But Daddy—"

"He left it to Lillian," I explain for the zillionth time. "Unless she's incapacitated, it's hers to invest or spend any way she sees fit. If she wants to throw it all into the ocean, she can."

The phone goes dead before I can finish speaking. Alicia has hung up on me.

* * *

A month later Alicia calls again, in hysterics. "I've just discovered that I'm not even *in* Lillian's will. She's leaving everything to the SPCA. Can she do that?"

"She can. Unless there's duress or fraud involved, she can leave the money to whomever she wants."

"But it's not fair."

Since I've had no luck explaining the limits of fairness to my children, I don't even try with Alicia.

"I want to contest the will," Alicia says.

"She's not dead yet. Besides, you have no grounds."

"There must be something you can do," Alicia wails. "Aren't you even going to try?"

"There's nothing to try."

She is silent a moment. "For what it's worth," she says icily, "you're fired."

I know I should feel regret, or at least a moment's disappointment, but what I honestly feel is relief.

*　　*　　*

JANUARY has slipped into June and the sun is warm on my shoulders as I return to the office from my noon-time walk. I have two message slips on my desk when I return—one from my dentist and one from Lillian Good-hue. I know what my dentist wants—I am overdue for a crown—but I'm perplexed by the call from Lillian.

"We met several months ago," she reminds me when I return the call. "You came to see me about Alicia."

I assure her that I remember. "What can I do for you?"

"I've decided to revise my will. Do you handle that sort of work?"

Mentally, I run through a conflict-of-interest analysis. To the extent that Alicia was ever my client, she isn't any longer. I've not heard a word from her six months, since the day she fired me.

"I'd be pleased to handle it." We set up an appointment for the following day.

The Lillian Goodhue who arrives in my office at nine o'clock the next morning looks ten years younger and far more vibrant than the woman I'd met earlier. She is dressed in a well-cut navy linen pantsuit with a white silk blouse. Chunky silver jewelry adorns her neck and earlobes, highlighting the silver in her now shiny and trimmed hair. What impresses me most, though, is the sparkle in her eye. If she's been taking vitamins and herbs, I want to know which ones.

Lillian surveys the office, which is modest in both size and decor. "Sized for humans," she says. "I like that. My last attorney had an office that made you feel like you were visiting the Vatican."

"You look wonderful."

She laughs. "I feel pretty good, too."

"I'm glad to hear it. I was afraid these changes you want to make, uh, that they might be tied to health problems."

"No, I'm just tidying up a few things." She takes a seat and spends a moment gazing out the window before continuing. "I want to leave a bequest to a young man by the name of Miles Quackenbush. I've got his social security number right here if you need it."

"That's not necessary, but it would help to have his address."

"He lives with me."

I must have raised a brow because she laughs again. "No, not the way you think—although I must say I wouldn't be averse to the idea. He's a lovely man and very attentive."

Immediately, red flags start flapping before my eyes. "How long has he been living there?"

"Let's see. He started working for me after the first of the year—"

"Working for you?"

"As a handyman. There were so many things that needed doing. Alicia thought that I was letting the place go. Of course she was worried about property values and money, but in the final analysis she was right." Lillian laughs conspiratorially. "Only I'd never give her the satisfaction of telling her so."

"And this Miles, he's still there, fixing things?"

"Oh yes, there's always something. But now he does other things, too. He helps me in the garden, and he's a wonderful cook." With a glint of amusement she adds, "He plays a mean hand of gin rummy, as well."

The red flags are now waving so fast and furiously I have trouble knowing how to best approach Lillian on the subject. "It's nice that you want to remember him in your will, but if you're already paying him . . ."

"I am. Quite well, too."

"And you haven't known him for long."

"Long enough. Sometimes you meet someone and it feels like you've known them forever."

And sometimes we make mistakes. I wonder how hard I should push the point. But what harm can come of leaving him a token of her appreciation?

"I'll need a copy of your existing will," I tell her.

"It's right here." She hands over a thick document. "I'm leaving a small bequest to Alicia because it seems only right. And I've added a few charities, but I want Miles to be well provided for. I was thinking something along the lines of a million."

I swallow my first response, which befits my children's vocabulary better than mine. "That's a lot of money," I say instead.

"I hope so. Miles is a lovely person."

A lovely person who will also be a wealthy person at some point. There are so many things wrong with this picture I can't think where to begin.

Outside a horn honks. Lillian stands and goes to the window. "Oh, there he is now." She waves, then turns to address me. "Miles drove me downtown so that I wouldn't have to worry about parking. Isn't that sweet?"

I move to the window and glimpse a surfer-blond head in a red Ferrari convertible. "Nice car he drives."

She laughs. "That's mine—well, his now. I bought it for him last week."

Oh, Lillian, I think. *You may have kept the upper hand in dealing with Alicia, but you've met your match in Miles.*

* * *

I spend the afternoon poring over Lillian's existing will. Despite the sums involved, it's a fairly straightforward document. The changes she wants to make will be easy to implement, but they feel as wrong as a yellow sky.

Several days later, I trump up an excuse to pay an unexpected visit. Once again, Lillian answers the door herself. Among his many roles, Miles apparently does not assume that of butler.

"That was quick," she says. "Are the changes finished already?"

"No, uh, I just needed to check a few details."

I look around but do not see Miles. What I do see are a big-screen television and a similarly sized sound system in the corner where during my last visit I'd seen a china cabinet.

Lillian again has a pot of tea brewing, only this time it's an odd-tasting herbal concoction. We settle in the den with our tea and freshly baked scones.

"Miles made these," she says proudly. "The tea, too, in fact. He's a wonderful cook, and so thoughtful."

"I was hoping I'd get a chance to meet him."

"You'd like him, I know. Unfortunately, he left to run by the hardware store just as you were pulling up. Here, have another scone."

Much as I hate to admit it, the scones are first rate—despite the fact that they are flecked with unidentifiable bits of green. "What is this?" I ask.

Lillian shakes her head. "Some kind of health supplement, I believe. Miles is very much into herbs."

I set my scone on the saucer. "Mrs. Goodhue, maybe

it isn't my place to ask, but just how much do you know about this young man?"

"He comes from back east originally, and he lived in Los Angeles for a couple of years trying to get established in the movie business. He played in a number of the popular television shows. Maybe you've seen him."

"So how did he get from movie star to handyman?"

"Well, he wasn't really a *star*. That's what he wanted, of course, but he ended up with little parts. As Miles says, a person can bang his head against the wall for only so long. He's so adaptable. That's one of his charms. When life gives you lemons, he says, make lemonade."

I can't believe what I'm hearing. Can't believe that Lillian herself can't see a few red flags. "Does he have any job aside from working for you?"

She chuckles. "Oh, I keep him plenty busy. He's been cultivating an herb garden out back. And yesterday he fixed the railing on the upper deck."

"It was loose?"

She frowns for a moment. "Not that I'd seen, but of course he knows more about these things than I do."

It's like a script from a bad movie. "And does he work on your car, too?"

Her face shows delight. "Yes, how did you know?"

"Just a hunch."

"Come," she says, rising from the sofa. "Let me show you the new cooktop. It's gas, like all the professional cooks use. I had electric before and I always hated it. But Walter thought it was cleaner so of course we stayed with the electric."

An accidental fall, failed brakes, deadly gas fumes. Images of Lillian's demise pound my brain like gunfire. I promise myself I will talk to Aaron before lifting a finger to change Lillian's will. Aaron has good insight and judgment. I'm hoping he will tell me I've let my imagination get out of hand.

"Oh, do be careful," Lillian cautions, reaching for the

knife resting at my elbow. "Miles keeps the knives very sharp. They'll cut right through anything."

"When do you suppose Miles will be back?" I ask uneasily.

"I don't know, dear. The hardware store might not have carried the kind of rat poison he wanted. He was very clear that it had to be a specific type."

"You have rats?"

"Not that I've noticed. But Miles thinks it's wise to take an aggressive approach."

I pull myself straight. "I'll need the address where Miles lived before he moved in with you. And I think it would be helpful if I had that social security number, after all."

Lillian looks perplexed. "I don't know his former address."

"Maybe it's among the papers in his room."

"I don't . . . I hate to go poking around."

"It's *your* house," I remind her.

"Yes, I suppose, but it doesn't seem . . ." She stops and gives me a sly look. "You don't believe me, do you? About there being nothing romantic between us. I'm flattered, but I assure you that he does have his own room. I'll show you."

Miles not only has his own room, it is the largest in the house, with its own bath and adjoining sitting room. It looks like the master bedroom and I say so.

Lillian nods. "It is. Or was. I sleep in a room on the main floor. That way I don't have to worry about all those stairs, and the heat there is better."

Okay, I tell myself, the important thing is to stay calm. Miles isn't going to do anything to harm Lillian until the will is changed and signed. At present, only the dogs and cats of San Francisco have reason to hasten Lillian's demise.

"Mrs. Goodhue, I think we need to talk."

"Yes, of course. I love visiting with you. Such a

change from that horrible man who was my former attorney." She goes to the window. "Take a look, from here you can see what Miles has done with the rose garden. Isn't it beautiful?"

I gaze in the direction she is pointing at a brick patio and arbor enveloped in rose blossoms. It is, indeed, a beautiful picture. And Lillian Goodhue seems radiant. How do I tell her she's being snookered?

*   *   *

"WHY not talk to her stepdaughter?" Aaron Stern suggests.

"Alicia? The two of them don't exactly get along."

"Still, she must have some sense of this young man."

I call Alicia several times before reaching her. Though I've left messages, she has ignored them. I explain my qualms without mentioning the pending changes to the will.

"It's her money," Alicia snaps. "You said so yourself."

"Yes, but I think this man might be taking advantage of her."

"I tried to tell you she's incapable of managing her own affairs." Alicia's tone is more vexed than smug.

"Have you met this Miles?"

"Of course."

"And what do you think?"

"What does it matter what I think? It's Lillian's money. I'm never going to see any of it, so why the hell should I care what she does?"

Before I can respond, she hangs up.

I go see Aaron again. "You say Lillian is happier," he notes wistfully.

I nod.

His eyes mist over. "It's hard to knock happiness."

"But—"

"There's no law against befriending someone. Even a wealthy widow."

"Unless she's mentally incompetent."

"But you told me she wasn't. He's not forcing her to make the changes, is he?"

"No, but it doesn't smell right to me."

Aaron closes his eyes a moment, lost in thought. "One man's folly, another man's grace. Suspicion isn't enough, Hannah, not without solid evidence. I understand why you are uncomfortable, but you can't deny Lillian Goodhue her happiness."

* * *

FOR two nights in a row, I am unable to sleep. I have called in a favor with a private investigator I know, but he is busy preparing for a big trial and doesn't know how soon he can get me information on Miles Quackenbush.

Wednesday morning, Lillian calls me at the office. "Is the will ready to be signed yet?"

"Not quite. We've, uh, had some technical problems with our software." It's an excuse that doesn't hold water, but I'm hoping Lillian Goodhue doesn't see that. "I can let you look at a draft, however. Why don't I bring it by this afternoon? And I'd so like to meet Miles."

Several hours later I am once again at Lillian's door. Fleetingly, I catch a glimpse of Miles as he slips down the back hallway from the kitchen.

Lillian pours me a cup of tea. Almond-flavored this time. As are the cookies. Once again she tells me what a whiz Miles is in the kitchen.

Mid-bite, I remember what that I've read about almond-tasting poison, and wonder if it's safe to swallow. Then I remind myself that the will isn't yet signed. Dogs and cats are still the clear winners.

There's a shuffling sound from the other room.

"Miles, dear, is that you?"

Silence.

"I don't know where he's gone to," Lillian says. "I told

him you were looking forward to meeting him." She sighs and looks over the papers I've handed her. "It looks to be in order. Shall I sign it?"

"This is just a draft." I point to the large DRAFT stamp at the top of the page.

"But if it's right . . ."

A door shuts and I hear footsteps approaching.

Lillian turns. "Is that you, Miles?"

"Sorry to be late. I had to take the bread from the oven."

"So you're Miles," I say without waiting for an introduction. "I've been hearing such nice things about you."

"Likewise." He looks me in the eye and smiles.

Up close, Miles Quackenbush looks smaller and slightly less the peacock he did from a distance. He has a full mouth that tweaks at the corners and his eyes are so blue I suspect he's wearing colored lenses. Despite my reservations, however, I am charmed.

"Mrs. Goodhue says you're a big help."

"I hope so. She's a peach." He glances her way and smiles.

"I understand you're an actor. You must miss being on camera."

"A little. But it's a tough field to break into."

"So now you're honing your skills."

He gives me a funny look. "To tell the truth, I've sort of given up."

"Too bad. I imagine you have real talent." I see the hint of blush on his face and decide that he's understood my meaning. "Do you have any family, Miles?"

"Family?"

"You know, parents, brothers, sisters."

Lillian pats his arm. "His parents are both deceased," she says. "The poor boy was shuttled from one foster home to another."

"On the East Coast," I say.

He nods.

"Where about?"

"Boston."

"Which high school?"

"A couple of different ones," he says vaguely. "I never did graduate."

I walk away with little new information to pass along to my investigator friend, but with renewed conviction that all is not what it seems.

* * *

A week later I am still spinning my wheels. My investigator friend has finally gotten back to me, but found little. Miles Quackenbush is real, as is his tale of foster homes and several high schools. He lived in Los Angeles for five years, chasing after bit parts and taking odd jobs to tide him over. No arrests, no big-time trouble except that he was a suspect in a hit-and-run four years earlier. He was cleared when a witness substantiated his alibi.

Finally, I decide there's nothing to do but lay out my suspicions for Lillian. I hope I can persuade her to hold off changing her will, at least for the short run. I call the house and Miles answers. He promises to give Lillian my message, but I have my doubts.

Surprisingly, she calls back within the hour.

"You've been such a dear. Send me the bill and add a little for all your extra effort."

"We're not finished yet."

"Oh, we are."

Has she decided against changing her will? Already, I am breathing easier.

"It's all signed. I had it witnessed at the bank."

My heart stops. "Mrs. Goodhue, that was a draft I left with you."

"But there weren't any changes to be made. We just photocopied the first page, whiting out the word DRAFT. Looks very professional."

I feel the walls closing in around me. "Does Miles know about the will?"

"Of course."

"Mrs. Goodhue, I'm worried. Now that he stands to benefit, he might . . . might kill you." The words sound melodramatic even to my own ears. But my heart is pounding with real fear.

"Don't be silly, dear. I wasn't born yesterday. Besides, it's been signed a whole week, and I'm still here, aren't I?" She laughs. "Don't forget the bill—and drop by any time for a chat. Except tomorrow afternoon. Alicia's coming to lunch."

*   *   *

ONCE again, I am awake all night, tossing and turning. In the morning, I take my fears to the police, who humor me by listening before explaining there is nothing they can do. I imagine they will have a good laugh at my expense the minute I depart.

Back at my office, I find the written report my investigator friend has dropped off. Flipping through it, I am jolted out of my seat. The witness substantiating Miles's alibi for the hit-and-run is none other than Alicia Goodhue.

It is suddenly clear to me what has happened. Alicia and Miles have a history. No doubt a long and colorful history. Knowing she wasn't going to inherit directly, Alicia has arranged for Miles to win Lillian's favor. Now that the will is signed, they have only to kill Lillian and split the money.

I glance at the clock and realize that Alicia is lunching there this very minute.

I dash into Aaron's office. "Quick, we have to get to Lillian Goodhue's. She's in danger."

"What?" Despite his aching joints, Aaron is nonetheless out of his seat in a flash.

"I'll explain on the way."

There is no answer when we knock on the door. We circle the house, peering through windows into the silent interior.

Panic seizes me. "I'm afraid we're too late."

Aaron grabs a brick and breaks a glass panel on the French doors.

"Hurry," I yell.

He reaches through the jagged glass, turns the lock and opens the door. The shriek of a house alarm pierces the air.

We run from room to room, finding no one. In the kitchen we see the remnants of lunch—a wild-mushroom quiche.

"Don't touch the food," I yell at him. "It's probably poisoned."

Just then we see a streak of red in the driveway. The Ferrari. And inside, Lillian and Miles.

My relief quickly gives way to embarrassment. I wonder how I'll explain. I wonder, too, if I'll be disbarred for breaking into her home.

But Lillian is too preoccupied to be angry. "Alicia's in the hospital," she says.

"Poisoned, no doubt," I add, understanding instantly that Miles has outfoxed the fox.

But I am wrong. It turns out that the fox has outfoxed herself.

Miles makes cappuccino for the four of us while he and Lillian explain.

Alicia did indeed approach Miles about currying favor with Lillian, but as he came to know her, he found instead the kind of warmth and companionship he'd always longed for.

"I never wanted to be a party to murder," Miles tell us as he hands us our coffee mugs. "But I needed a place to live. I thought I'd play the role for a month or so and

then split. It never crossed my mind she'd actually change
her will."

"A little inheritance seemed only fair," Lillian adds,
"after all he did. Miles pulled me from despair and taught
me to feel joy again. It's been a godsend having him
here."

Miles sips his coffee. "I told Alicia months ago that I
wasn't going to do anything illegal, but she wouldn't take
no for an answer. Finally, she took matters into her own
hands by slipping poison into Lillian's wine."

"Only I rarely drink anymore," Lillian says. "So I
poured my wine into Miles's glass."

"Then how—"

"By this time, Alicia no longer trusted me," Miles explains. "So instead of drinking her own wine, she
switched her glass with mine. Alicia ended up poisoning
herself."

I am feeling drained and revved at the same time. I
glance at Aaron to see how he's holding up, and find that
he's got eyes only for Lillian.

"What about this hit-and-run you were suspected of?"
I ask, still not satisfied. "You and Alicia were both tied
into that. She provided you with an alibi."

He nods. "She was driving my car that night. The police thought I was involved even though I was on the other
side of town at the time."

"Why not tell them the truth?" I ask.

Miles drops his gaze. "I was spending the night with
a Republican presidential contender. His career would
have been ruined."

His career. I realize I'm watching for Lillian's reaction.
But it's not what I expect. She is gazing back at Aaron
with the same lovestruck look he's giving her.

*   *   *

SIX months later I get an invitation to the wedding.
"A celebration of new beginnings," Aaron says,

still slightly dazed by the wonder of it all. "Who'd have thought."

Indeed, I agree silently, who'd have thought.

Miles, who is now happily ensconced as the firm's administrative assistant, will give the bride away. Alicia, who is not so happily awaiting trial, will miss the ceremony, but she'll no doubt have ample time to reflect on her new life in prison.

As for myself, I have decided that I'm better suited to matchmaking than rainmaking. And while you won't find that term on the bar exam either, it certainly can't hurt to have a happy senior partner.

Restitution

Taffy Cannon

Taffy Cannon's Nan Robinson is a California bar investigator whose thankless task is to weed out corrupt and unethical attorneys. Needless to say, her job often involves her in murder. Cannon's new series, the Irish Eyes travel mysteries, debuted with Guns and Roses, *set in Colonial Williamsburg.*

S HE could hardly claim to be too busy.

That was Nan Robinson's first reaction as she listened to the fussy little lawyer outline her late neighbor's bewildering request. Her second thought was more basic.

"Why me?"

Rupert MacDonald squared his sagging shoulders and steepled his fingers on an oak desk not quite old enough to be classified antique. Enough July sun fought its way through the smog-streaked windows of his dreary second-story Santa Monica walkup to make the room unbearably stuffy. Nan could feel perspiration seeping into the dry-clean-only silk shirt she wore under her once-crisp summer navy lawyer's suit.

"I must confess that I asked Mrs. Dupree the same question," the elderly attorney said. He'd described himself as semi-retired, and the secretarial desk in his outer office lacked a computer or any signs of recent habitation. "She was adamant that you were the appropriate person to handle this matter, because she admired that your work involves the administration of justice." He offered a thin-lipped smile. "Or, anyway, that it did when she made these arrangements."

Ah. Administration of justice. Well, *that* certainly didn't apply anymore. As of two weeks ago, Nan's job—and nearly all attorney discipline in the state of California—had ceased to exist. She no longer investigated and prosecuted errant lawyers as part of the state bar Trial Counsel's office, striving to keep the evil and the negligent and the incompetent away from an unsuspecting public.

She was, in fact, unemployed.

He nodded. "Oh, yes. I'm well aware of the fate of your little operation at the state bar."

"Dead as a doornail," Nan agreed cheerfully. "Though I have to say I was hopeful till the very end."

Blindly optimistic was more like it. The governor was mad at the state bar for being too involved in political issues, and had consequently vetoed the bill authorizing its funding. State bar officials had failed to find a compromise over the previous nine months. And that was that. Crooked lawyers from Eureka to San Ysidro were dancing with joy.

"I can't say that I was personally sorry to see the bar shut down," MacDonald went on. His wispy hair was neatly cemented to his scalp with what looked like aerosol adhesive. "I've paid in tens of thousands of dollars over the years and never gotten anything but aggravation in return. There isn't even an 800 number for attorneys, only one for whiners who want to complain. But that's neither here nor there."

How many other lawyers felt the same way? The governor had called the state bar "bloated, arrogant, oblivious, and unresponsive." Nan hadn't realized, until the bar and her job bit the dust, just how intensely disliked both were.

"I barely knew Eleanor Dupree," Nan said now, trying

to return to the business at hand. Whatever exactly it might be. "She was my next-door neighbor for several years in Venice, and I know she lived there a long time before I moved in, but we rarely spoke. I was only inside her house once that I can recall."

And a strange interlude *that* had been: coffee in Wedgewood cups while Nan perched uneasily on a club-footed loveseat in a room crammed with elaborate doilies and an eerie collection of glass and ceramic clowns that grimaced from two illuminated hutches and every available surface. Small talk. Instant coffee. A mason jar of Mrs. Dupree's spectacular roses to take home when the awkward meeting ended.

"What Mrs. Dupree wishes you to do is really quite simple," the attorney explained now. "Her property has been sold and the expenses of her final illness and burial have been met. She had only one living relative, a son, John, who's incarcerated up at Pelican Bay. He is specifically disinherited. The remainder of her estate is to go to three people living in Corsicana and one in Santee. I have cashier's checks for these people, and an investigator has determined that each is at the address given. You are to deliver the checks personally, with regards and apologies from Mrs. Dupree. On completion of this task, you will be paid seven-thousand five-hundred dollars for your services."

He handed Nan the four checks and she stared at them, dumbfounded. *Regards and apologies.* Three checks for $27,845 each, payable to Susan Finnegan, Matilda Smithson, and Joseph Doolittle. One check for $55,690, payable to Elizabeth Barnstable. Nearly $150,000, when you added in Nan's fee. Which was $7,500 more than anybody had offered her in a long time.

"Restitution?" Dumb question. What else could *regards and apologies* possibly mean? But why would a little old lady who starched her antimacassars feel the need for posthumous restitution? And where was Corsicana, anyway?

Rupert MacDonald wasn't giving up anything. "I'm authorized only to tell you what I already have. Mrs. Dupree was equally adamant on that point. I can hold the checks until you make your travel arrangements."

* * *

O N the way home, Nan splurged on an early-bird special at a favorite Thai restaurant. She'd stopped eating restaurant meals months earlier when the threat of unemployment first loomed seriously, simultaneously refinancing her house at a lower interest rate and cutting all discretionary spending to the bone.

Back in Venice, she carried a Molson Golden into her bougainvillea arbor and stared for a while at Eleanor Dupree's little bungalow, now freshly painted a pastel yellow. When Eleanor died of cancer in March, Nan had been surprised to learn that the woman was only sixty-seven. The house had been recently bought by a young couple with a perennially squalling infant, and the rose blooms were puny compared to previous years, the foliage skeletonized by bugs.

When the baby started bellowing, she went inside, feeling a renewed sense of purpose, even if she didn't understand what it was about.

* * *

T HE next morning, she phoned the district attorney's office and asked her friend Andrea Westbrook to check on John Dupree. Late that afternoon, Andrea called back with disquieting—if unsurprising—news.

"Hope you don't have designs on this fellow, Nan, 'cause the chances of his ever being released to fulfill his conjugal duties are somewhere between slim and nonexistent."

Nan laughed. "I already knew he didn't get sent to Pelican Bay for shoplifting." Despite its bucolic name, the prison was an isolated fortress housing the nastiest of the nasty, felons who could never hope to repay their debt to society and weren't interested anyway. "What's his story?"

"Grim. White male; forty-seven years old; last outside address, Santee, California. Had a minor record—car theft, D and D, that sort of stuff—till he killed somebody in a barroom brawl. Went up to San Quentin on manslaughter twenty-three years ago, hooked up with the Aryan Brotherhood and killed a couple of brothers who didn't like his politics. That bought him a one-way ticket to Pelican Bay."

"Who'd he kill the first time?"

"You mean the first time we know about," Andrea corrected. Like most DAs of Nan's acquaintance, her outlook on life was bleak. "A guy named Leo Stokely. This help any?"

"I'm not sure," Nan told her. "But thanks. I guess."

*   *   *

I T was nice to have something specific to do.

Nan wasn't used to unstructured time. She'd gone from high school to college, college to law school, law school to McSweeney Lane, McSweeney Lane to the state bar—all without taking more than a brief interim vacation.

For the moment, she had deliberately avoided making a decision about her future. She was closing in on forty, or maybe forty was closing in on her. Either way, she didn't have nearly enough experience with indolence.

So initially when the Trial Counsel's office shut down, Nan told herself she was on vacation. She slept late, went to the beach, puttered around the house. By the end of the second week, however, indolence was wearing thin, and Rupert MacDonald's call a welcome diversion.

*   *   *

Two days later, Nan set out an extra-full bowl of kitty krunchies for Nefertiti, picked up the checks and releases from MacDonald, and pointed her '67 Mustang south, passing through Orange County and cutting inland on Highway 78, up into the mountains east of San Diego.

Corsicana had turned out to be on the Anza-Borrego side of Julian, and was nearly as old as its neighbor town, though nowhere near as tourist-savvy. Where Julian bustled with antique stores and apple pie shoppes nestled into groves of tall trees, Corsicana squatted, sullen and defiant, at the edge of the desert, short on vegetation and charm, long on heat.

The grandly overnamed Corsicana Inn sat nearly empty at the eastern end of Main Street, with a gleaming Harley-Davidson parked beside the office. Nan cruised the cross streets to locate the two other addresses she was seeking, then checked into the motel.

The bored young man at the front desk set aside a motorcycle magazine to register her and brightened only once, when he caught a glimpse of the Mustang and asked a staccato series of technical questions about its specs. He gave a little chuckle when Nan asked for a quiet room—which seemed, on reflection, a rather gratuitous request—and volunteered that the ice machine was broken. He handed over the key to unit 15, on the end, and picked up his magazine again.

Unit 15 seemed to be furnished with Camp Pendleton barracks castoffs, complete to a set of unsavory stains on the brown bedspread that resembled camouflage fatigues. She cranked the air conditioning unit to the max and decided that with a little bit of luck, maybe she could check out without spending a night here.

Santee couldn't possibly be worse. Hell might not be worse, and might even be cooler.

To play Jane Beresford Tipton, Nan had opted for khaki slacks and a burgundy blazer, though she hadn't realized how hot it would be here on the summer desert's edge. She started to remove the Susan Finnegan file from her briefcase, then considered a moment and decided to leave nothing more valuable than her toothbrush unattended in the room. She headed for the office.

"I'd like to speak with Susan Finnegan," she told her sullen young buddy at the desk. He sighed mightily and ran stubby fingers through thick, too-long hair. Each nail was neatly ringed with permanent grease-stains. "Is she available?"

He stood up, opened a door behind the counter and bellowed, "Ma!"

A moment later, a middle-aged woman in a Padres T-shirt and faded jeans slouched through the same door. She was thin without seeming fit, carrying a lot of wrinkles that makeup wasn't hiding particularly well. Her straight dark hair was starting to streak silver, and for an inn-keeper, she didn't look the least bit hospitable.

"You need something?" she asked, brown eyes flat and lifeless.

Nan introduced herself. "Is there somewhere we could speak privately on a business matter?"

"I'm not buying anything," Susan Finnegan announced irritably. Aha! The source of Sonny Boy's etiquette training.

"That's fine," Nan answered with what she hoped was a disarming smile, "because I'm not selling anything."

Susan Finnegan frowned, shrugged, then lifted a section of the Formica counter. Nan followed her into what seemed to be her living room. A dirty braided rug covered most of the linoleum floor and an oversized TV played a muted soap opera in front of pair of vinyl Barcaloungers. Susan Finnegan clearly hadn't become an innkeeper to provide an outlet for a decorating jones, but at least it was cooler in here.

Nan had mentally rehearsed her meetings with the four people on Eleanor Dupree's list, but the reality was a lot harder than the concept. She was assuming that Eleanor's wish to provide restitution was related to her no-account son, but it hadn't occurred to her that she herself might not be welcome. Of course Susan Finnegan wasn't yet aware that Nan was handing out money, and this looked like a place that could absorb twenty-seven grand without a hiccup.

"I'm here on behalf of Eleanor Dupree," Nan began neutrally. The name registered, no question. Susan Finnegan's features tightened and her eyes narrowed. Not an auspicious beginning. "Mrs. Dupree lived next door to me in Los Angeles until she passed away recently, and she left you a bequest in her will." The eyes widened and Finnegan's jaw opened slightly as she leaned forward, moving her head slowly from side to side.

Nan snapped open the briefcase, removed the file and handed over the check. Finnegan took it and gaped.

"Is this some kind of a joke?" she asked finally.

"Not at all. I take it you're familiar with Mrs. Dupree?"

Finnegan turned the check over and over in her hands and gave a short, bitter laugh. "It's been a long time. But yeah, I remember her. Is this for real?"

"Absolutely. I was instructed to give you the check with Mrs. Dupree's regards and apologies."

"Too late for both," Finnegan muttered, continuing to fondle the check. "So I can just take this to a bank?"

"Yes, ma'am." Nan hesitated. "Did Mrs. Dupree live here in Corsicana?"

Susan Finnegan nodded. "Till they sent Johnny away, anyhow."

"Her son?"

"One and the same." She stood up abruptly. "Look, I don't want to talk about this."

"Perfectly all right with me," Nan lied. She'd been hoping that a woman watching soaps before noon would be a willing gossip. "I just need for you to sign that you've received the check." She passed over Rupert Mac-Donald's release form and retrieved it after the woman affixed a hasty scrawl. "I'll be here at the motel tonight if you have any more questions."

"Just one," the gracious innkeeper said. "When are you leaving?"

* * *

THE second check was for Joseph Doolittle, who operated a combination real estate/insurance office on D Street, just off Main. A few sun-faded property listings were taped inside the front window, curling at the edges.

When Nan walked in, a bell *bing-bong*ed and a bespectacled man looked up from one of two desks in the office. The other was unoccupied and piled with file folders. His own was tidy and uncluttered with anything resembling work. He set aside the sports page of the *San Diego Union-Tribune* and stood with an effort. He was as heavy as Susan Finnegan had been thin, wearing his pants belted high like Humpty-Dumpty.

"I know we've never met," he announced jovially, extending a hand, "because I never forget a pretty face. Joe Doolittle. What can I do for you this fine July morning?"

Once again, Nan introduced herself, altering her spiel slightly, watching his eyes. "I'm an attorney, here on behalf of Eleanor Dupree."

He was a born salesman, didn't flinch. "Eleanor Dupree! Well, whaddaya know! Haven't heard that name in years." But he clearly remembered it, just as Susan Finnegan had. "And how *is* Mrs. Dupree, anyhow? Haven't seen her in half of forever."

"I'm afraid Mrs. Dupree passed away in March," Nan told him, watching his expression. It seemed to brighten a bit at the news. What in God's name had Eleanor Dupree—or, more probably, her son—done to the people in this town to make them hate her so?

Joe Doolittle blathered condolences for a moment or two, then sat back puzzled, as if he knew his turn was over. Nan explained why she was there, and brought out the second check and release form. Doolittle looked at them closely, then propped the check on his coffee cup. "I don't get it," he said finally.

Nan smiled. "Neither do I, Mr. Doolittle."

"Joe," he corrected quickly, the salesman in him rising automatically.

"Joe. Actually, I was hoping you might be able to explain it to me."

He considered for a moment. "No, I don't think so," he said finally. He signed the release, handed it back and showed her to the door.

*   *   *

Two checks, two strikes. She'd earned $3,750 and felt dirtied by her efforts. It was definitely time to regroup. She walked across Main to what seemed to be the only restaurant in town, an uncharacteristically cheerful and cool place with pink eyelet curtains and a friendly waitress named Maggie, who steered her away from the chef's salad but promised that the vegetable soup was excellent. The soup was chunked with fresh vegetables and barley, and Nan had a second bowl, then finished with a slice of apple pie from Julian.

Maggie was chatty, but Nan decided not to pursue her curiosity here, even though it was probably the gossip nerve center of Corsicana. She tipped heavily, determined that she'd have to go to Julian if she wanted dinner, and set out for her third visit.

Matilda Smithson's duplex was on F, and a painted plywood cat directed Nan to the rear apartment, which featured a wheelchair ramp and a window box of rugged scarlet geraniums.

Braced for hostility by now, Nan was startled to see Matilda Smithson's clear blue eyes light up when she explained who she was and that she was visiting at the behest of Eleanor Dupree.

"Do come in, my dear," Matilda told her, wheeling her

chair smartly backwards and gesturing into a sparsely furnished unit designed to accommodate her chair. "Can I offer you some refreshment?"

Nan shook her head. "I just had lunch, but thank you."

"Then come out to the kitchen and tell me all about Eleanor. Is she well?"

Finally, somebody who cared.

"I'm afraid I have sad news, Mrs. Smithson. She passed away this spring."

Matilda shook her head in dismay. "How dreadful! And she was so young, so very young." Matilda herself looked nearly ninety, but it was still a reach to think of the stooped and unhappy old lady who had tended the Venice rose bushes as young. "Such a tragic life."

Nan had found her gossip.

"I taught for fifty-three years," Matilda Smithson explained, "and I came to realize after a while that there were some kids I was simply never going to be able to reach. I don't believe in evil, necessarily, but now and again I'd have a student who made me seriously consider the possibility. Johnny Dupree was that kind of student, incorrigible from the very beginning."

Sitting in a captain's chair across from Matilda Smithson in a bright red-and-white kitchen, Nan felt comfortable for the first time since she'd driven into town. Matilda Smithson exuded an easy charm and seemed delighted to have company. She was not a Mrs., she'd explained, just an old-maid schoolmarm who didn't like *Ms.* and wanted Nan to call her Matilda anyway.

"I'd love to hear more about him," Nan told her, "but first I need to tell you exactly why I'm here." She explained the bequest and brought out Matilda's check, careful to mention the regards and apologies.

"Why, I can't imagine . . ." As her voice trailed off, it seemed obvious that Matilda knew exactly why she'd been remembered. "She understood I never blamed her for what Johnny did."

"He seems to have made a great many people unhappy," Nan said carefully.

Matilda nodded. "That was his special gift. The last I heard he was in San Quentin, but that was quite some time ago."

Nan brought her up to date on John Dupree's criminal resume. "I didn't even realize Eleanor had a son, though I didn't know her well."

"When Eleanor left here, it was to get away from people who knew about Johnny, who blamed her for Johnny."

"People like Susan Finnegan and Joe Doolittle?" Nan told her about the other bequests, and about the reception she'd gotten so far.

"Susie Lewis got pregnant in high school," Matilda said. "She'd been quite a nice girl up till then, a good student, cheerleader, all those sorts of things. The kind of nice girl who'd be easily taken in by a good-looking fast-talker like Johnny Dupree. She said Johnny was the father, but when her family tried to get him to do the right thing, he spread such horrible stories about her that her reputation was absolutely destroyed. Susie went off and had the baby and eventually she came back after a couple of divorces, but she was never the same again."

"That young man working the desk at the motel? Was he Johnny's son?"

"Oh, no. She gave up that first baby, the way girls did back then. Davey's last name is Rockwell, but nobody here ever did meet a Mr. Rockwell. I've heard that Davey's involved with drugs, but that could just be loose talk. I don't think Susie would have come back to Corsicana at all, except that her father died and left her the motel."

In which her son was probably manufacturing crystal meth. And maybe sharing with Mum.

"Well, that explains why she was so unhappy to see

me, I guess. What about Joe Doolittle?" Surely Johnny Dupree hadn't knocked *him* up.

"Poor little Joe! He was always a chubby boy, and Johnny just teased him mercilessly, year after year. All Johnny had to do was look at Joe and he'd start blubbering. I lost track of the number of times that I personally had to discipline Johnny for picking on Joe.

"They were classmates, and it wasn't a big enough class to separate them too far. Though eventually we did hold Johnny back a year." She smiled. "Fortunately not the year I had him. One year was quite enough."

Nan hesitated. "It's none of my business, of course, but I can't help wondering—what did Johnny do to you that made Mrs. Dupree include you on her restitution list?"

Matilda patted her right hip. "He iced my sidewalk one January. We get hard freezes up here in the mountains, and I'd disciplined Johnny for some reason or another the previous week. It was the year he was in my class, fifth grade. He came by here in the middle of the night and poured water on my steps and walkway. It froze slick as glass and when I came out to go to school the next morning, I went head over heels. Broke this hip for the first time that morning, and it never did get quite right again. You young girls are all warned about osteoporosis now, but back then, all we knew was that some ladies got dowager's humps and the lucky ones didn't. I managed to avoid the hump, but I've got bones like matchsticks."

"It was definitely Johnny who iced the walkway?"

Matilda laughed. "No doubt whatsoever. He was too much of a braggart to let it go without taking credit. I hadn't even gotten to the hospital when it was all over town who was responsible. Not that *responsible* was a word much associated with young Johnny Dupree." She shook her head. "He left a lot of unhappy people in his wake, I must say that. I'm surprised you only came for the three of us."

"Actually, there's one more person," Nan admitted, "but she's in Santee. Elizabeth Barnstable." No need to tell Matilda that Ms. Barnstable's check was twice as large as her own, particularly since Matilda had immediately announced her intention of donating hers to charity.

"Elizabeth Barnstable?" Matilda frowned. "That name isn't familiar. I was thinking it might be some relative of the man that Johnny killed, of course, but I'm sure his name wasn't Barnstable. Stokes? . . . No, Stokely, that was it. Leo Stokely. I believe he left a widow."

"I'll find out tomorrow," Nan told her, suddenly exhausted. Cruising the ruinous wake left by Johnny Dupree was no fun at all. "That's soon enough, I guess."

"Are you going down to Santee tonight?"

Nan shook her head. "I have a room at the Corsicana Inn, though I can't say I feel particularly welcome. But I understand I have to go to Julian to get any dinner."

"Why don't you stay for supper with me?" Matilda pointed to the check on the table. "I don't do any fancy cooking anymore, but I have a freezer and I can certainly afford to feed you."

"I have a better idea. Why don't you come with me over to Julian? That wheelchair folds up, doesn't it? And this will definitely be my treat."

*   *   *

NAN left town the next morning without bothering to stop in the office and check out of the Corsicana Inn. Many times the night before she had seriously regretted declining the offer of Matilda Smithson's fold-out sofa. She had tossed and turned on a mattress that managed to squeak endlessly despite an apparent lack of springs. The dinner in Julian, complete with more apple pie, was the high point of the trip so far, and she'd promised to let Matilda know what happened in Santee.

Elizabeth Barnstable wasn't home when Nan rang the bell at her well-tended split-level house in a pleasant

neighborhood with full-grown trees. A teenage girl playing with several young children in a nearby yard called
out that Liz was at work. Apparently Nan looked respectable, or maybe this was just a trustingly anachronistic
neighborhood. Nobody in Venice would offer information
on anybody else's whereabouts. Ever.

Nan debated waiting till Liz Barnstable got home. She
was being amply paid for her time, after all. On the other
hand, Santee was nearly as hot as Corsicana had been,
and the girl had helpfully offered directions to the orthodontist's office where her neighbor worked.

Liz Barnstable was getting twice as much money as
Susan Finnegan and Joe Doolittle. If she hated Johnny
Dupree twice as much as they did, Nan might just as well
get the delivery over with and go home.

The orthodontist's waiting room was jammed. Nan told
the receptionist that she'd like to see Liz Barnstable when
she had a moment free, and that she'd wait. She flipped
through *Ranger Rick* and watched the patients play and
jabber, awaiting their appointments with no apparent
dread. Some of them seemed to be barely of school age,
far too young for braces. Back when Nan was a kid, you
waited till you were in high school and then got wired
into about fifteen pounds of shiny, spiky steel. But apart
from one middle-aged woman who kept her mouth
clamped tightly shut, the patients waiting here were all
under the age of twelve, most sporting appliances in rain-
bow colors.

It was half an hour before Liz Barnstable came out,
and mindful of their audience, Nan told her only that she
was an attorney from Los Angeles who wanted to speak
privately.

"My God, I'm not being sued, am I?" She was about
Nan's age, a perky blonde with freckles and a tiny waist
and a natural rapport with the kids in the waiting room.

"Absolutely not," Nan assured her. "This is something
else altogether."

"Then could you come back at noon? We're absolutely swamped today, but we close down for an hour at lunch."

Nan looked at her watch. Just a little over an hour. She suddenly realized that the upbeat energy of this office was the perfect antidote to her depressing early experiences in Corsicana yesterday. "I'll wait," she said. "Take your time and if you'd like, I'll buy you lunch."

It was quarter after twelve by the time Liz Barnstable emerged again. Nan had watched countless kids pass in and out of the office, nearly all of them happy. Liz suggested the Denny's down the road, and she made peppy small talk till after they'd ordered.

"Okay," she said finally, "if I'm really not being sued, then what's going on? Did somebody leave me a million bucks?"

Nan smiled. "Not quite a million. Fifty-five thousand."

"You're joking!" Liz Barnstable clapped her hands to her face. "You *are* joking, aren't you? I know I was."

"Not at all. I'm authorized to give you a cashier's check from the estate of Eleanor Dupree, with regards and apologies." Nan pulled out the envelope with the check and release form and passed it across the table.

"I don't get it." And she didn't. The name sparked no recognition at all. "Eleanor *who?*"

"Dupree." Nan swallowed anxiously and waited while the waitress dropped off glasses of iced tea. "You may have known her son, Johnny."

Now she knew. Recognition rose in her eyes and she leaned back in the booth. Nan waited for her to snatch the check and split. "You mean John Dupree who killed my husband, Leo?"

Nan nodded.

"And his *mother* left me money in her will?"

Nan nodded again.

"You know, I may be the densest person in the world, but I still don't understand what's going on here. Are you sure this is real?" She pointed to the cashier's check, which she had yet to touch.

"Absolutely. Mrs. Dupree was a neighbor of mine, you see. And apparently when she passed away, she wanted to compensate some of the people that her son had wronged. As the widow of the man he killed, you were on that list."

Liz Barnstable's face crinkled into an enormous grin. "Do I have to do anything to get this? Make some kind of statement or something about how awful it was that Leo got killed?"

"Just sign the release, that's all."

"And then the money is mine?"

"And then the money is yours." Nan put the release in front of her and watched as Liz Barnstable scribbled exuberantly, then straightened the check in front of her.

She was still grinning. "I went to the trial, you know. For John Dupree. It seemed like the right thing to do, Leo being my husband and all. But I've gotta tell you something. I'm too honest not to, I guess. Leo Stokely was a drunk and a bum and he used to beat me when he got drunk, which was just about every night. It took two weeks after he died before the last bruises cleared away. I was scared to death of Leo and I hated him.

"I'm married now to a guy who treats me like a queen and we have a couple of kids who God willing are going to turn out okay, and I like my job and I have a nice house and a good life.

"Johnny Dupree did me a favor, killing Leo. He probably saved my life while he was at it." She looked at the check. "And now this. *Incredible*. Tell you what. Lunch is on me. And let's have hot fudge sundaes for dessert."

Strange Bedfellows

Michael A. Kahn

A trial lawyer practicing in St. Louis, Kahn is the creator of the clever, witty Rachel Gold mystery series, which explores the lighter side of the legal profession in such novels as Bearing Witness and Sheer Gall. His short stories have appeared in such diverse collections as Legal Briefs and Mystery Midrash, an anthology of Jewish tales.

"OH, Benny," I groaned, "how did I *ever* let you talk me into this case?"

"Talk you into it?" he said, incredulous. "Talk you into it? My God, Rachel, you should be sending flowers to my office, planting trees in my honor in Israel. When are you ever going to find a case like this again?"

"Hopefully never."

We were heading west on Highway 70, about forty miles outside St. Louis. The Warrenton exit was ten miles ahead. Benny had directions from there to the ranch, where we were going to meet my newest clients, Maggie and Sara. Sara's younger brother, Paul, was a first-year law student in Benny's contracts class. One day after class last week Paul told Benny about a lawsuit involving his sister—a truly preposterous case, and thus one that immediately appealed to Benny, who'd driven right over to my office to enlist my help.

Had he been any other law school professor in the

United States, I would have said no. But of course he wasn't any other law school professor in the United States. He was Benny Goldberg, unique by any standard: vulgar, fat, gluttonous, and obnoxious. But also ferociously loyal, wonderfully funny, and—most important—my very best friend in the whole world. I loved him like the brother I never had, although he bore as much resemblance to my fantasy brother as, appropriately enough, an ostrich does to an eagle. We met as junior associates in the Chicago offices of Abbott & Windsor. A few years later, we both escaped that LaSalle Street sweatshop—Benny to teach law at DePaul, me to go solo as Rachel Gold, Attorney at Law. Different reasons brought us to St. Louis. For Benny, it was an offer he couldn't refuse from Washington University. For me, it was a yearning to live closer to my mother after my father died.

"Come on, woman," Benny said. "We gotta focus on the big picture."

"Focus me."

"Do ostriches have dicks?"

I turned toward him with raised eyebrows. "Pardon?"

"We're talking schlongs here, and if the answer is yes, then we're not talking ordinary bird schlongs. We're talking big swinging ones. So that's the issue, woman. Do ostriches have 'em?"

"I have no idea."

"Then we better find out pronto, eh? I mean, what's going on down there between Big Bird's legs? We talking Ken doll or we talking Burger King?"

I gave him a dubious look. "Burger King?"

He winked. "Home of the Whopper."

I sighed and shook my head. "I can't believe this."

"Come on, Rachel, this is a great case. These women pay ten grand for a genetically superior stud and instead they get the Slobodan Milosevic of the ostrich world."

We drove for awhile in silence. I glanced over and shrugged. "I have no idea."

"Huh?"

"I just assumed that birds had them."

"Not so, O provincial one. Ducks do, but most don't. Canaries and parakeets definitely don't."

"Benny, how in the world do you know this?"

"I worked in a pet store in high school."

"If they don't have penises," I asked, "how do they do it?"

"Ah," he said, segueing into his impression of the narrator in a cheesy documentary, "join me on a voyage into the strange and wondrous world of ornithological amour, to that magic moment the experts call the 'cloacal kiss.' "

"Which is?"

"Basically," he said, switching back to his standard New Jersey, "they press their butts together."

"Come on."

"I'm serious. The male's sex organs are inside his butt, and the female's are inside hers. When birds get some booty, we're talking booty squared."

"Are you making this up, Benny?"

"Would I make something like that up?"

"Absolutely."

The sign ahead read *Warrenton Next Exit*.

I mulled it over, recalling some of the material I'd read in preparation for today's meeting. "Those birds are humongous," I said. "They can weigh three hundred and fifty pounds. Penis or not, that's a lot of ostrich to fight off."

We drove in silence for awhile.

I shook my head in disbelief. "Could this case possibly be any stranger?"

"Actually," he said, pausing.

I shot him a look. "What?"

He gave me a sheepish grin. "Your clients—the two women."

"What about them?"

"Well, they're—you know."

"They're what?"

"Lezzies."

"Huh?"

"Daughters of Sappho."

"Whose daughters?" I asked, pulling ahead of a truck and into the right lane.

"Sappho. Sappho? Good grief, Rachel," he said in exasperation, "you may have showgirl legs, but don't ever try to win Ben Stein's money. Your clients are lesbians."

"So? I've got no problem with that."

"I know *you* don't. I'm not talking about you."

I looked over with a frown. "What do you mean?"

"Charlie Blackwell. He's the breeder who sold them the ostrich. That's his explanation."

"What are you talking about?"

"The women demanded their money back. Blackwell refused. Wait till you see his lawsuit. He claims that up until his breeding cock arrived at their ranch it was perfectly normal—presumably a caring, tender, romantic, sensitive lover. He claims the two women messed him up. He accuses them of incompetence and inexperience, and he also blames their lesbianism."

I turned to him, flabbergasted. "Are you serious?"

"There's more. He claims he's suffering mental anguish over the damage to his bird. That's why he's seeking punitive damages."

I could feel my litigator's pulse quicken. "That is absolutely outrageous."

Benny chuckled. "You go, girl."

I took the Warrenton exit and followed Benny's instructions along the state highway. He had, by now, switched topics to one far dearer to his heart: barbecue.

"I don't care how long they smoke them," I said with a shudder. "I'm not eating noses."

"Not noses, you Philistine. Snouts. Actually, we pig

proboscis aficionados call them snoots. Believe me, woman, you ain't done St. Louis barbecue 'til you scarf down a bucket of hickory-smoked snoots at C and K Restaurant bathed in sweet . . ." His voice trailed off. "Sweet Jesus, check it out."

I slowed the car. "Wow."

It was an astounding sight, made even more so here in the middle of the middle of America. We'd been driving past typical farmland vistas: grazing cattle, red barns, fields of soybean, metal silos, and green rows of corn stretching to the horizon. And then suddenly a pasture with a flock of ostriches running parallel to our car. The adults were enormous, all easily over seven feet tall, loping in graceful rhythm on long, skinny legs that thickened near the top to massive drumsticks. Their black-feathered torsos were balanced above their pumping legs while their little white wings flapped absurdly, as if they were a garden party of maiden aunts escaping a sudden shower. Their tiny beaked heads were perched on long, reddish necks that seemed to undulate in time with their gait. Scampering behind were about twenty chicks, some the size of adult geese, others the size of third-graders, all looking even more prehistoric than the parents, with their ridged heads and protruding black eyes and juvenile feathers that resembled spiky bristles.

"Whoa," Benny said, peering out the window, "welcome to Jurassic Park."

Maggie Lane and Sara Freed were seated together on the porch swing, each sipping a glass of lemonade, as we pulled up to the snug farmhouse. They came down to greet us.

Simpatico. That's what I felt the moment I met them. Maggie was in her late forties—a tall, slender brunette with the strong, elegant face, wise eyes, and wavy hair of a British stage actress. Her last name could have been

Redgrave. Sara was in her late twenties, stood maybe an inch over five feet, and had a sturdy build. She was a perky All-American type: blond hair, blue eyes, lots of freckles, cheerful smile. Both women wore jeans, work shirts, and boots.

We joined them on the porch, where there were chairs for us and a big pitcher of fresh-squeezed lemonade. They filled me in on the background of the lawsuit. Maggie explained that ostriches had been bred and raised in captivity for more than a century. Originally marketed for their feathers and leather, they were increasingly valued as food. Indeed, the recent boom in ostrich ranching had been fueled by the belief that ostrich steaks—an excellent source of low-fat, low-cholesterol protein—would be the health meat of the twenty-first century. Newborn chicks weighed two pounds and stood ten inches tall. They grew fast and reached processing size in a little over a year.

"Luckily," Maggie said, "we're in the middle of breeding season."

"Luckily?" I asked.

She nodded. "You're likely to see one of our pairs mate. It'll give you something to compare to Big Red."

"Big Red?" Benny perked up. "Great name, eh?"

I went over the lawsuit basics with Maggie and Sara, explaining that I'd be able to tell them more once I saw the court papers. Then it was time for the tour. We started in the barn, where a portion of the interior had been turned into a hatchery. There were two incubators, each resembling a double-sized white refrigerator, sitting side by side on an immaculate cement floor. Maggie pulled open one of the double doors to reveal dozens of huge eggs in rows in seven stainless steel bins.

"Here," she said, reaching into one of the bins and carefully lifting out an egg with both hands. She placed it into my hands. The egg was smooth and warm and weighed almost five pounds. I could feel a slight movement inside of it.

"Wow," I said softly, cradling the egg in my hands as I gave it back to Maggie.

From the hatchery we moved to the nursery, which took up part of the barn and extended into a fenced-off pen outside. Milling around were about a dozen brown-and-black baby chicks and a little white goat. The chicks resembled furry, prehistoric ducks.

"Goats are like nannies," Sara explained as she kneeled down by the fence. "This one's Rita. The chicks learn to eat and drink and avoid the rain by following her around." The little goat trotted over on stiff, pigeon-toed legs. She was adorable—little brown horns, loppy ears, a short, up-turned tail, and a streak of black fur running down the middle of her back. Sara put her hand through the fence to nuzzle it against the goat's neck.

We moved on to what Maggie called the breeding colony, which presently consisted of ten adult females (known as hens), two adult males, and about two dozen juveniles. They lived in a fenced-off area about three times the size of a football field. They were milling around and pecking at the grass as we approached.

Maggie scanned the pasture. "Oh, there's Tracy." She turned to us. "Let's go say hi. She's a doll."

We followed Maggie and Sara across the pasture. As we approached, the bird turned to face us.

"Jesus," Benny said under his breath, "look at the size of that chicken."

Tracy was immense, standing every bit of eight feet tall, her tiny head perched atop a long, rubbery neck. From a distance her long legs had merely looked skinny; but up close there were thick tendons and muscles visible beneath her rough skin—muscles and tendons powerful enough to propel three hundred and fifty pounds of ostrich at speeds of up to forty miles per hour. I stared down at her feet. They were thin and callused—almost human, but with two toes instead of five. One of the toes was huge, with what looked like a sharpened toenail. It reminded me of another thing I'd read in the materials: ostriches use their feet as weapons.

I took a wary step back, but it was quickly apparent that Tracy was no kick-boxer. She was delighted to see Maggie, and started rubbing up against her with her wings spread. Maggie gave her a hug around her neck, and Tracy pecked playfully at Maggie's shirt buttons. She took a step toward me, tilting her head to stare.

"Hi, Tracy," I said, smiling.

She lowered her head for a better look. Her huge dark eyes were framed by impossibly long lashes. As she studied me, there was a deep, booming roar off in the distance. Tracy quickly straightened and turned to look.

"What the hell was that?" Benny asked.

"Oh, good," Maggie said, shading her eyes as she stared at a pair of ostriches who were slowly circling each other about fifty yards away. "It's Hillary and Bill."

I burst into laughter. "Really?"

Maggie turned to me with a smile. "They're about to mate. You'll be able to see the way it's supposed to be done. We have Big Red on video."

"On video?" Benny asked.

Sara turned to him and nodded triumphantly. "It'll be Rachel's best trial exhibit. The jury will go crazy when they see it."

My God, I thought, trying to imagine how to present this bizarre case to a jury.

Another booming roar.

"Come on," Maggie said. "We can get a little closer."

As we approached, one of the ostriches—presumably Bill—seemed to kick his mating dance into high gear. Standing in front of Hillary, he began shimmying his shoulders like some massive go-go dancer on speed. He dropped to his hocks and fanned his wings rapidly. Another bellow, and then he scrambled back to his feet and started rocking forward as if he were *davening* in synagogue.

"This is foreplay?" Benny mumbled.

Apparently so. Hillary had been watching Bill impassively through the early phase of his fan dance, but now she was fluttering her own wings and batting her eyelashes. Suddenly she spun away from Bill and dropped to the ground, her head extended, her rump slightly raised. Bill moved in quickly.

I felt embarrassed watching, but Bill was oblivious, totally caught up in his act. Fifteen seconds, a grunt, and curtains. He stood, stretched his neck, and sauntered off without a look back.

Fifteen seconds, a grunt, and curtains, I thought with a rueful smile, feeling a stab of solidarity as I watched Hillary stagger to her feet in dust.

* * *

"Y OU see it?"

Despite myself, I smiled. "Yes, Benny, I saw it."

"Peculiar-looking, wasn't it?"

We were heading east on Highway 70, the sun setting behind us.

I looked over and shrugged. "To be honest, Benny, they're all kind of peculiar looking."

"But did you see those grooves? What's that all about? It looked like a goddamn NASA docking device."

"Probably the same design principle at work."

* * *

T HE following morning I read for the first time the petition in *Blackwell Breeders LLC and Charlie Blackwell v. Maggie Lane and Sara Freed.* Blackwell alleged that my clients "acquired sole custody and control of said ostrich at an especially sensitive stage in its development." He claimed that "if said ostrich has any alleged defect, then the proximate cause of said defect is the negligent animal husbandry procedures, general incompetence, and degenerate lifestyles of said defendants."

But the document saved its most unpleasant surprise for the signature block at the end, which read *MacReynold Armour, Attorney for Plaintiffs.*

"Oh, great," I groaned aloud.

Mack Armour, a.k.a. Mack the Knife, was the kind of litigator who made opponents consider career changes— that is, when they weren't considering ethics complaints and contract hits. Although I'd never faced him before, I knew his reputation. What he lacked in legal talent he more than made up in deceitfulness and sheer gall. Over the years, he'd bullied his way through hundreds of law-suits, building a lucrative practice with clients who be-lieved that the best lawyer was a belligerent lawyer. The book on him was to be patient and hang in there. Al-though he curried favor with the trial judges—drinking with them after hours, hunting and golfing with them on the weekends—the breaks they gave him in the courtroom rarely survived scrutiny on appeal. But the catch was that few lawyers, and even fewer clients, had the stomach or the wallet to endure Mack the Knife through a trial and an appeal. Most chose to settle.

That was obviously his strategy here. Blackwell Breed-ers should have been the defendant in the case, but Ar-mour jumped the starting gun and filed first, seeking a declaratory judgment that his client didn't have to refund a penny. As an added bargaining chip, he tacked on Char-lie Blackwell's ludicrous claim for mental anguish. His goal: scare off my clients.

They didn't scare easy.

"We're not backing down," Maggie told me over the phone after I'd described Mack the Knife.

"He'll drag your personal lives into it, Maggie. He'll try to turn the case into a freak show."

"We understand," she said calmly. "This is a matter of principle. Mr. Blackwell cheated us. He should have done the right thing on his own, but he refused, so now we'll ask a judge to make him do it. That's why we're going to court. We're not looking for sympathy, Rachel, and we're not looking for favors. We're looking for justice."

"You won't always find it in a courtroom."

"We know that. If we lose, we lose. We can deal with it. We're big girls."

*   *   *

"I'M here on the motion in *Blackwell Breeders*," I told Judge Hogan's clerk.

She paused in filing her nails and glanced down at the calendar. "You Rachel Gold?"

"I am."

"Knock on the door. The judge is ready."

"Has plaintiffs' counsel arrived?"

"Oh, yeah. He's in there already."

Of course, I said to myself, trying to control my irritation. Five months into the case, and this was the fourth time I'd found Mack the Knife already inside the judge's chambers when I arrived for a court appearance. I rapped on the door and opened it just as Armour was delivering what sounded like the punch line to a dirty joke.

". . . and don't ride your bike for a week."

Judge Hogan was seated behind his desk, leaning back in the chair, his arms crossed over his ample gut. He chuckled and leaned forward, waving me in. "That's a good one, Mack. Hello, counsel, come on in."

"Good morning, Your Honor."

Armour got up from his chair to face me, his eyes doing a quick body scan. "Miss Gold," he said, nodding curtly.

I returned the nod. "Mr. Armour."

Mack the Knife was a burly, athletic man in his late forties. He had a golf tan, a smooth shaved scalp, slate-gray eyes, and a neatly trimmed black mustache. In his khaki suit, crisp white shirt, and gleaming brown loafers, he reminded me of a cynical CIA operative in a Latin American capital. Judge Lamar Hogan, by contrast, was the jowly, heavy-lidded deer hunter from rural Missouri. Neither saint nor sinner, Judge Hogan was just another insurance defense lawyer in his late fifties who'd used Republican Party connections to get appointed to the bench. His demeanor was affable, his rulings unimaginative, and his workday short. He was rarely reversed on appeal because he was rarely bold at trial.

"This is your motion, Miss Gold?" Judge Hogan asked.

"It is, Your Honor."

"What's it seek?" he asked, paging through the file. As usual, Judge Hogan had read none of the motion papers and done nothing to prepare for the argument.

"As the court knows," I explained, "my clients seek a full refund on the male ostrich they purchased from Blackwell Breeders. They also seek compensation for injuries inflicted upon several of the hens. I'm here today asking the court to dismiss Mr. Blackwell's claim. He alleges that he suffers emotional distress from the thought of his ostrich residing on my clients' farm. Frankly, Your Honor, the claim is absurd on its face."

The judge turned to Armour. "Mack?"

Armour snorted. "Judge, my client sold those gals a normal, heterosexual stud cock—the kind of animal that's happiest when he's putting the lumber to some hen." He became solemn. "Except now he's stuck out there in Kinkyland with—"

"That's ridiculous," I snapped, immediately regretting my interruption, knowing Armour would take advantage of it.

"Your Honor," he said, pointedly ignoring me, "I'm simply attempting to answer the court's question. May I continue?"

"Please do."

He glanced at me. "Without further interruption?"

"Get on with it," I said through clenched teeth.

"These women," Armour said, shaking his head sternly, "concealed their inexperience and their incompetence and, even worse, their perverted lesbian lifestyle from my client at the time of the sale. Mr. Blackwell is overwhelmed by feelings of guilt and remorse over what he's done to that poor ostrich. When Miss Gold has the opportunity to look him in the eye, she will feel his pain."

"Your Honor, I've already looked Mr. Blackwell in the eye at his deposition. He could barely keep a straight face."

"Smiling through his tears," Armour answered. "The man is devastated. He's entitled to compensation."

"Your Honor," I said, trying to contain my anger, "the only reason Mr. Armour put that ludicrous claim in the lawsuit is to confuse and prejudice the jury. It should be dismissed for that reason alone. More important, the claim has no scientific basis."

Judge Hogan turned to him. "What about that, Mack?"

Armour smiled as he unclicked his briefcase. "She wants science, I'll give it to her in spades." He started pulling scientific journals out of his briefcase and piling them, one by one, onto the judge's desk. I skimmed the titles as they dropped onto the desk—*Journal of Animal Behavior, Field Studies in Evolutionary Biology, Animal Husbandry Quarterly, Zoological Record.*

When he completed his stack, Armour leaned back and triumphantly crossed his arms over his chest. "How's that for starters?"

"How's what?" I responded. "What are these?"

"Scientific studies of animal behavior. And there's plenty more where that came from."

I started to answer when the judge held up his hand. "You make some good points, Miss Gold, but I think we'd all agree this is a case of first impression. The safest route here is let the jury take a crack at it. We can clean up any miscues in the post-trial motions."

*   *   *

"LAST chance," Armour told me as we emerged from the courthouse. "Settle now or this trial's gonna put those gals on the cover of the *National Enquirer*."

"What's your proposal?" I responded frostily.

"Well," he said, scratching his mustache thoughtfully, "I might be willing to recommend a dog fall."

I stared at him. "You drop your claims and we drop ours? You call that a good-faith offer?"

"Not an offer yet. I said it's what I'd be willing to *recommend*."

"Forget it, Mack. Your offer is as ridiculous as your lawsuit."

"Suit yourself, counselor, but you're living in a fantasy world." He chuckled. "The only ridiculous thing here is someone who thinks a St. Louis jury is going to award one red cent to a pair of muff divers."

I stared at him as a bunch of possible responses flashed through my head—all at the playground level, none that good. Oh, where is Benny Goldberg when you need him?

*   *   *

"UNBELIEVABLE," Benny said, shaking his head as he sliced off another hunk of smoked ham. "What did you say to him?"

"Nothing. I just walked away."

"Nothing?" Benny took a big chug of beer. "Nothing?"

I shrugged. "What would you have said?"

"Easy," he said, putting down the bottle and stifling a belch, which rumbled ominously in his belly. He jabbed his finger at an imaginary Mack Armour. "I'd say, 'Watch your mouth, bullet-head, 'cause I got chunks of guys like you in my stool.' "

I smiled and shook my head. "Works better coming from you."

He gestured toward the cutting board. "You sure you don't want some more?"

I held up my hands. "I'm stuffed."

It was late afternoon. Benny had come by my office for a surprise happy hour. Though he had a hot dinner date in two hours, he'd stopped at his favorite Italian deli for a "light snack"—an entire smoked ham, a thick slab of cheese, a jar of pickled onions, an Italian bread, and a truly repulsive sausage composed of semi-identifiable animal parts suspended in a pink gelatinous goo.

"When's the trial?" he asked, pausing to take a bite out of a sausage, onion, and ham concoction he'd piled on a slice of bread.

"One week from Monday." I leaned back in my chair and sighed. "I just want it to be over, Benny. Armour's been a complete jerk—hid documents from me, lied to the judge, hired an investigator to harass two of Maggie's former lovers. I feel like I'm stuck in an endless backstreet brawl with that guy. Each day brings a new dirty trick. This morning he dumped a pile of scientific journals on the judge's desk, supposedly to support his contention that my clients' actions could have changed that ostrich's behavior."

"And?"

"There was nothing even remotely close in there." I shook my head in exasperation. "Just another sleazy stunt."

"You ready for trial?" he asked, chewing.

I sighed. "I'm still poking around. Blackwell's operation is near Crystal City. I hired an investigator down there. He found two possible witnesses—ex-employees of Blackwell."

"What do they know?"

"No idea." I frowned. "Neither of them would talk to him, but he told me both left Blackwell Breeders under hushed circumstances."

"Really? What happened?"

"Don't know. That's why I'm driving down there tomorrow."

*   *   *

THE first was Rudy Witherspoon, a gaunt man in his sixties with pendulous ears and a leathery, creased face. We met during his afternoon break at the Mc-Donald's near the Home Depot where he now worked. Three years ago, he'd been in charge of machinery maintenance for Blackwell Breeders.

Although he disliked Charlie Blackwell, I quickly realized that Witherspoon was worthless as a witness. First off, he'd left Blackwell Breeders before Big Red hatched. Moreover, his animosity stemmed solely from his belief that his former boss had cheated him out of $135 in a poker game one night after work.

"I stomped out to my pickup and sat there in the dark," he told me, pausing to rub an age-spotted hand back and forth across his chin. "I waited till his cousin Bob drove off, and then I grabbed me a length of pipe out of the back and busted in every damn window on the son-of-a-bitch's Eldorado. That was my last day working for Mr. Charlie."

And my last hope for him as a witness.

My expectations were only slightly higher for Milly Eversole. The good news was that Milly's three years at Blackwell Breeders included the fourteen-month period during which Big Red was reared and delivered to my clients. She'd quit about nine months ago and now worked as a bank teller. The bad news: she refused to talk about her years with Blackwell or her reasons for leaving. Only the threat of a deposition subpoena had persuaded her to give me fifteen minutes today.

I'd parked my car with a clear line of sight to her late-model Ford Escort, which was in the lot behind the bank. I'd brought a file of pretrial materials to work on while I waited for the bank to close, but I couldn't concentrate. I desperately wanted to win this case—for my clients, of course, and also because I despised the other side. Although the evidence—at least the relevant evidence—favored my clients, victory can be tricky to define in civil litigation. My clients had paid ten thousand dollars for Big Red. That was a lot of money to them, but chump change to Charlie Blackwell. He was the one with the deep pockets here, and he'd used them to fund Armour's scorched-earth tactics. As a result, my legal fees would exceed Big Red's price tag. A true victory meant finding a way to get my clients much more than just a refund. But try concentrating on that goal while fighting off ridiculous allegations about lifestyles and animal husbandry techniques. Suffice to say, I hadn't had a good night's sleep in weeks.

Employees began emerging from the building shortly after five. Although I'd never seen Milly Eversole, I recognized her the moment she stepped onto the parking lot, shading her eyes from the late-afternoon sunshine. She was a slender woman in her twenties with mousy brown hair and horn-rimmed glasses. Her outfit was bank-teller conservative: white blouse, navy skirt, navy flats. She moved across the lot in a hesitant manner. Pausing at her car door, she scanned the street. I started my car and revved the engine once. Our eyes briefly met, and then she glanced around, as if afraid someone were watching.

I followed her through town and onto Highway 55. We headed south, took the second exit, drove along country roads, and pulled into a small park overlooking the Mississippi River. Ours were the only two cars in the parking area. I joined her on a wood bench facing the water. Her hands were folded on her lap, her head bowed.

"Miss Eversole," I said softly, "I'm Rachel Gold. Thank you for agreeing to meet with me."

She nodded, still looking down at her hands.

"I represent two women," I told her. "They own an ostrich ranch. During the time you worked at Blackwell Breeders, they bought a male ostrich. You would have known him as Big Red."

She looked up at the sound of the name, and then she turned toward the river with a frown. I tried to gauge her mental state.

"You remember him?" I asked gently.

She nodded, still looking toward the river.

"Did you see any indication that he might have behavioral problems?"

"What kind of problems?"

"Was he overly aggressive? Violent?"

She hesitated, and then shrugged. "Maybe." She turned to me. "Why?"

"Let me tell you about the lawsuit."

As I described the case I could see her interest grow. By the time I finished she was staring at me raptly.

"What did Mr. Blackwell say?" she asked.

I shook my head. "He refused to refund their money, and then"—I paused—"he sued them."

She looked puzzled. "Why?"

"He claimed it was their fault."

"How?"

I glanced at the silver cross dangling from her necklace. "My clients are lesbians."

She squinted at me from behind her glasses. "So?"

"Charlie Blackwell blames their lifestyle, along with their inexperience in raising ostriches. He claims Big Red was perfectly normal when they took him. I know it sounds ridiculous, Milly, but he claims that at least part of the ostrich's problems results from exposure to my clients' sex life."

Her cheeks flushed with anger. "He said that?"

I nodded. "Even worse, he's suing *them* for damages. He claims he's suffering mental anguish over the thought of his ostrich living on their farm."

Milly stared at the ground. She was visibly upset, her breathing irregular. Her hands twisted and clenched in her lap. I waited.

She turned to me with a pained look. "He's a bad man."

I nodded. "He is."

"So's his lawyer."

"Mack Armour?"

"I hate them." There were tears in her eyes. "I hate them both."

"How do you know Mack Armour?" I asked softly, surprised and concerned.

She looked down at her hands. Her lips were quivering. I waited. A tear trickled down her cheek.

I reached over and placed my arm around her shoulder. "It's okay, Milly," I whispered, pulling her closer to me. "It's okay."

* * *

WE were in chambers—the final pause before opening statements. Jimmy, the judge's elderly bailiff, was standing by the door, waiting.

"Counsel," Judge Hogan said as he buttoned up his judicial robe, "Jimmy's about to bring in our jury. Sure there's no chance of getting this thing settled?"

I looked at Armour and shrugged. "Our demand hasn't changed, Mack. Give my clients their money back and we'll drop the other claims."

Armour chuckled. "That's a no-brainer. Let's raise the curtain and bring on the dancing dykes."

* * *

MACK Armour's opening statement was every bit as misleading and offensive as I expected. He roamed from New Testament quotes wrenched from context to an animal behavior "study" published in a supermarket tabloid. He ended with a jab at what he labeled the "feminazi cult of political correctness."

"What next?" he said, acting astounded. "Does the animal kingdom come flocking to our courts, one by one, seeking redress for their place in God's plan? Will the heirs of the male black widow sue Big Momma for wrongful death because she killed Daddy after they mated? Will the mare sue the stallion for assault for biting her on the neck during sex? And what about that poor praying mantis?" He paused, hand on his heart in mock sympathy. A few of the jurors were smiling. "As soon as he ejaculates the female bites off his head and eats it. Talk about bad sex. Gotta be a claim there, eh?

"Of course not," he said with a sneer. "We're all God's creatures. Each of us does what God designed us to do. It's called natural reproduction—a path, ironically enough, that Miss Gold's clients spurn in their own lives. If these two women are looking around for someone to blame, someone to hold accountable, then I suggest they look in a mirror." With a triumphant about-face, Mack Armour turned from the jury and gave me a wink as he returned to his seat.

"Miss Gold?" the judge said.

I stood and faced the jury. "Mr. Armour and I will agree on little during this trial," I started, aiming for a low-key tone, "but we do agree that Mother Nature has devised an amazing array of reproductive strategies. The black widow, the horse, the praying mantis, and, as you will soon learn, even the ostrich—each species performs the sexual act in a way that seems strange or even shocking to us. But what Mr. Armour ignores is that the end result of each of these mating rituals—*every single one of them*—is the creation of new life. Here, though, the end result was terror."

I paused, trying to read the jurors' facial expressions— about as helpful as trying to read tea leaves. At least they seemed to be listening.

"Here," I continued, "the end result was serious injury. And in one case, it was death. Not once did this ostrich engage in the mating dance of his species. Not once did this ostrich complete a sex act with any hen. Not once did this ostrich create new life."

I moved back to counsel's table and stood behind my clients, a hand resting on each one's shoulder. "These women," I said, "paid a lot of money for a breeding ostrich. Blackwell agreed to sell them a stud. Instead, he sold them a dud. And a lethal one at that. They're entitled to compensation."

I came around from behind the table and stopped in front of the jury. "Mr. Armour talks about God's creatures flocking to this courthouse with frivolous claims. As the evidence will demonstrate, only one of God's creatures tried that ploy here." I turned toward counsel's table and gestured at Charlie Blackwell. "He's sitting right there."

* * *

I cross-examined Charlie Blackwell late that afternoon. Armour had run him briskly through his paces in what was obviously—to me, at least, and hopefully to the jury—a well-rehearsed two hours of direct. As I got to my feet, I could see Blackwell hunker down for what he no doubt assumed would be a grueling, comprehensive, several-hour cross-examination. I had other plans.

"Good afternoon, Mr. Blackwell."

"Affer-noon, ma'am," he answered in his high-pitched nasal twang. *May-yam.*

Charlie Blackwell had spiffed himself up considerably since I'd taken his deposition a month ago. He had on a starched white cowboy shirt stretched tight against his belly, black Sansabelt slacks, a bolo tie, and black cowboy boots polished to a high sheen. His gray hair was slicked back, his face clean shaven, and his complexion ruddy.

"Let me make sure I understand your testimony, sir. You believe that the sexual practices of the humans who handle an ostrich during its formative years will affect its future behavior, correct?"

Eyeing me warily, Blackwell nodded. "Yes, ma'am. At least in part."

"And you believe that the formative years for a male ostrich are the first two years, correct?"

"Yes, ma'am."

"Even though they're basically full-grown after twelve months?"

"On the outside, yep. But they still got some growing to do on the inside. Your males are particularly sensitive, you see. They gotta be brung along careful or they'll go bad on you."

As he spoke, I moved along the jury box toward the back, resting my arm against the railing. Now he'd be forced to look at the jurors when he answered my next questions.

"Nevertheless, your company raised that ostrich for the first fourteen months, right?"

"Yes, ma'am."

"Getting back to the sexual practices of the human handlers. You claim that they'll influence the ostrich's behavior even if he doesn't witness them having sex?"

"I'm saying it's possible, yep."

"The ostrich just kind of senses it, eh?"

"You could say that, yep."

"But what if he actually witnessed them in the act?"

He chuckled. "That'd be even worse."

"Oh? And why is that?"

"To actually see an unnatural act, well, that could mess him up real bad. Matter of fact," he mused, his eyebrows raised, "I bet that happened here. Sure could explain a lot, yep."

Mack Armour snickered behind me.

"You say that could explain a lot?" I repeated.

"Yep." Blackwell was grinning. He glanced over at his attorney and then back at me. "Sure could."

"What if there was violence, too?" I asked.

"You mean during the act?"

"Yes."

He nodded. "Oh, boy, that'd make things even worse."

"Really?"

"Mess him up real bad, yep."

"Thank you, Mr. Blackstone. No further questions."

*   *   *

S ECOND day of trial.

"Call your next witness, Miss Gold."

I stood and took a deep breath. I'd been up until four in the morning preparing for this next encounter, trying to anticipate every possible scenario and my response. Armour was the wild card, of course. I glanced over at him. He leaned back, his arms folded over his chest. He was smirking. *It's show time, Rachel.* I turned toward the back of the courtroom and nodded to the bailiff, who opened the courtroom door.

"Defendants call Milly Eversole," I announced.

Armour jumped to his feet. "What the—objection!"

Millie entered the courtroom, escorted by Benny Goldberg. Coming in behind them was Ruthie Silverstein, looking severe as usual. Our eyes met as she came up the aisle. She snuck me a wink. I could have kissed her.

"This is ridiculous," Armour muttered. "May I approach, Your Honor?"

I joined him for the sidebar.

"What kind of carnival stunt is this?" Armour demanded, pausing to glare at Milly as she filed past, eyes averted, toward the witness stand.

I said, "Miss Eversole worked in the nursery at Blackwell Breeders from the time this ostrich hatched until my clients bought him. Based on my cross-examination of Mr. Blackwell yesterday, I believe her testimony is highly relevant."

"You're out of luck, lady," Armour said. "There's not going to be any testimony. That girl signed a confidentiality agreement. Her lips are sealed."

"Not according to her attorney," I said.

"Her attorney?" Armour turned to me, his eyes ablaze. "Who's that?"

I pointed. "There."

Armour turned toward Benny, who'd taken a seat in the front row. Benny winked and gave him a thumbs-up. Armour glowered at him for a moment, and then glanced at Ruthie, who'd taken a seat alongside Benny in the front row. Armour knew who she was. We all did. Ruthie had been a prosecutor in the sex crimes division for more than thirty years. Shrewd and relentless, she had the highest conviction rate in the office.

"What the hell is *she* doing here?" Armour demanded, gesturing toward Ruthie.

Ignoring his question, I turned to the judge. "Your Honor, may I proceed with the witness?"

"Hold it," Armour said. "Can we get the jury out of here and sort this out?"

Judge Hogan nodded wanly.

I turned toward Ruthie as the jury filed out. She and Benny and I had gone over this very possibility last night in my kitchen. I was ready for him and hoped they were, too.

As the door closed behind the final juror, Armour spun toward the judge. "That girl," he said, pointing at Milly, who flinched in the witness box, "is getting dragged down the primrose path by Miss Gold. Milly had an employment dispute with my client. My client settled with her. A very generous settlement, Judge. He gave her a five-grand severance payment with one condition: if she *ever* disclosed the terms of the settlement agreement to *anyone*, she'd have to refund the full amount *and* pay my client an additional five grand. Miss Gold's little grandstand play here is going to cost that girl a pretty penny."

"Hey, Curly," Benny interrupted, "Rachel isn't her lawyer. I am."

Armour spun toward him. "Really? Do you have any grasp of the financial impact of this on your client?"

Benny smiled. "I have a pretty good idea what it would take to settle it right now."

"Oh, is that so?" Armour said. "And what is it?"

"About a million from that redneck cretin over there, another two hundred grand from you."

"Have you lost your mind?" Armour asked.

"No," Benny answered, "but you may lose your license."

"Hey," Armour said, taking a menacing step toward Benny, "watch your mouth, buster, 'cause I got chunks of guys like you in my stool."

Benny glanced at me, a twinkle in his eye. He turned to Armour, feigning confusion. "Chunks of what in your stool?"

Armour thrust his chin forward. "Guys like you."

"Don't lose hope," Benny said, shaking his head sadly. "They may yet find a cure."

"For what?" Armour asked.

"For your eating disorder, you poor bastard."

"Hold on, gentlemen," Judge Hogan said, trying to recapture control of his courtroom. He turned toward Ruthie. "First things first. Ms. Silverstein, are you here on a matter?"

She stood. "I am."

"Let's take care of you first, then. Which matter?"

"This one."

"This case?" Judge Hogan looked puzzled. "Why?"

"At Rachel Gold's request, I interviewed Miss Eversole yesterday," she said, nodding toward Milly. "Based on that interview, there is probable cause for the perpetration of at least four felonies."

"Aw, shit," Charlie Blackwell groaned in the background.

"I don't understand," Judge Hogan said.

Ruthie started ticking them off on her fingers. "One count of forcible rape and one count of forcible sodomy. Both criminal acts perpetrated by Mr. Blackwell during working hours inside the nursery barn at Blackwell Breeding. Miss Eversole was the victim both times."

There was a long pause as Ruthie stood there with two fingers raised.

"Uh, you mentioned four," Judge Hogan finally said.

"Two counts of concealing an offense," Ruthie answered.

Judge Hogan frowned. "Pardon?"

"Section 575.020 of the Missouri criminal code makes it a felony to agree to confer a financial benefit on any person in consideration for that person's agreement to conceal a crime or to refrain from initiating the prosecution of a crime."

"Mr. Blackwell did that?" Judge Hogan asked.

"Actually," Ruthie said, turning toward Armour, "this man did. He not only worked out the financial details, prepared the papers, and had the victim sign them, but he also issued his own highly inflammatory threat."

In the hushed courtroom, Ruthie stared up at Armour like a butcher eyeing a steer.

*   *   *

"THAT'S why I ought to be a judge," Benny said. "Mack the Knife is the perfect example."

Benny and I were in a blues bar on Laclede's Landing. From our table you could see the Arch in the distance through the window.

Almost two weeks had elapsed since the abrupt end of the ostrich trial. As so often happens, the threat of criminal prosecution forced a quick resolution of the civil case. Charlie Blackwell surrendered that afternoon in the judge's chambers. With Ruthie standing behind me and glaring down at Blackwell, the judge wrote out the terms of the agreed settlement order: my clients would receive a full refund of their money (with interest), an additional $25,000 in compensation for injuries to the other ostriches, and payment of all of their legal expenses. A week later, Blackwell agreed to a plea bargain on the criminal charges. That deal included time in a minimum-security prison, $250,000 in restitution to Milly Eversole, and an agreement to cooperate in the prosecution of Mack the Knife, who'd already retained a team of defense attorneys for the criminal case and the disbarment proceedings.

Maggie and Sara threw a celebration party at their ranch that Saturday night. Millie drove up from Crystal City with her mom and her sister. Benny arrived with one arm around a St. Louis Rams cheerleader (don't ask) and the other around a big bucket of barbecued snoots. We told stories and sang songs and drank several toasts to the ostriches, who looked on curiously. Much later in the evening Benny somehow coaxed all of us, including Hillary and Bill, to sample the snoots. They're not bad.

"You should be a judge?" I said to Benny, bemused. "Why?"

"Creative sentencing. Make the punishment fit the crime. That'd be my mantra."

"Enlighten me, O learned judge. What sort of punishment would fit Mack's crime?"

"That's easy. Book the weekend special at the Honeymoon Hotel. Strip him naked, spray him with ostrich musk, and lock him inside with Big Red. Talk about your rehabilitation—damn, by the time you open that door on Monday morning you'll have either a compassionate, New Age attorney ready to champion the rights of women or . . ."

"Or what?"

Benny winked. ". . . or Big Red's favorite boy toy."

Mortmain

Claire Youmans

The author of Rough Justice, *Youmans lives on a forty-three-foot sailboat when she's not practicing law in Seattle. Appropriately enough, she is also the author of* How to Live Aboard and Like It.

THE night Serafina died, I took my children—Rags, thirteen, and Alec, eight—and our au pair, Cherry, to Carlo's Italian Restaurant in Seattle's Pioneer Square for dinner. It had been a favorite of ours long before I met Serafina Baldi shortly after Carlo's tragic death in a railroad crossing accident some years before. I handled the wrongful death action for Serafina and she became a friend.

Serafina was the epitome of an Italian matriarch, exercising complete control over her family. It surprised me when she turned over the restaurant to Carl, her son, and gave an equivalent amount to her daughter, the concert pianist and rising composer, Carolina. Amy Centioli, Carl's wife, took over as executive chef, and the business prospered and grew. Carl, a jovial, unambitious man, would have been happy riding his father's coattails.

A few months ago, Serafina had a stroke. When Serafina wanted to review her estate plan, I referred her to the lawyer who handled my husband's estate.

"Sandy Whitacre!" Carl said, a grin spreading across his patrician features as he extended a powerful hand to clasp mine.

"Nice to see you, Carl," I said, introducing him to Cherry.

"How's your mother?" I asked him, after he'd greeted the children.

Dejection emanated from every inch of his stocky frame. "Not well," he said, shrugging. "You've visited her. Now the doctors say it's only a matter of time."

"I'm so sorry to hear that." I decided to visit Serafina again soon.

"Thanks," Carl said, then added, "You know Carolina's come home to stay?"

I was surprised to hear that his sister had gone off the concert circuit and said so.

"It's an Italian thing," Carl said. "We take care of our own. Amy's there now and I'm going at nine." He shook himself and became a gracious host once more. "We have a wonderful new pastry chef," he told Cherry and the kids. "You'd never know she's actually—" he leaned down and whispered "I—Irish. Moira O'Connell's her name. But don't tell anybody." I grinned. I was sure he was telling every customer he spoke to exactly the same thing, so it wouldn't be a secret for long. He said he'd send out one of her specialties for us—his treat. We thanked him; then Carl went off to greet other customers.

So I was thinking of Serafina that night, and of Carl and Amy, and of Carolina, a dark exotic beauty, both talented and spoiled. I knew she loved Serafina, but did she really want to be home, or was she just there out of duty?

*   *   *

EARLY riser Cherry took the call.

"Mrs. Whitacre?" Cherry can't seem to get her

mouth around *Ms.*, much to the children's amusement. "Phone for you. It's a Mrs. Baldi. She says it's important."

Serafina? I thought as I said, "Okay, got it," grabbed the phone, and noted it was just before seven o'clock.

"Sandy Whitacre," I said.

"Sandy, it's Carolina Baldi." Right. No *Ms.* from Cherry. "I have bad news. Mother's passed away."

I sat up and shook my short red hair out of my eyes. "I'm so sorry," I said. "When did this happen?"

"Just now," Carolina said. "We just found her this morning. Sandy, the police are coming. Can you come over?"

"Why the police?" I said. Cherry tapped on the door and came in with coffee. She put it on the bedside table. I mouthed heartfelt thanks.

"Oh, Sandy, it looks like she committed suicide." Carolina's rich voice choked with tears.

"Suicide? Serafina?" Devout Catholics don't commit suicide, I knew. It's a mortal sin; sends you right to hell. The hope of a last-second repentance is often held out to the survivors as a kindness, as is the concept of "unsound mind."

"It looks like she took pills and put a plastic bag over her head."

"Carolina, I'm so very sorry," I told her. How could Serafina, paralyzed except for some limited movement in her upper body and arms, have managed the plastic bag trick? "You want me to come?"

"Yes. We need somebody to tell us what's going on."

"Half an hour," I said. "Don't talk to the police until I get there."

We hung up. Quickly, I showered and pulled on a navy blue suit. The matching heels bring me up to about five foot two. My hair fluffs into place and I rarely wear makeup, so I was pulling Hal's Mercedes 560 SL convertible, now mine, into the Baldi driveway on Capitol Hill by seven thirty-two.

Carl looked grim when he let me in.

The original house was enormous and old. Carl and Amy lived in a modern house Serafina had built for them on the other side of her property. Carl led me into the morning room, where Amy and Carolina waited. We exchanged somber greetings.

"Mrs. Rogers, the housekeeper, found Mother this morning," Carolina said. "She gets—got—Mother up in the morning. She came for me. I called nine-one-one."

"And they've gone?"

"Yes," Amy said. "They say the—the body can't be moved until the police get here." Tears left ugly red splotches on Amy's pale skin. Her blond hair was disarrayed.

"The police need to see the scene, and the medical examiner needs to look at the body," I explained.

"An autopsy?" Carl was outraged. "They want an autopsy?"

"Probably. It's an unexplained death, you see. It's required."

"But . . . it's horrible," Carl went on.

"Don't think about it," Amy interrupted sharply.

"Serafina's gone," I said gently. "To join your father in heaven, I'm sure. What's left is simply dust."

" 'Ashes to ashes, dust to dust,' " Carolina's beautiful voice resonated with the quote. She swung her long dark hair forward to hide her face.

Monica Rogers, the housekeeper, came in with a coffee tray just as the doorbell rang. She, too, had been crying. She set the tray down and went to answer the door, returning with a tall fair man, mid-forties, well built, but softening slightly around the middle.

"This is Detective Tremaine," Mrs. Rogers announced.

Carl performed introductions. At first, the interview elicited only what I already knew. Then Tremaine asked about money.

"We all have good careers," Carl said. "Plus, after my

father died, Mother gave me the restaurant—Carlo's in Pioneer Square?" Tremaine obviously knew it. Carl continued, "She also gave my sister seed money for a music festival and retreat she wants to build. The money's split between us but we don't need it."

Uh-oh. I'd better speak up. "Carl, you must not know that Serafina redid her estate plan after her stroke."

"None of us did," Carolina said, leaning forward, obviously—and naturally—interested.

"I'd better tell you." Serafina's motives in changing her will, I had thought disapprovingly, had to do more with *mortmain*—the "dead hand" controlling from beyond the grave—than the expected tax savings. I nonetheless began, "To save taxes, after a few cash bequests—like to the Rogerses—everything goes into a trust. The trustee uses an objective standard to make distributions. At your deaths," I gestured to Carl and Carolina, "the balance is divided equally among your children."

Carl had been getting redder and redder in the face as I spoke. As soon as I finished, he blurted, "Exactly what the hell does—"

Carolina exploded, leaping to her feet. "How dare she? She's been after me to produce grandchildren *forever,* and then when she hauls me home to take care of her so I haven't a prayer of actually doing it, she leaves her money to children she's made sure I'll never have! Damn her!" Carolina stalked over to the long window, pain and indignation vibrating from her.

"What is this 'objective standard' stuff?" Carl asked, returning to his point as if his sister's outburst hadn't happened.

"We're expanding the business," Amy told me. "I want Carl to add another vineyard, a big one, and start marketing the wines commercially." The Baldi Family private-label wines were sold only in the restaurant. Carl was an excellent winemaker. "And there's the grocery store line, too," Amy went on. "Sauces, pastas, calzones, and pizzas, for the deli sections."

I saw Tremaine watching, interested and amused.

I could guess what was coming.

"The bank won't loan us enough to do both projects at once." Carl elaborated. "Amy figures we'd do better faster if we did the wine and the food at the same time. We wanted Mom to lend us some of the money, or at least guarantee it for us."

"You never told me that," Carolina said from the window, her back still turned.

"Never came up." Carl shrugged.

"Right," Carolina replied with dripping sarcasm.

"Can we borrow from this trust? Can it be our guarantor?" Amy asked.

"This isn't the time or place to discuss that," I said. They weren't my clients—Serafina's estate was—but I had been asked to help. I balanced an ethical tightrope. "I'm sure Detective Tremaine doesn't need to hear this."

"One last thing," Carolina said, turning from the window and returning to her seat. "Who's the trustee?"

"I am."

"Did you draft the will, Ms. Whitacre?" Tremaine asked.

"No. Lauren Bigler did. Mrs. Baldi asked me to be her executrix and trustee. Here." I wrote Bigler's name and phone number on the back of a business card and passed it to the detective. He asked about Serafina's state of mind, suicidal ideation, and relationships, then informed the family that there would be a routine investigation and autopsy. He went off to the kitchen to talk to Mrs. Rogers, who had found the body.

"Why you?" Carolina asked as soon as the detective left. "I don't mean to be rude, but she had us."

"Sometimes people don't want to burden their children. When a professional handles the business side, the family is free to deal with real life." I'd said this a hundred times.

What Serafina had actually said was, "If I put one in charge, the other would hate and resent it. If I put them both in charge, they'd just fight. Carl's conservative and Carolina's headstrong. You know what she wants now? She wants me to finance that festival thing for next summer! You haven't earned it, I told her. When you can get some outside financing, we can talk. But Carolina—" Serafina shook her head, smiled indulgently and patted my hand in a characteristic gesture—"she wants everything yesterday."

The next thing I told them was how to set up funeral arrangements and explained the access I'd need to Serafina's papers. "You tend to yourselves and your loss," I finished, "and let me worry about the business. That's what I'm for." I ended with the customary disclaimer, describing my current role and advising them that they could get personal attorneys.

"But our *house*." Amy Centioli's voice shook. I handed her coffee, with milk and real sugar.

"Drink this," I said.

"The title is in Serafina's name." Amy ignored the coffee. Some color returned to her pale face, but that wasn't good. "She *built* it for us," Amy wailed, "but it's not ours. I was sure . . ."

"Don't worry about that, Amy." My mind raced over possible scenarios that would allow Carl's family to keep its home without penalizing Carolina. *Serafina, dammit, you could at least have left them their house,* I thought. Instead, where Carl and Amy would live had become my problem. "Something can be worked out."

Carl scootched over beside his wife and put his arm around her. "Amy designed our house," Carl said. "We can't lose it. It's our *home*."

I reassured them. "I'm certain something can be worked out. Now I'd better go see Detective Tremaine." I issued the standard warnings about the police and left to find Tremaine.

I found him at the kitchen table, sharing a plate of biscuits with Lou Rogers, the groundskeeper, and the housekeeper's husband. My stomach growled. Mrs. Rogers sat me down with a fresh cup of coffee and a biscuit, hot, split, and buttered with jam, on a plate before me. I dug in, listening to Tremaine.

"She left you something in her will, Mrs. Baldi did," he said with a sidelong glance at me.

"She did? Both of us?" Mr. Rogers said unbelievingly.

"Ask counsel, here," Tremaine said, indicating me.

"Each of you," I said around biscuit smothered by superb homemade plum jam. "You each get fifty thousand dollars."

"I don't believe it," Lou Rogers whispered.

"He didn't know," Monica Rogers said. "But I did. Mrs. Baldi said she wanted us to have something to go on with. It's separate because that's how I wanted it. My first husband gambled us into bankruptcy. I manage the money now, and I won't tolerate debt, but I want money that's mine, not ours. Mrs. Baldi completely agreed."

I almost laughed. Serafina had kept every cent of the family money under her iron control. Naturally, she'd agreed!

"How was Mrs. Baldi recently?" I asked.

Mrs. Rogers frowned. "She's better off now, sad to say. She seemed to be bearing up well enough, but it was a trial for her. Nothing had changed since the last time you saw her. She needed total care, and she hated it, even from me. Knowing she was only going to get worse must have been the last straw for her."

"You think she wanted to die?" Tremaine asked.

"Of course. Wouldn't you? Having to have someone feed you, bathe you, clean up your excrement? Everybody dies sometime. Why prolong suffering when there's nothing to look forward to?"

"You're not Catholic, Mrs. Rogers?"

"Not me. Those people are crazy, keeping old people

and sick people alive and suffering. They'll do more for a pet than they will for a person."

I disagreed. I felt a gut-level repugnance at the idea of ending any life deliberately. I see life as a process, with a purpose behind it, though I'm not quite sure what it is. If one cuts the process short, for any reason, doesn't one also short-circuit the plan? How can we predict the consequences of that? *Oh, Serafina,* I thought, allowing myself a moment of the feeling my professional self had to suppress as the tragedy of her terrible choice washed over me, *how horrid it must have been for you!*

"I better get upstairs," Tremaine said, stuffing the last of a biscuit into his mouth. "I might come talk to you later." The Rogerses nodded assent.

"I'd like to see the body," I said, rising. "Serafina was a friend of mine," I added by way of dubious explanation.

Tremaine looked like he was about to say no, but then cocked his head to one side and reconsidered.

"I know who you are," he said suddenly. "You were married to that treasury agent—Bailey, Harold Bailey, right?"

I nodded. I'd just as soon not be recognized as the avenging widow of the murdered treasury agent. It's embarrassing.

"Not much bothers you, I guess," he said. "Come ahead."

Tremaine was wrong about things not bothering me, but as a lawyer, and especially as a woman lawyer, I'd learned to keep my feelings and reactions hidden until I had a chance to do them justice privately.

Upstairs, the medical examiner, a young African-American woman in white coveralls, led us to the body.

"There are some apparent anomalies here," she said, pointing.

The plastic bag was a grocery store produce bag. The rubber band was a giant red one, like you find on the Sunday paper. It had left a mark on Serafina's neck. Serafina's face was peaceful in death, as dead faces almost always are. Her body seemed to have shrunk, a visible sign that life in leaving the body takes with it the weighty substance of the soul. Her luxurious white hair looked incongruously vibrant.

I almost cried. Serafina looked so fragile, so helpless, so gone. I reached out to touch her dead hand, as she had so often touched mine. I snatched it back a split second before the ME could reprimand me.

"Everybody says there were only three capsules left in this bottle," the medical examiner told Tremaine. "The pharmacy had another ready to deliver today. There isn't another bottle anywhere in the house. They only give out a month's supply at a time. She couldn't hoard them."

"Three would have put her out," Tremaine said.

"Two would have knocked her cold. But then she'd die of asphyxiation, as she did," the ME said. "This method is for people who want to go out from the pills. They hear it's easy that way, though it isn't always. People know asphyxiation's hard. The body fights it. Your hands might rip that bag right off, conscious or not."

"Not necessarily," Tremaine said.

"You wouldn't want to take that chance," the ME retorted. "She'd wait another day for a full bottle of pills."

A scientist examined the plastic bag. "Look here."

Tremaine and I did.

"These are cotton fibers, consistent with the gloves on the night table."

I glanced over and spotted the kind of gloves you sleep in, after rubbing in cream. Serafina's hands were bare.

"Find all the gloves so I can make an exact match. What you'd do," the ME explained, "is put the bag on just before you passed out. You wouldn't be able to take off your gloves after that."

I said, "Detective, Mrs. Baldi was paralyzed except for limited use of her upper body. Her right hand was pretty good. She might just have managed the bag, but I don't think she could have gotten the gloves on or off."

Tremaine nodded, issued instructions to the assorted crime scene personnel, and told the ME she could move the body. I followed him into the hall.

"You know what this means, don't you?" Tremaine said. I slapped on my court face and waited for him to say it.

"This death," he said, "is a probable homicide."

*   *   *

FIRST, I told the family. Then I put Mark Carlisle, one of the city's best criminal defense lawyers, on call. I passed on what Mark said, then started on the probate by making an appointment with Lauren Bigler, who had drafted the will and who would be attorney for the estate, with me as executrix.

"Hot damn," she said. I walked into her office as she hung up the phone. She smiled radiantly and tossed her long salt-and-pepper hair. "I just settled with the IRS on Louis Rogers. You don't have any problem with advancing him enough to pay them off, do you?"

"Lou Rogers? Serafina's groundskeeper?" I sat down.

"The very same," Lauren told me. "Amy Centioli sent him to a CPA who sent him to me. This was a while ago. I worked out a payment plan once the back tax returns were filed. Now that he's coming into some money, I made them an offer and they jumped at it."

"Glad to hear it." I remembered what Monica Rogers had said about debt. "Does his wife know about this?"

"Not on a bet." Lauren scrawled a note on a yellow pad, tore the sheet off and tucked it into the file. "She'd kill him if she found out he let his taxes go. When they got married, he had to come clean because they'd be filing joint returns. It's been a real job making sure she doesn't find out." She gave me a look. Now Lauren walked an ethical fence. I wouldn't push her off if I could help it.

"How's he going to explain to her why he doesn't have the whole amount of the legacy?"

She grimaced. "I've been telling him he'll have to let her in on it eventually. Now that it's all taken care of, she can't get too pissed."

"Hmmm," I said, wondering where Lou Rogers had found the money to make the payments without Monica's knowledge as Lauren pulled out the estate file.

Later, I went up to the Baldi house to sort Serafina's papers. Carolina drifted in while I was trying to figure out which bank accounts were still current. She said hello, then wandered over to the window. I looked after her. Carl and Lou Rogers were standing not far from the house, under a tree. Carl passed something to Lou.

"Carl's a fool," Carolina spat. "He's paying Rogers off, I don't know why. Ever since I've been here, I've noticed it. It's not salary. The paychecks are on automatic deposit."

"Why would Carl pay anybody off?"

"Carl doesn't tell me anything." Carolina came over to the desk where I was working.

"Sandy," she said, taking a deep breath, "I've made a decision. Since you're the trustee, you should be the first—no, the second," she said, "to know. I'm going on tour with my new music. I'm also going to get pregnant. The Desert Music Festival will begin as soon as I'm too pregnant to tour."

"I thought you needed money to start the festival."

"I thought I did, too. What I realized is that I don't need to be married to have a child, and I don't need to be rich to start the festival. I have a friend—he's gay—who wants a child, too. We can do the festival together, be parents together, raise this child together, and if either of us meets someone, it won't be a problem."

"Is he a musician, too?"

"Voila. We'll be partners. He has some money; so do

I. We'll have to start small, and it's going to take time, but I am going to do this."

"What brought this about?" This was a big change from the Carolina Baldi I knew. It sounded like an improvement, even though she seemed to have forgotten the murder investigation.

"Mother." Carolina fell into one of the leather chairs flanking the oak desk. "Everything. You can't buy loyalty. You can buy care, but not love. Mother didn't think she had much to live for, but even now she's still giving. This is what she wanted me to do. To think and act for myself. The money just doesn't matter anymore." She rose, gave me a sweet, Madonna-like smile, and floated off. *Where did that come from?* I wondered as I went back to work.

After I finished, I went to find Louis Rogers.

He was working on a riding mower in a shop attached to the garage. He jumped up when I marched in.

"Why is Carl Baldi paying you off?" I demanded.

"Who? No . . ."

"I've got a witness who says he is. Are you using it to pay off the IRS?"

"How did you find out about that?" The man looked terrified. It could have been funny, him so large and me so small, but force of personality goes a long way. He was ready to crack.

"How did you expect to get an advance from Mrs. Baldi's estate to pay them off without me knowing about it? C'mon, Lou. It's either me or your wife."

"God, don't tell Monica. She *hates* debt, wants to pay our bills before they're due. She scrimps and saves until I bet she's about as rich as Mrs. Baldi. She says it's for that inn she wants to open, but it's really because she's scared of being poor again. I love her," he said, pleading. "I don't want to lose her."

"Why is Carl giving you money?" I was implacable. His defenses visibly collapsed.

"He has a girlfriend. I caught them outside the restaurant one night, necking in the alley. If Ms. Centioli finds out, she'll leave him for sure, and then he loses his executive chef, and you know what a reputation she's got. But he can't give up Moira, either."

The pastry chef? I confirmed it. Was Carl out of his mind? Amy was a shining star in Seattle's firmament of chefs, and Carlo's was her culinary turf. Amy would fight tooth and nail for her home and her career. She'd lose the house since they didn't own it, but with a good divorce lawyer, she could wind up owning Carlo's. Was Carl simply hormone-crazed or was he sure enough of his mother's imminent death, which he thought would bring him enough money to buy Amy off, to jump the gun by bringing his sweetie right into the restaurant?

"You're going to have to tell your wife about the IRS."

He hung his head. "I know. I don't know what she's going to do." He looked up, hangdog. "What are *you* going to do?"

The man was practically trembling. I wondered at the ability of his wife to inspire this level of devotion—or fear.

"Nothing, now. You'll have to tell the police what you know. And stop putting the bite on Carl. If I look too closely, I might see extortion." I left.

Carolina might have planned her pregnancy and tour long ago, only to be derailed by Serafina's illness. Her revelations might be a way of claiming her goal. Ignoring the murder investigation didn't make her seem too tightly wrapped, and many killers come apart after the fact. Carl might have needed money to pay off Amy so he could marry his pastry chef. Amy clearly wanted to expand the business and didn't have a clue about Moira. Lou Rogers would stoop to damned near anything to keep his Monica. Monica Rogers herself could be a typical "mercy killer," not incidentally picking up a tidy bundle to add to her monetary security blanket.

I called Tremaine and offered to buy him a drink. He

chose a small, elegant bar in Madison Park, an expensive residential area on the shores of Lake Washington. He ordered a glass of merlot. I joined him.

After repeating that I was not attorney for the family, and as executrix deserved his cooperation, I passed on Carolina's revelations.

"It could be a legitimate change of heart," he offered.

"Or the fulfillment of her real plan. She was the only other person sleeping in the house. Were there signs of forced entry?"

"No. But Mrs. Rogers found the back door unlocked in the morning. That's not unusual. There's a perimeter alarm around the whole place, but the houses aren't wired, and they all go back and forth."

"She could have unlocked it herself. You heard her in the kitchen. She knew she'd get a chunk of money. She could tell herself it was a mercy killing. They often do."

"She and Lou swear they walked home together after Mrs. Baldi was settled and were together until six-thirty the following morning. By that time, Mrs. Baldi was long dead."

"Speaking of husbands and wives?"

"Carl and Amy walked home together, too, and were together until Carolina woke them."

"Carolina?"

"Went to bed and went to sleep, until Mrs. Rogers woke her."

"Nobody has an alibi that's worth a damn," I said. "You're certain now it was homicide?"

"Absolutely. The fibers are from a pair of cotton gloves found in the laundry room, near the back door. Also, the ME says the asphyxiation was quick, quicker than the bag would account for. She thinks the other pillow on the bed was pressed down over the bag."

I hated to think about it, couldn't think about it, had to think about it. Whose hands pressed that pillow down?

"What happened the night before?" I asked.

"Amy Centioli went home at six. The nanny was off. She fed the kids, got them settled, and went over to visit Serafina. Carolina came in about nine. They visited until ten-thirty. Mrs. Rogers made cocoa for everyone at ten; her husband brought it up. Mrs. Baldi's cup was a special one with a straw. The Rogerses left then, through the back door. She thinks he locked it. Ms. Centioli and Ms. Baldi both remember one sleeping pill in a paper cup by the bed, which Mrs. Baldi took. Neither of them looked in the bottle, which was on the bedside table as usual."

"That's how you found it, right?"

"Yes. The paper cup was in the wastebasket. Carl came in when Mrs. Baldi was settled to say good-night. Carolina went to her room and the other two left, together, through the side door, which is the way they usually go. Ms. Centioli took the cocoa tray to the kitchen while Mr. Baldi locked the side door. It was still locked in the morning. The alarm was on, according to both Ms. Baldi and Mr. Rogers. He sets it when he goes to bed; whoever is up first turns it off. They all have electronic bypass keys for the gates. All keys are accounted for."

My mind caught something he'd said earlier. All at once, I could see the shadowy figure pulling on the white gloves, sliding the bag over Serafina's sleeping head, fastening the red rubber band around her neck. I could see the pillow pressing down, Serafina's body jerking involuntarily until, at last, all movement ceased. I could see the figure taking a fresh pair of gloves from the drawer and tossing them artlessly on the night table. Throwing the second pair into the laundry. I thought I knew who it was, who it had to be. I told Tremaine.

"There's no proof. There's not even enough for a warrant," he objected.

"I might be able to get that far," I said. "With your help."

Two days later, we both attended Serafina Baldi's funeral. It was a mark of Serafina's stature in the community that the gigantic sanctuary of St. James' Cathedral didn't dwarf the crowd. I let the Mass of the Resurrection wash over me. I needed an almost meditative state for what I was about to do. For what I had to do.

Naturally, the huge house was packed with sympathizers. The restaurant catered and served food, cases of Baldi Family wines were broached, and the talk, in English and Italian, looked as if it would go on well into the night. Kent—Tremaine and I had graduated to Sandy and Kent— kept me company in a corner from which we watched the proceedings and talked to passers-by. Finally, I checked my watch. "Excuse us, please. We have some legal business to discuss." I stood up, and collected my briefcase "I'll be in the library," I told Kent.

Kent got Carl, Amy, Carolina, and the Rogerses into the room and settled. I sat behind the desk and, with solemn legality, read the will.

"Anyone who commits a crime can't legally profit from it," I said when I'd finished. "That's why we must find the person responsible for Serafina's death. You wanted me to read the will; you know it's not a formal necessity. I agreed because I want to find out who killed Serafina."

"Mother killed herself, Sandy, you know that," Carolina said. So that was how she was avoiding murder.

"Not true, Carolina. Someone, someone in this room, deliberately smothered your mother."

Kent nodded even as Carl barked, "Someone climbed a tree and jumped over the wall. That wouldn't set off the alarm. She woke up when he was searching her room; he panicked and smothered her. Then he tried to make it look like suicide, and was so scared he left without taking anything."

"Won't wash, Carl. Forensics show the pillow was on top of the bag, not the other way around."

Carolina looked shaken; Carl wary. Amy was impassive, except for her hands, tightly clenched in her lap.

Monica Rogers looked righteous. Her husband looked scared.

"We now believe this is what happened." I related my nightmare vision of the shadowy white-gloved figure. "But whose hands? You all had motives."

"I loved my mother," Carolina shot back.

"You resented her for calling you home. That cut off your life. You say you didn't know about the will, but that doesn't matter. You did know you were trapped, indefinitely, while your biological clock kept ticking and your ambitions faded away. With Serafina dead, you could go ahead with everything you planned—a child out of wedlock with a gay father—Serafina would have loved that—and your music festival. You figured you could talk me out of money, more than Serafina would have given you, especially once you had a bastard child on the way."

"That's not true!" Carolina leapt to her feet in outrage.

"Who put Serafina's evening pills into that paper cup that night?"

"Mrs. Rogers, I assume," she said, puzzled.

"Yes, it was me," Monica Rogers said. "I always put the pills out at seven. Ms. Centioli was right there."

"And you made the cocoa?"

"I made it for everyone. Lou and I had some."

"How did you serve it?"

"How did I—in the silver chocolate pot. I put the cups around it on the tray with a plate of cookies."

"Was Mrs. Baldi's special cup full or empty?"

"Empty."

"Did you look in it? Wash it?"

"I didn't have to. I took it right out of the dishwasher."

"You were in charge of Mrs. Baldi's medications. You prepared the cocoa. Your husband says you were with him all night, but you could have gone out while he slept. You have a key to every door in the place."

"So does everybody else," she said, holding her ground.

"You won't be poor again. You save every penny. You want to start an inn. You knew you were getting capital from Mrs. Baldi. And you believe in mercy killing."

"I do not believe in murder."

I was getting nowhere. She was too hard a target. Time to switch. Carolina helped me out.

"What about him?" She pointed at Louis Rogers. "He carried the cocoa upstairs. If he wouldn't have known his wife had gone out during the night, she wouldn't know if *he* had. He needed money, too. I know you were bleeding Carl. What about that?"

"I was going to tell you, Monica." Lou Rogers extended his hands, beseeching his wife. "I didn't know how. A long time ago, I didn't pay my taxes. I knew I had to fix it when we got married. The accountant and lawyer got the total down, but it was still a lot of money. I didn't have any way to pay it without you finding out. Mr. Baldi helped me."

"And you could have slipped the extra drugs into the cup on the way up the stairs," Carolina said triumphantly. "Amy would never have noticed when she opened the cup to pour."

"Carl." I took command. "What was Lou blackmailing you about?" He balked. "I know what it was," I went on, "and so does he. You better come out with it."

"I never thought it would come to this," he said, glancing at Amy. "All I did was fall in love." Amy's eyes widened and her mouth dropped open. Her facial muscles began to work. "I know Amy. She loves the house, loves her work. She's a lot more ambitious than I am. If she left me, she'd take everything I owned unless I had enough money to pay her enough to open her own place, start her own deli line. How was I going to get that kind of money? But Moira . . ."

"You son-of-a-bitch!" Amy cried, lunging for him. "I did it for you, you bastard. So, we could have *our* future. You bastard," she cried, dissolving into tears and collapsing onto the floor as Carl watched, horrified. "I did it for you."

"Shut up, Amy." I strode across the room, pulled her to her feet and shoved her back into her chair. "Not another word until Mark Carlisle gets here." Monica Rogers, ever efficient, went to find him. He must have been lurking; they were back in seconds. Mark gave me a dirty look before switching his gaze to Carl.

"It's Amy," Carl said, looking exhausted and sounding defeated. "Amy did it."

"I want time alone with my client," Carlisle said, moving into position next to her.

"She could have done it," Carl said as though hypnotized. "I slept like a rock that night, like I'd been drugged. Maybe I was," he added, sounding surprised. "I woke up once. Wanted the bathroom. But Amy was in the shower, so I went back to sleep. But you weren't in the shower, were you? The door was closed and the water was running, but you were gone, weren't you? Weren't you, Amy?"

She hissed at him, but Mark's hand on her shoulder forestalled further reply.

Kent Tremaine said, "Amy Centioli, you are under arrest for the murder of Serafina Baldi. You have the right . . ."

LATER, after the guests were all gone, Amy had been taken away and a badly shaken Carl had brushed off his Moira and gone home to talk to his children. Carolina poured us both brandy and sat down in front of the library fire with me.

"How did this happen?" she asked. "How did you know?"

"Amy and Carl approached Serafina about money for the expansion." I said. "Serafina said no. Carl was stuck with Amy unless he could afford to buy her off. Amy's

the ambitious one. She's the one who made Carlo's even
more successful than it was when Carlo was alive. She
pushed Carl into winemaking. Carl was happy with the
restaurant the way it was. He just doesn't have her kind
of ambition.

"You all had motives. You all had opportunity. In the
end, it came down to character. Who had the drive, the
guts, the ambition, the thwarted dream?"

"Why not me?" Carolina wanted to know.

"Not your style. If what you want isn't forthcoming,
you try to talk or sulk your way into it. That's been your
strategy, and it's always worked. That first day, when you
blew up, you showed the way your mind works. But
you're smart. You figured out another way to get what
you want. That's what Serafina wanted you to do. She
might not have liked the details, but she would have respected you for coming up with a solution."

Carolina nodded. "What about the Rogerses?"

"He had things set up perfectly. He had an agreement
to pay his back taxes, with Carl making the payments. He
didn't want things to change. Serafina's death screwed
him up. As for her, belief in suicide or even voluntary
euthanasia isn't the same as doing it. She has strong moral
fiber, and she's no gambler. Murder is always a gamble."

"What was going on in Amy's mind? How could she
actually do it?"

"She's the flip side of Monica Rogers. She told herself
she was putting Serafina out of her misery. The fact that
she thought she'd get a pile of money became a side issue.
Doing it was easy, once she'd made up her mind."

"What's going to happen?"

I'd been unsatisfied and restless, sad for Serafina, and
disturbed by this outcome. Suddenly, I felt a curious
peace, almost as if Serafina had laid a reassuring hand on
me.

"You've blossomed," I said. "Serafina would be proud.
She'd be proud of Carl, too. Running the business alone

and being a single parent will make him stop coasting and start growing."

"He'll never go back to Amy," Carolina agreed.

"He'll dump Moira, too. He won't be able to look at her."

"What about Amy?"

I had to think about that for a second. Not that I didn't know, but how did I feel about it?

"Her confession is inadmissible. Carl can't testify against her. Mark will have her plead to some lesser charge. I doubt she'll serve a day in jail."

"But that's awful. No one will ever know she killed Mother. She's going to get away with it!"

"No," I said. "She won't. If she doesn't give up any claim to the children or to any property settlement from Carl, I'll file a civil suit. The burden of proof is different; I think I could win it. Even if I didn't, the suit would make what really happened public. She'll blink. She couldn't live with publicity. She won't be able to live with it anyway. Her conscience is going to eat at her every day for the rest of her life. That's the worst punishment of all, I think."

"It's so hard to believe that someone would actually kill another person—just for money."

"People do it," I said. "Every single day."

As I drove home, I figured out what Serafina had wanted me to know. Who am I to sit in judgment of the unfolding of the universe? Maybe her death was untimely; maybe it was not. Perhaps the dead hand only rules when it is meant to, and releases only when its work is done.

CRIMINAL DOCKET:
THE PROSECUTORS

"You Win Some . . ."

Rochelle Krich

*Rochelle Krich (www.rochellekrich.com) won the Anthony
Award for* Where's Mommy Now? *(filmed as* Perfect Alibi).
*Her mysteries include the Jessie Drake series (the most re-
cent is* Dead Air; *forthcoming in August 2001 is* Shadows of
Sin). *She extended her formidable talent as a suspense writer
into the legal thriller with* Speak No Evil, *which centers on a
lawyer's worst nightmare: not only are female lawyers being
murdered, but what is worse, their tongues are cut out. Truly
a fate worse than death.*

WALT gave her the Silver case because no one else
wanted it. He tried to sweeten it, said she was the
one who could pull it off.

"Everybody knows Jane Palmer always gets her man."
He smiled broadly at her while acknowledging nods of
relief, masquerading as approval, from the three other assistant DAs sitting in his office. "You proved that with
Oberman."

She'd won a maximum sentence for Oberman, that
slimy Armani-suited bastard who had romanced and
bilked five women who should have known better of their
life savings and dignity. She'd celebrated with dinner and
drinks with her best friend, Tim, a defense attorney she'd
known since law school. And she'd slept exceptionally
well that night, picturing Oberman in his ugly blue prison
uniform.

Jane knew that flattery was to some degree manipula-
tive but was pleased by Walt's compliment. She was a

damn good prosecutor, and she usually *did* get her man.

She would get Ned Silver, too.

It would be a hard sell, persuading a jury to convict Silver, she thought as she walked to her tiny cubicle of an office. He was good looking even by L.A. standards: Mel Gibson–blue eyes, a winning smile, dimples that made him look like a Boy Scout with a sexy hint of the rogue.

A charming rogue—that was the problem. Over the past eight months he'd allegedly stolen almost a dozen cars from people who drove them recklessly while under the influence, people who deserved, at a minimum, to have their licenses yanked and their cars confiscated. But not by Ned Silver.

Jane hated with a passion drunk drivers and the impotence of the laws that allowed them to walk out of court with barely a slap on the wrist. But she disapproved of people like Ned Silver, who took the law into their own hands. You were on one side of the law or the other, she'd learned from her family-court-judge mother, who had raised Jane alone from the age of six after Jane's father had skipped "to pursue his dreams." The fabric of social order, Edith Palmer had taught her young daughter, is delicate. One snag, and it unravels.

The press didn't share Jane's views, or her mother's. According to a recent poll, neither did the American people. To them, Silver was a hero.

His first target had been an Acura; the second, an Infiniti; the third, a Lexus. Police didn't connect the thefts until eight cars later, when Leonard Roth, the owner of a Porsche, reluctantly told the truth:

Roth had been half a mile from his house, driving home from a party where he'd had a few drinks, when Silver, dressed like a motorcycle cop, had pulled him over.

He'd ordered Roth to take a field sobriety test, told him he'd failed. "I see this isn't your first time," Silver had said after pretending to radio the station. "I take you in, you'll lose your license. You know that, don't you?"

He'd made Roth sweat a while, listened to him sputter excuses, then suddenly relented and sent him home.

On foot.

"Let this be a warning," Silver had said, handing a perspiring and grateful Roth the keys to the Porsche. "Come back in a few hours, or in the morning, when you're sober. And don't make me stop you again."

Two hours later when Roth returned, his car was gone.

They never found it. It had been either sold to someone over the border, or reduced in ten minutes by a chop shop into pieces worth considerably more than the whole.

And within days of the theft, police later learned, MADD—Mothers Against Drunk Driving—had received a significant anonymous cash donation.

With Roth's information, detectives eventually coaxed the same uncomfortable truth from ten other victims and realized that one man was responsible for all the thefts. And, presumably, for the subsequent anonymous gifts made to MADD and to the victims of the drunk drivers.

Naturally, the media jumped on the story. Jane had to admit that it made for great copy and great headlines:

DRUNK DRIVERS SCARED SOBER

DUI'S TAKEN FOR A RIDE

MADD IS MAD FOR MYSTERY THIEF

They labeled him the DUI Demon and compared him to Robin Hood, Zorro, Superman. Leno and Letterman and Conan joked about him, their barbs laced with admiration and envy. He was the hot topic on Rosie and *The View*. They adored him, speculated about his identity and his story, wondered what he looked like and prayed they wouldn't be disappointed when, like all heroes, he finally revealed himself.

All over the city, including here in the DA's office, there had been betting pools: he would stop now that his MO had been broadcast and his prey would be less gullible. He would strike again, undaunted by the fear of capture.

They had placed bets on what kind of car he would snatch next.

And then they caught him—compliments of a suspected chop shop employee's girlfriend lured by the big bucks offered by the *Inside Scoop*. The tabloid gave the police two hours to make their arrest before it identified the thief as Ned Silver, a thirty-eight-year-old accountant with a Wharton MBA who, a year ago, had closed a lucrative practice and picked up a brush and palette.

HI YO, SILVER, AWAY! THE LONE RANGER RIDES NO MORE!

"Didn't part of you want him to get away?" Tim had asked Jane the morning of Silver's capture. She'd admitted to herself, but not to Tim, that she'd felt a twinge of surprising regret when she'd read the *Times* headlines.

But the feeling had quickly passed. Edith Palmer's daughter wasn't someone who saw nobility in vigilantism. The law was the law, and Jane would bring him down.

*   *   *

JUDGE Baylor had banned cameras from his courtroom, and Jane was grateful. She glanced to her right at the impaneled jury and suppressed a sigh. Two men and ten women, seven of them young; all yearning, no doubt, to fill the role of Maid Marian to Silver's Robin Hood. Male jurors were more likely to be critical of Silver, and envious. But Geraldine Cotter, Silver's gray-haired, brown-suited, schoolmarm attorney, had managed to dismiss most of the males from the jury pool.

Yesterday Jane had met with Silver and his attorney and offered again a minimal sentence in return for a guilty plea. Walt wanted to avoid a trial, which Jane agreed was a lose-lose situation. If Silver walked, critics would claim they'd been soft on him because they'd pandered to popular opinion, and other would-be vigilantes might be inspired to act. If he was convicted, they'd be vilified by a public that wanted to put a halo on Silver's head, not lock him up.

Jane had met with Silver twice before—once prior to the indictment, the second time three weeks ago. Each time she'd prickled with annoyance as he flashed those baby blues at her, no doubt hoping that, like most of the world, she'd be taken in by his smile.

She saw why women responded to him. He had a sexy vulnerability that made you want to take him home, bake cookies for him, and bed him. Her mother had married a man like Ned Silver. Two years ago, when Jane was thirty-three, she'd almost done the same. Common sense and her mother's counsel had stopped her, although Tim, with whom she'd had a brief romantic fling that had shifted into a comfortable friendship, had told her she'd blown it. Sometimes, when she allowed herself, she wondered if he was right.

Silver had smiled at her yesterday, too. She'd been momentarily unsettled by the sympathy in his eyes and the wistful, knowing turn of his lips, as if he felt sorry for her, instead of the other way around. As if he knew the loneliness that was her companion most nights. Other women would have melted under the intense intimacy of his gaze, but she'd reminded herself that he had impersonated a cop and stolen eleven cars.

"We have the evidence to convict you," she'd told him, looking confident. She had a great poker face, Tim said.

Their star witness was Mandy Blank, the suspected chop shop employee's girlfriend—now his ex—who could place Silver at the auto shop. The ex-boyfriend, one nervous Artie Lamb, claimed he'd never met Silver but had heard around town "from no one in particular" that he was the guy snatching cars from DUIs, more power to him, man.

Lamb's boss, Vincent Renaldo, the owner of the shop, insisted that he ran a bona fide auto shop and had never heard of Silver. Jane promised Renaldo immunity if he talked. He refused. He didn't flinch, not even when Jane, eyeing him coolly, threatened to subpoena all his books and prove the illicit nature of his business.

"I'll lock you up and throw away the key unless you give me a name," she warned. To which he said, "Go ahead, lady. You won't find nothing." Protecting not Silver, she assumed, but his own business and contacts. Profit and fear.

She subpoenaed Renaldo's books and found what he'd promised. Nada.

She had the testimony of Silver's victims, which demonstrated a consistent MO, but she didn't have a single untainted identification, thanks to the *Inside Scoop*, which ran Silver's photo when it broke the story and consequently made a lineup virtually useless, thank you very much. And Silver had apparently changed his appearance with each victim. He had curly, long blond hair. He had short brown hair. He was bald. He had a mustache. He had a beard. He wore glasses. He had a scar.

He was a chameleon.

And meticulous: he'd left no fingerprints or other evidence in any of the cars he'd stolen. *Once an accountant . . .* , Jane had thought meanly. Not that he looked like one.

There had been no sign in his apartment of any of the facial disguises he'd used. He'd probably disposed of everything once the media speculation had begun. The police *did* have Silver's motorcycle, which by itself proved nothing but might score points with the jury. And in his closet they'd found a cop's uniform, which he claimed he'd bought at a flea market, but didn't remember where or when.

So they had means and opportunity. Silver lived alone and had no alibi for any of the times the cars in question had been stolen. And they had motive: a year and a half ago, a drunk driver in a Mercedes had killed Ned Silver's widowed mother, sister, and fiancée on their way home from the fiancée's bridal shower. The driver, a wealthy second-time offender, had received probation and been ordered to undergo counseling and perform community service.

A horrific tragedy of Sophoclean proportions, one that gave Silver a hell of a motive. But it was a double-edged sword. Jane could convince a jury that a devastated Silver had avenged the deaths of his loved ones by targeting other drunk drivers who had eluded justice. But would the jury be swayed to convict or to commiserate? She had been moved to tears herself, had found it hard to look at him with the dispassionate objectivity with which she regarded every defendant.

Maybe that explained Silver's confidence. He had turned down the plea yesterday, as he had before. Or maybe he *wanted* the trial so that his victims would be forced to tell their shameful stories for everyone to hear.

Jane glanced at him now. His attorney had dressed him wisely—a navy suit, pale blue shirt, a conservative striped tie. His dark brown hair was neatly combed, but a lock fell, Superman-like, onto his forehead. No accident, Jane decided.

She had dressed with care, too, keenly aware that she would be the object of media scrutiny, like Marcia Clark, who had changed her hairdo and her wardrobe while prosecuting O. J. Simpson. This morning Jane had worn her shoulder-length, wavy dark blond hair loose instead of pinning it up and had softened her tailored cranberry suit with a lacy camisole. She wasn't vain, but didn't relish being cut by the papers (PLAIN JANE, they'd say; the epithet had haunted her in her gawky junior high years), or described as a hardhearted bitch determined to topple a hero.

"All rise for the Honorable Judge Wendell Baylor," the bailiff intoned.

Ten minutes later Jane approached the jury box and gave her opening statement.

*   *   *

GERALDINE Cotter blasted the testimony of a pouting, big-breasted Mandy Blank, who swore that Artie Lamb had told her Silver was the DUI Demon.

"This is hearsay, Your Honor," Cotter exclaimed with heaving indignation after approaching the bench with Jane. "I ask Your Honor to have it stricken from the record."

Judge Baylor lowered his bifocals and frowned at Jane. "I don't know what you were thinking, Ms. Palmer. Have you forgotten the basic rules of testimony?"

"Her ex-boyfriend, Artie Lamb, is a hostile witness, Your Honor. So is his boss, Vincent Renaldo, the owner of the body shop that we think is the chop shop where most of the cars Mr. Silver stole ended up. Ms. Blank links the shop to the defendant."

"No, she doesn't, Ms. Palmer. Not in this court. I'm having her testimony stricken. You can proceed to examine the witness, but I don't want any more hearsay."

Geraldine Cotter's thin smile was lofty with disdain. Jane shrugged her shoulders in polite defeat and repressed her own smile as the judge instructed the jury to disregard Mandy Blank's testimony. Not an easy thing to do, Jane knew.

"Ms. Blank," Jane asked, "did you ever meet the defendant before today?"

"Yeah, I did. At VR Auto Repair."

"Can you tell the court the circumstances of that meeting?"

"It wasn't exactly a meeting. I went there one night to see what was holding Artie up. When I got there, I saw this dark green Land Cruiser pulling into the shop, with custom plates. HRT2HRT. Heart to heart. A guy got out and started talking to Artie. So I got out of my car and walked over."

"Did Artie introduce you to this man?"

"Nope. But I heard Artie call him Ned. Artie looked nervous when he saw me. He told me he'd come to my place after he drove this guy home. When Artie showed up, I asked why did the guy come late at night. Artie snapped at me, said the guy works late hours, he's a good customer, so what's the big deal?"

"Then what happened, Ms. Blank?"

"I heard on TV about this guy they call the DUI Demon, and they described all the cars he stole. One was a green Land Cruiser, with the same custom plates. Heart to heart."

"Did you say anything to Mr. Lamb?"

"Sure." Mandy nodded vigorously. "He said the car I saw at the shop was a different one. I told him I knew what I saw, and if he couldn't trust me, it was over between us." She paused. "So Artie says, yeah, he's the guy. But he made me swear not to say anything, or the cops would come down on him."

"Objection! Hearsay!"

"Sustained. The jury will disregard the witness's last statement." The judge frowned at Jane.

"I'm sorry, Your Honor." Her smile was contrite. "Ms. Blank, did you go to the police with the information you had about the man you saw at the body shop with the green Land Cruiser?"

"No, I didn't. I didn't want to get Artie in trouble."

"What *did* you do?"

Mandy Blank had the grace to blush. "I phoned the *Inside Scoop* and sold them information about the DUI Demon."

"How much money did you get paid?"

"A hundred thousand dollars." Half embarrassed, half proud.

"Did you tell Mr. Lamb what you'd done?"

"No. I knew he'd be mad. But I heard that reporters don't snitch on their sources, even if it means going to jail. So I wasn't worried that he'd find out, or that the cops would bother him."

"Did you tell anyone else, besides the *Inside Scoop*, about what you had seen?"

"Yeah, my sister." Mandy snorted. "I wish I'd known she had such a big fat mouth."

Lucky for the police. The tabloid reporter had fully intended to protect his source. "Ms. Lamb, is the man you saw driving the Land Cruiser with the plates HRT2HRT sitting in this courtroom today?"

"Yeah, that's him." Mandy pointed at the defendant.

Jane was pleased with Mandy Blank's testimony, and even more pleased when the woman held her own under Geraldine Cotter's aggressive cross-examination.

Lamb was next. He had slicked back his black hair and doused himself with aftershave. He fidgeted in his shiny gray suit, frequently craning his neck, red where it chafed against the knot of his tie.

Jane spent a few minutes establishing Lamb's identity, place of work, and relationship with Mandy Blank. "So you're no longer involved with Ms. Blank, is that right?"

"Yeah, that's right. Things didn't work out."

"By 'things' you mean the fact that Ms. Blank sold information about Ned Silver to the *Inside Scoop*."

"Objection!" Cotter rose. "Leading the witness."

"He's a hostile witness, Your Honor," Jane said.

"Answer the question, Mr. Lamb," the judge ordered.

The defense attorney resumed her seat.

Lamb narrowed his eyes. "I didn't appreciate having the cops breathing down my neck, like I had somethin' to do with all this."

"Ms. Blank testified that you told her Ned Silver was the person the media have labeled the DUI Demon."

Lamb shook his head. "No way did I say that."

Jane arched a brow. "So she came up with his name

out of the blue? The name for which she was paid a hundred thousand dollars? Is that what you want this jury to believe?" Jane was frowning, as if insulted on behalf of the jurors, whose intelligence was being attacked.

Lamb flushed. He darted a nervous glance at the jury, just as Jane had hoped he would, then back at her. "I might've said his name. I heard it in a bar."

"You *might've* said his name?"

"I said it." Lamb nodded, unhappy. "But I never met Silver. I heard his name from some guy in a bar."

"Which guy? Which bar?"

Lamb shrugged. "I don't remember."

"Funny that this nameless guy in this nameless bar didn't go to the *Inside Scoop* himself with that hundred-thousand-dollar information." Jane paused. "Mr. Lamb, there's more than one Ned Silver in the Los Angeles area. How did Ms. Blank know which Ned Silver would be worth a hundred thousand to the *Inside Scoop*?"

Lamb hesitated. "I heard this Silver used to be an accountant, then gave it up to paint. I heard he lived in Santa Monica. I must've told Mandy."

"Where did you hear all this? From that same guy in that same bar you can't remember?"

"That's right. I don't have a regular place to go to, like Cheers, where everybody knows your name." He smirked.

"You're lying under oath, Mr. Lamb," Jane said, her voice like steel. "Not very funny. Isn't it true that you've known Mr. Silver for quite some time?"

"I never met the guy."

"He *never* brought his car to be serviced at your shop?"

"Not that I know. If Mandy says she saw him, she's wrong. She saw another guy."

"Another man named Ned," Jane said sarcastically.

Lamb nodded. "That's right." Very smug now.

"What's the last name of this Ned that Ms. Blank saw?"

"I don't know. He came in just the once, wanted an

estimate on some body work. Guess the price was too high." Lamb shrugged.

"You just met him, and you called him by his first name?"

"He was a friendly guy. That's how he introduced himself."

"According to Ms. Blank's testimony, you told her he was a regular, and you drove him home before going to her apartment."

"Didn't happen. I said that 'cause I don't like being grilled. 'Why this, why that?' " Lamb mimicked a whine, then grunted. "I don't have to punch no clock." He looked at the jury for affirmation.

Jane faced the judge. "Your Honor, I'd like to submit this as People's Exhibit C." She showed the judge a book, then received permission to approach Lamb and hand the book to him. "Mr. Lamb, can you please identify the book you're holding?"

He darted a look at the defense table, where Ned Silver was sitting. "It's a high school yearbook."

"It's *your* high school yearbook, is that correct?"

"Yes." He arched his neck, adjusted his tie.

"Please open it to page eighty-nine." She waited while Lamb found the page. "Can you identify the person in the professional photo?"

"Yeah. That's me." Grudging.

"On the bottom of the page there's another candid snapshot of two young men. Can you identify them?"

The jury's attention, Jane saw, was riveted on Lamb. He stared at Jane but didn't respond.

"Answer the question, Mr. Lamb," the judge directed.

"Me and Ned Silver." His voice sounded strangled.

"Can you please read the caption underneath the photo?"

"Best buds," he mumbled.

"Best buds," Jane repeated. "Do you want to change your earlier statement, Mr. Lamb?"

Lamb sighed. "Okay, so I know Ned Silver. But he had nothing to do with stealing those cars. Mandy was mistaken about what she thought she saw. That's the honest truth."

"Is that what best buds do, Mr. Lamb? Lie for each other? Help each other break the law?"

She ended her questioning of Lamb, and after he was cross-examined, she called Vincent Renaldo to the stand. He was laconic and belligerent, glowering at Jane and the jury. She had gleaned no further information from either man, but she was gratified. She sensed she'd convinced the ten women and two men that Renaldo and Lamb were lying and involved in more than brake alignments and lube jobs. She hoped some of their unsavoriness would attach itself like pond scum to Ned Silver and tarnish his halo.

Jane and Walt had debated the merit of putting on the stand the owners of the vehicles Silver had allegedly stolen. Now, feeling good after Lamb and Renaldo, she decided against it. None of them could give an irrefutable identification, and Silver's attorney would be certain, on cross-examination, to air their shameful records of drunk driving, arousing the indignation of the jury and confusing the roles of victim and perpetrator.

To avoid that same confusion, Jane had begun the state's case by calling to the stand the detective heading the Silver case. In a clear, objective recitation, he'd listed the eleven stolen cars and described the identical method the thief had used to trick the cars' owners.

"Was there anything similar about the people whose cars were stolen?" Jane had asked, knowing that if she didn't, Geraldine Cotter would raise the point on the cross and imply that Jane had tried to hide it from the jury.

"Yes. All these people had previously been convicted of driving under the influence."

"And during the course of your investigation, did you

discover anything about the defendant that led you to believe he was responsible for these thefts?"

"We learned that his mother, sister, and fiancée were killed by a drunk driver," the detective said solemnly.

Geraldine Cotter had tried, on her cross, to dwell on the DUI convictions of the victims, but the judge had sharply cut her off. And all that had taken place two days ago. By this time, Jane hoped, the victims' guilt had been overshadowed by Mandy Blank's and Artie Lamb's testimony.

Now Jane had the jury listen to the crisp testimony of the detective who had searched Silver's apartment and found, along with his motorcycle, a police uniform.

The jury looked unhappy, like the family of a patient forced to confront bad news. A perfect note, Jane thought, on which to rest the prosecution's case.

GERALDINE Cotter introduced a host of witnesses who testified to Ned Silver's sterling character and good deeds: the senior partner of an accounting firm who had given Silver his first job swore to his integrity and respect for the law, as did several former clients from Silver's now-defunct practice. The nurse in the burn unit where he had been volunteering for over a year talked about Silver's selflessness and compassion for others.

The jury, casting accusatory glances in Jane's direction, was impressed by the witnesses' portrait of Silver. So was Jane. She chose not to cross-examine the senior partner and former clients, none of whom had been in contact with Silver during the last year. The nurse, on the other hand, might prove useful.

Jane approached her. "Ms. Lompost, did Mr. Silver ever discuss the death of his mother, sister, and fiancée?"

"Objection!" Geraldine Cotter stood. "This question has no relevance to testimony given during the direct examination of this witness."

"Sustained."

A fair call. "Ms. Lompost, did Mr. Silver tell you why he chose to do volunteer work in your burn unit?"

Cotter frowned. She opened her mouth to say something, then clamped her lips together.

"He said his sister had been critically burned in the accident that eventually took her life, unlike his mother and fiancée. They died immediately." The woman sighed. "He said the staff who cared for his sister tried hard to ease her pain. He wanted to repay their kindness."

"Did Mr. Silver ever discuss the accident that took his loved ones' lives?"

The nurse glanced at the judge.

"You may answer the question, Ms. Lompost."

She faced Jane again. "Once in a while. This was after I got to know him."

"What did he say?"

"How ironic it was that drunk drivers usually left the scene of the accident with little more than a scratch."

"Did he sound angry about drunk drivers?"

"Objection. Calls for speculation."

"Sustained."

Jane could have argued the point, but thought it simpler to try another tack. "Did Mr. Silver make any comments about the law in regard to drunk drivers?"

The nurse pursed her lips. "We all make comments about drunk drivers. We see their victims all the time in the hospital, those who are lucky enough to live."

"Of course. But I'd like you to try to remember whether Mr. Silver made any comment." Jane spoke gently, careful not to arouse the animosity of the witness, and the jury.

"He said that the law was a joke, that drunk drivers acted as if their cars were harmless toys." The woman hesitated. "He said somebody should take their toys away."

Jane paused to let the jury absorb the statement. "To

the best of your recollection, when did he say that?"

The witness thought for a moment. "It was right after New Year's, when we had a lot of car accident victims."

"Nine months ago, just before the first car was stolen by the man known as the DUI Demon," Jane said. "Thank you, Ms. Lompost." Thank you very much. "No more questions."

"Ms. Lompost," Geraldine Cotter said on redirect, "when Mr. Silver suggested that somebody should take away drunk drivers' cars, did you think he meant he wanted to be that somebody?"

"Not at all. It sounded to me like wishful thinking."

Jane stole a glance at the jury members' faces. Inscrutable, every one of them.

*   *   *

ON the third day of the trial Geraldine Cotter called Ned Silver to the stand. There was a hush in the courtroom as he arranged his lanky form onto the chair, an almost palpable air of tense expectation. To Jane, he looked serious but calm. She was frankly surprised that Cotter was having him testify and was wondering what he was thinking, when suddenly he was looking straight at her with that same knowing sympathy. She flushed and averted her eyes.

Jane had spent a restless night. She'd wrestled with her pillow, trying to fall asleep, her mind preoccupied with worry about the jury, about the ambiguity of the whole case. In the middle of the night, for the first time in ages, she'd dreamed about her father.

The morning headlines had cheered her—D.A. PALMER LEADS LAMB TO SLAUGHTER—but she was irritated and cranky and wished the damn trial were over. So did Walt, who was continually moaning about the bad press the trial was generating for the department.

Geraldine Cotter elicited the usual background information that would transform Ned Silver in the jury's eyes from a defendant into a fellow human being—someone's son, brother. Almost someone's husband, until a drunk driver had killed his fiancée.

"Mr. Silver, in its opening statement the prosecution contended that the deaths of your loved ones turned you into a vengeful man. Is that true?"

"No. I don't consider myself a vengeful man."

"But the deaths had a profound effect on you, is that right?"

"Yes. I realized how fleeting life is. Not a big revelation to most people, I know." His smile was self-deprecating, ironic. "But I decided to give up my accounting practice, which I'd enjoyed, so that I could pursue painting, something for which I'd always had a passion."

"Mr. Silver, do you know Artie Lamb?"

"Yes. We were good friends in high school."

Uh-huh, Jane thought wryly. No point denying it now.

"Have you ever visited the premises of VR Auto Repair?"

"I take my car there for repairs. The prices are reasonable, and Artie does good work."

"Have you ever met Vincent Renaldo?"

"I may have. But mostly I deal with Artie."

Jane glanced at the jury. One of the men, and most of the women, were nodding. They were happy to accept these half-truths to fit their picture of the hero. But what would they do with Mandy Blank's testimony?

"Mr. Silver, do you own a motorcycle?" Cotter asked.

"Yes, I do. That was another passion I had. My mom thought it was too dangerous." A brief, sad smile. "I'm careful, though, and I always wear a helmet."

"Detectives found a police uniform in your apartment. Can you explain how that came to be in your possession?"

Now his smile was sheepish. "That's a funny thing. When I was a kid, I wanted to be a cop. So one time I came across this uniform in a flea market and I bought it."

"You don't remember where this was?"

"No, I really don't. And I don't remember when. It wasn't all that important."

"Did you tell Nurse Lompost that somebody should take away drunk drivers' cars? You called them 'toys.' "

"Yes, I did."

"What did you mean by that?"

"I meant that the police should confiscate the cars of anyone driving under the influence of alcohol or drugs."

Strong nods now from the jury.

"You didn't mean you were personally going to do that?"

"No, of course not."

"Mr. Silver, one last question. Do you consider yourself someone who respects the law?"

"Yes, I do."

Jane scribbled a note on her legal pad, then stood and approached the witness stand. "Mr. Silver, where were you on the night of February seventh of this year?"

"To the best of my recollection, I was home."

"The entire evening?"

"Most of it. I don't remember going out."

"Was anyone with you?"

"No, I was alone."

"So you have no one to verify where you were. What about the night of March second?"

"I was home."

"Home alone again?" she said with deliberate skepticism.

"Yes. I don't mind solitude, Ms. Palmer. It gives me the luxury of introspection, and time to paint."

Jane ran through the dates when the other cars had been stolen. Silver had no alibi for any of them but seemed unruffled by the fact.

"Mr. Silver, you testified that you bought the police

uniform because as a kid, you wanted to be a cop. You were never interested in other uniforms?"

"No."

She smiled. "You never hankered for a fireman's uniform?"

"No."

"A soldier's fatigues?"

"No."

"But you *had* to have this policeman's uniform?"

He shrugged and smiled. "It appealed to me."

"What were you planning to do with it?"

"Nothing, really. I just got a kick out of owning it."

"Did you ever put it on and go outside in it?"

"No."

She tilted her head. "You had this great uniform and you never pretended to be a cop?"

"No."

"So you bought it just to keep it in your closet?" she asked, her voice heavy with sarcasm.

"That's right."

She glanced at her notes to give the jury time to reflect on the uniform, then looked up. "Mr. Silver, you stated that you respect the law. Do you believe there are times when a person is justified in taking the law into his own hands?"

"Objection."

"Overruled. You opened the door, counselor. Answer the question, Mr. Silver."

"I could understand that person's actions, although I don't know if I would consider them justified."

"You're equivocating, Mr. Silver."

"No, I'm not. I'm trying to answer honestly, but your question is so hypothetical."

Jane smiled. "Let me make it more specific, Mr. Silver. Do you think a person is justified in stealing the vehicles of people convicted of drunk driving?"

"Optimally, the law should confiscate these individuals' cars so that they can't harm innocent people."

"This isn't hypothetical, Mr. Silver, and you're still equivocating."

Silver sighed. "I would have to say I approve of that person's actions."

"Because he's helping society?"

"That's correct."

"Even though he's committing a felony?"

"He may be preventing someone's death."

"Assuming that this person were apprehended, do you think he should be held responsible for his actions?"

"Objection."

"Overruled. Answer the question, Mr. Silver."

"I suppose so, yes. He should be held responsible."

"So if you were sitting on a jury at this person's trial, even though you understood his motives, would you vote to acquit or convict?" She had the jurors' rapt attention, she saw as she stood half facing them.

"I would have to vote to convict only if the evidence supported the prosecution's case beyond a reasonable doubt."

Smart, Jane thought. "Even though you sympathized with this person's actions?"

"Yes."

"Even though your vote might send him to prison?"

"Yes."

"Because your job would be to obey the law, isn't that correct?" she asked softly.

"Yes. I would assume, Ms. Palmer, that this person probably realized he might be apprehended and imprisoned."

The jury was with her now. She could see it, could almost savor the tantalizingly sweet taste of victory within her reach. "But he stole the cars anyway?"

"Yes."

"He risked his freedom for the greater good of others?"

"You might say that, yes."

Silver looked puzzled. So did the jury. Walt, sitting in the spectators' gallery, was probably wondering where the hell she was going with this line of questioning.

"So this thief is noble?" Jane asked. "Is that your view?"

"In my opinion, yes."

"What if he stole cars for the thrill of it, Mr. Silver? Would you still regard his motives as noble?"

Silver frowned. "No. Of course not."

"What if you discovered that as a young man, this person stealing cars from drunk drivers had a thing for other people's cars?"

"Objection!"

"What if you discovered that he'd hot-wired a car and taken it for a joyride?" With his best bud, Artie Lamb. That had been interesting.

"Objection! Approach, Your Honor?"

The judge nodded. A moment later the two attorneys stood in front of the bench.

Cotter said, "This is clear grounds for dismissal, Your Honor. Ms. Palmer has just irremediably prejudiced this jury against my client."

"Only if your client was convicted of hot-wiring a car. *Was* he?"

"He was, Your Honor. Ms. Palmer knows she can't refer to his previous conviction." The attorney smiled at Jane, triumphant.

"One would think so," the judge said, scowling.

Jane flushed. Walt was no doubt seething. "Your Honor, my comments were hypothetical. The jury will regard them as such."

"The jury, Ms. Palmer, will wonder, as I did. Ms. Cotter is correct. You've prejudiced this jury, and you leave me no recourse."

"Your Honor—"

"I'm dismissing all charges against the defendant."

And that was it.

* * *

JANE was nursing a Tom Collins at a bar she frequented when she looked up and saw him walking toward her. Her heart pounded.

"Can I join you?" Ned Silver asked.

She cocked her head. "How did you know where to find me?"

"I asked around."

Tim, she decided. Everyone, including Silver's attorney, knew that he and Jane were close. "I suppose you're here to gloat."

"Not at all. Okay if we sit at a booth? I'd like to talk privately."

She hesitated, then slipped off the stool and, taking her drink with her, walked on legs that felt like jelly to a booth at the end of the long, narrow room. He sat down across from her.

"I've been thinking a lot about what happened last week," he said. "I imagine your boss wasn't thrilled."

She smiled thinly. "Hardly."

"What the hell were you thinking?" Walt had yelled. He'd been unmollified even after she'd explained she'd wanted to make sure the jury didn't buy into the romance of the vigilante, and had barely spoken to her all week.

"I'm sorry," Ned Silver said.

"I'll survive." Eventually, things would be okay. Especially if she won the next case, which she would. "How about you? Staying out of trouble?"

"Hypothetical or real?" He smiled. "I was trying to figure out where you were going with the questioning. And all of a sudden you sprang that stuff from my past."

"I didn't want the jury to be blinded by emotion."

He narrowed his eyes, then shook his head. "You're smart. You know courtroom law. You knew the judge would dismiss the case. What I can't figure out is why you did it."

"You're wrong," she said coolly, her cheeks on fire. "I was overzealous and screwed up." She'd wondered if he'd figure it out, had half hoped he would. She was certain that Walt knew, that the yelling and silent treatment had been for public effect.

"That's what my attorney said." Ned leaned closer. "Hypothetically, though. Why would an experienced prosecutor make an error like that?"

"Hypothetically?" She took a long sip of her drink. "Maybe she decided the defendant didn't belong in prison," she finally said. "Maybe she sympathized with this guy who put drunk drivers out of commission. Maybe she isn't all that sure *why* she did it." Maybe it was the honesty and compassion in his eyes that had drawn her to him from the start, that had, for the first time, made winning not so important.

You fell for him, didn't you? her mother had demanded scornfully. What will you do, throw your career away for a car thief?

I'm not throwing away my career, Mom. I'll probably never see him again.

He'll leave you, just like your father left me. Haven't I taught you anything?

"Would she have regrets?" Ned asked, his blue eyes serious.

"Some, definitely. And she'd be devastated if he did anything like that again." She eyed him solemnly.

"He won't."

She wanted to believe him. She took another long sip. "My turn. Hypothetically, where would a person get a police uniform?"

A smile pulled at the corners of his lips. "Maybe he was painting sets for a studio where they were filming a police show. He always *did* want to be a cop, you know. Put the bad guys away." Ned sounded wistful. "What about you?"

"I always wanted to put the bad guys away, too."

Sometimes it was hard to figure out who they were. She sighed.

"I feel I owe you something," he said. "Dinner, at least."

She shook her head. She wasn't interested in gratitude. "You don't owe me anything."

"How about dinner anyway? We start fresh, no priors." He gazed at her intently. "Unless you think being seen with me will compromise your job."

Her mother would probably disown her. "I'm not all that worried." She smiled. "Dinner would be nice." For starters.

There would be talk, and then it would die down. And if it didn't, there were other jobs. She was very good at what she did.

"Jane Palmer always gets her man," Walt said all the time.

She hoped so.

Blind

Carroll Lachnit

In Carroll Lachnit's first Hannah Barlow mystery, Murder in Brief, *a former homicide detective turned law student discovered that the competitive world of law school is more dangerous than the mean streets. Lachnit uses her journalistic background to explore such cutting-edge issues as child molester registration laws* (Janie's Law) *and independent adoptions* (Akin to Death).

In fictional time, this story takes place after the events of the first Hannah Barlow novel, Murder in Brief, *and before the second book,* A Blessed Death. *As in* Murder in Brief, *Hannah is a law student, grappling with which direction her life should take professionally and personally. "Blind" was inspired by a case I covered as a newspaper reporter in Orange County, California, but the characters in this story are purely fictional.*

HANNAH heard Daniel Benavides before she saw him. A wooden cane clicked unsteadily, a faulty metronome. Rubber-soled shoes yelped on the linoleum in the hallway. She went to the office door and watched him approach, a tall, thick boy with a shaved head and slick Oakley sunglasses. He drifted left toward the courtroom doorways and then right toward the benches built into the wall. It made Hannah think of a sailboat with a novice at the tiller, unable to make the craft hold its course.

The file said Daniel was five-ten, a hundred and fifty pounds. Clipped to the folder was his picture: slim, elegantly dressed for a prom, his arms wrapped around a pretty, dark-eyed girl. The kid in the hallway had an extra forty pounds under his Mighty Ducks T-shirt and denim overalls.

On the phone, Daniel's mother, Berta, said he ate all the time—asking for big meaty sandwiches at lunch, and then, as he sat with her during the afternoon soap operas, he went after the Hershey's Kisses. He fished them out of the little glass bowl on the coffee table, unwrapped them, and pitched them into his mouth, one after the other. She didn't want to scold him, to tell him that he was getting so fat. Not after all that had happened to him.

He had been in the hospital for three weeks after the shooting. Since then, he had been at home, refusing to go back to school, not even for a visit. After a few sessions in the Braille Institute's program for adjusting to sudden blindness, he quit, telling them to stuff their damn talking clock. He refused friends' suggestions to come out for drives or hang on the sidelines of the weekend basketball games at the park. His sight had been taken, and Daniel had further compressed his world until it was a bleak, tiny cinder of what it had been.

He was angling away from Hannah now, headed for the door of Judge Bedsworth's courtroom. Hannah crossed the hall, touched Daniel's elbow and felt the muscles in his arm jump.

"I'm Hannah Barlow. It's good to meet you." His hand floated up and she shook it. "My office is over here."

He nodded and turned toward the sound of her voice. Hannah could see the scatter of shotgun pellets that still lay embedded under his nearly naked scalp.

"Okay," he said. His voice was polite, but flat.

Hannah heard the clatter of heels behind them. A

woman paused at the top of the stairs, her face tense with
worry.

"Daniel, I asked you to wait. You could have fallen
or . . ."

"I'm fine, Mom," he said. And then under his breath,
"Jesus."

She slid smoothly to his side. He started to resist the
hand she put under his elbow, but then let her guide him
through the door. They sat on the sun-bleached plastic
sofa, under the pictures of the Orange County DA and the
board of supervisors, and waited for Hannah's interrogation to begin.

So far, she had worked on two cases during the summer
clerkship with the DA's office: a first-degree burglary and
an armed robbery. This was her first homicide case—a
187, in penal-code lingo. They usually kept the law students away from those, the bosses believing there was too
much at stake to risk a reversal caused by some rookie
mistake. But Hannah's background as a cop apparently
made her different.

She'd read the file several times now, but wanted to
hear Daniel tell the story. About how he'd seen nothing
other than a brown Nova. About not seeing the sawed-off
shotgun or the faces of the people who blinded him and
killed his friend Bennett. In short, she was going to talk
to him about the last things he *didn't* see.

Futile? Her boss, Palafox, hadn't exactly said so when
he asked her to interview Daniel. The Las Almas police
had done what they could, but they were fresh out of
leads. The Nova had been stolen a few hours before the
shooting from a Denny's parking lot. Police in Long
Beach, just over the county line, found the car abandoned
in front of a Cambodian video store on Anaheim Street a
few days later. There were two fingerprints on the steering
wheel, but they didn't match up to anything in Cal-ID or

the federal database. Bennett's parents saw nothing. The
neighbors were blind, too. Fear did that to them, however.
Not shotgun pellets.

The gang prosecution unit, a macho enclave, already
had tried various approaches with Daniel, thinking he was
holding something back. There was the big-brother chat,
the blood-vengeance ploy, and the be-a-good-citizen
speech. All failed. Hannah figured Palafox had given her
a shot because she was a woman, and women were supposed to possess some kind of mysterious empathetic voodoo. Maybe he thought Hannah would mother-love the
truth out of Daniel. She tried not to take offense at the
idea.

Hannah opened the file and looked again at the pictures
taken at the hospital a few hours after the shooting.

In them, Daniel's pellet-wounded, swollen eyes bulged
from their sockets. The shot left tiny craters in his puffed-
out cheeks. His front teeth were shattered, jagged shards.
Through the blood and the grotesque swelling, Hannah
saw the terror on his face.

Daniel had taken his sunglasses off, and Hannah could
see the scars the pellets had left behind. As though he
knew she was examining his eyes, he tentatively fluttered
the lids open and clenched them shut again. Hannah could
not imagine what that would be like: to open your eyes
and see only darkness.

She pulled her chair around and sat down in front of
him. "I know you've talked about the shooting with the
police and some of the deputy DAs. But I wanted to hear
it from you directly."

"I'm not lying," he said. His voice was tight, sullen.
"I didn't see who shot me."

"Has anyone called you a liar?"

"They think we all lie."

"Who all lies?"

"Us. The supposed *vatos*. Homies. You know."

"My boy is not in a gang," Berta said. Anger darkened

her cheeks. Hannah glanced at the police report to double-check the age. It said Berta Benavides was thirty-six. The charcoal rings under her eyes, the drawn skin at the corners of her mouth and the gray-streaked hair added years to her face. Palafox said she'd been widowed for ten years. A construction-site trench collapse had killed Daniel's father.

"I think we need to clear the air," Hannah said. "To begin with, nobody thinks Daniel is a gang member. We aren't so stupid as to believe that just because you know people who live in a gang neighborhood, or live in one yourself, that you are automatically in a gang." Hannah knew she was lying. Cops and deputy DAs of her acquaintance believed exactly that. "Okay?"

"Yes. Good." Berta seemed slightly mollified. Daniel said nothing.

"The Las Almas police don't even have a field interview card on you, Daniel," Hannah said. "You steered clear of a lot of trouble in your time."

"Yeah, well, my luck ran out, didn't it? Could be worse, though."

"You could be dead," his mother said.

He let out a harsh laugh. "You think that's worse than this?"

"Daniel," Hannah said. "Let's just go through this once more, okay? I know it's not easy to think about, but the more detail you can give me, the fewer questions I'll have to ask."

He began, and there were details aplenty: the concert—Wu-Tang Clan—was kick-ass. The drive home was fine—hot June night, open windows, cold Cokes. Bennett kept a little stash of dope—really good, sticky stuff—in his room, and they smoked a joint there, with all the windows closed and a towel tucked under the door. Bennett would air it out later, after his dad was in bed. His mother already was at work. Night-shift LVN at UCI Medical Center.

But it was stifling hot in the house, so they decided to go outside. Bennett said it was okay, things were cool on his block. They first saw the Nova as it slowly cruised by, but not so slowly that it made them suspicious. They were a little high, but not stoned stupid. They knew what had been going on in Bennett's neighborhood.

"Tell me about that," Hannah said.

Daniel laid it down, describing it in the detail that PBS lavished on the Civil War. Bennett and his folks had lived for a couple years in an area coveted by the Fruit City Crips. The mixed-race gang—Latino and black kids—had their eye on Bennett's block, which had traditionally been held by the Third Street Playboys, an almost extinct group, thanks to shootings, prison, and heroin overdoses. The leftover Playboys were lazy, didn't police their turf like they should. That made things iffy, Daniel said, because the F.C. Crips weren't the only ones who liked the real estate. The Mala Sangre boys held the neighborhoods on the other side of the Playboys' territory. Things escalated when one of the Mala Sangres, a kid fresh from the Youth Authority, moved in next door to Bennett's house. Bennett's folks were worried, felt the pressure like a pipe ready to burst. They were working on getting a down payment together for a house in Moreno Valley, hoping to get out before the shit hit.

But they couldn't get out fast enough. The Mala Sangre homesteader invited his cousin over for a visit, and he brought some friends. The resulting skirmish with a half-dozen Fruit City boys later that night was brief, but bloody. The new kid on the block was wounded, and a retaliatory war was fought in short, brutish bursts, followed by periods of unnatural calm. Bennett mistook one such period for a truce.

"It had been cool for weeks, Bennett said," Daniel told Hannah. "No shooting, just peaceful, like."

So maybe that's why their guard was down, he said. And maybe it was the dope. Whatever it was, they didn't go inside when the saw the car coming a second time. They were too busy laughing, as Daniel tried to explain to Bennett why *pendejo*—literally, pubic hair—meant crazy in Spanish slang.

"That multicultural stuff really cracked Bennett up," Daniel said.

And then, boom, the car was right there, idling in the street, and there was the hand signal. And the sound and the light. And then the dark.

"I couldn't see nothing," Daniel said, his voice soft, disbelieving. "I heard Bennett screaming, screaming, and it sounded, like, real far away. I couldn't get up, so I crawled, and I didn't even know which way I was going."

Then the rest of it: Bennett's dad on the phone to 911. The cops and the ambulance and the hospital.

"He died right there, in the street."

"Bennett was a good friend," Hannah said.

Daniel nodded. "I couldn't do nothing for him. Still can't."

Hannah tried a few questions, but Daniel's attention to detail began to dry up. It seemed as though he could no longer make out the fine points of that night. He just saw a hand, he said. A hand throwing a sign.

"Can you remember how it looked?" Hannah asked, although she knew it was probably a waste of time. The gang cops in Las Almas knew every sign, read them like semaphore. They'd undoubtedly been over this ground with him.

"I don't know the damn Fruit City signs," he spat. "I'm not part of their shit. I said that."

She hadn't said anything about Fruit City. "What about Mala Sangre's signs?"

He hesitated. "Don't know them, either."

"So who do you think it was? Bennett's black, you're Latino, so . . ."

"Chicano," Daniel said, interrupting her. "There's a difference. I'm homegrown Mexican-American. Ever see

Born in East L.A.? Cheech, man. He is some funny guy."

"Missed that one," Hannah said, thinking it interesting that Daniel was suddenly so chatty. "In any event, it's not likely that Fruit City thought you two were Mala Sangre. Mala Sangre doesn't take black kids, right?"

It was Berta who was nodding, but she stopped herself when she saw Hannah watching her.

"So probably not Fruit City," Hannah said. "But Mala Sangre could have taken you for a two-tone Fruit City unit, about to hassle the Sangre outpost next door to Bennett's house."

Daniel shrugged. "Shit if I know."

It went on like that for a while. His answers dwindled to mumbled syllables. Then he stopped speaking altogether, opting for shrugs and shakes of the head.

Hannah thumbed the file for a moment, saw a report card littered with incompletes.

"What's up with school? Did you go back for part of the year?"

"Nah. A teacher came with assignments. My mom read them to me and I, you know, listened and stuff. I didn't miss much, I don't think."

Berta looked away and then back at Hannah, shaking her head. She folded a tissue into smaller and smaller squares and dabbed her eyes with it.

"What about your friends?" Hannah said. "Are they coming by?"

"They're pretty busy and stuff now. They've got summer jobs and all. And there's college, for some of them, in the fall."

Hannah closed the file and looked at the picture clipped to the cover.

"The girl you took to the junior prom is pretty," she said. "Do you still see her?"

The words hung there for a moment. God, Hannah thought, how stupid can I be? "I'm sorry," she said.

"It's okay." Then, Daniel slowly smiled, showing off

newly capped teeth. Palafox had quietly seen to that: a way of winning Daniel's trust, Hannah supposed. "I *can* see Sylvia, just like in that picture," he said. "You tell me if I miss anything."

He tilted back his head and described the girl's dark brown eyes, her strong nose. Her mouth, small but full. The little scar on her chin, from when she was seven and fell off her bike. Her hair, long and so straight that it could have been a black waterfall. Her dress, a swirl of pale orange.

"What's that color called? Some kind of fruit," he said, frowning as he tried to remember it. "Apricot. That's it."

Hannah looked down at the picture. The dress was beaded pink silk. Sylvia's hair was short. Maybe she'd worn her hair long once, but not for this dance. Daniel had forgotten what should have been an unforgettable evening. What else had disappeared from his memory? Was everything about the night of the drive-by gone, too?

"Sylvia's going into Las Almas City College's nursing program in the fall," Berta said. "You've been going out with her how long, Daniel?"

"We went out. Two years." Past tense.

"When did that end?" Hannah said.

"After that night. I decided," he said curtly.

"What did she think about that?"

He shrugged. "Didn't matter. I wasn't going to drag her through this, that's all."

Hannah pondered that for a moment. "I don't think I would have been so noble."

Daniel suddenly was on his feet. "Are we done here?" He kicked the table as he lumbered to the door, frantic as a bull in a chute. "I'm starved."

Hannah walked them to the door. Berta reached for her son's elbow, but he pulled away from her and lurched down the hall, swinging the cane furiously in front of him. It hit a bench, swiped the wall and finally struck the metal balustrade. The harsh clang rang in the air, then fell silent.

*   *   *

AFTER Hannah got Sylvia's last name and ran it
through the DMV for her address, she went to the
crazy-quilt map in the conference room. A legend at the
bottom explained the shaded squares and rectangles: red
was Mala Sangre territory. Dark brown belonged to Fruit
City Crips. The yellow strip at the west edge of town was
the Saigon Boyz. The white islands were unclaimed turf.
Hannah shook her head. The gang unit certainly didn't
waste its imagination on politically correct color-coding.

Daniel and his mother lived in one of those white islands. Sylvia Gonzalez's street was solidly in Mala
Sangreland.

Hannah found Palafox in his office, cramming a sandwich in his mouth with one hand and jotting notes with
the other. The phone was jammed between his shoulder
and ear, and he made affirmative grunts as the caller
talked.

When he'd hung up, Hannah told him about the interview and the girl's neighborhood.

Palafox shrugged and packed up the leftovers from
lunch. "You think it's Sharks and Jets and Maria and
Tony? That Mala Sangre thought Daniel was with Fruit
City and went after him? We checked. It wouldn't have
mattered if he was with Fruit City. Sylvia's not down with
Mala Sangre. She can date whoever she wants."

"He broke up with her, after the shooting," Hannah
said.

"Sure. Pre-emptive strike," Palafox said. "If I had been
Daniel, that's what I'd have done, too. Better to be the
dumper than the dumped."

"Why was he so sure she'd dump him?"

"She's seventeen," he said. "What would you have
done at that age?"

Hannah thought back on her own alternating impulses:
intense selfishness one minute, unbridled altruism the

next. "I'd have been Florence Nightingale for about six months, then found a way to get out."

"There you are," Palafox said, grabbing for the other half of his sandwich. "Daniel might not be able to see, but he ain't blind."

*   *   *

IF the gang map had been subtler, the Gonzalezes' block would have been washed in a lighter shade—rose perhaps. As Hannah stood in front of Sylvia's house late that afternoon, waiting for someone to answer the doorbell, she saw that Mala Sangre did not own the street. Not yet. There were fresh gang *placas* on a cinderblock wall at the end of the street, but here was a middle-aged man with a can of white paint, hurriedly running a roller over them. There was actually a neighborhood watch sign—free of bullet holes—on one of the light poles. Most of the lawns were well-tended, planted with roses and lantana. But there were also thick burglar bars on windows, and high walls that turned some of the homes into compounds. And except for the painter, there was no one out. No pickup ball games in the street, no folks sitting on their porches, chatting. Living was what you did inside, where it was safe. Out here, you took your chances.

SYLVIA Gonzalez answered the bell, but didn't open the door. She looked at Hannah through the heavy grate like a postulant peering out from the cloister. After Hannah explained who she was, Sylvia hesitated.

"If my dad hears me talking about Daniel, he'll freak."

"Why?"

"After the shooting, somebody threw a dead cat on the porch. It meant I should shut up. But Daniel never told me anything, and I told the police that. Wait a second."

She disappeared, and came back with two cans of Diet Coke. Hannah followed her up the driveway, into the back yard. There was a kid's swing set there. Sylvia sat on one rusty metal seat, and Hannah took the other. The chains creaked, and Sylvia looked for a moment as though she wanted to launch herself into the summer sky, be seven again.

Her hair was long again, and she twisted it through her fingers as they talked. Even without her prom gown, just in her shorts and YWCA swim-team T-shirt, she was a beautiful girl. And Daniel had thrown her away.

"I thought I knew what Daniel was doing," she said. "He didn't want me to feel like I had to call him, to come over. But I wanted to be with him."

"And now?" Hannah said.

"I don't call him anymore. He was so—mean. He wasn't like that before."

"He didn't say anything about the shooting to you? Ever?"

She shook her head. "Just that he didn't want to think about it."

"Do you think he knows something he's not telling the police?"

"Why would he do that? Those assholes blinded him." Sylvia's voice was venomous. "I'd want somebody to get theirs, if it happened to me. The Bible even says it, right? Eye for an eye."

The back door slammed. A boy in a parochial-school uniform, carrying a backpack, ran through the yard, picked up a fallen bike, and threw open a gate into the alley. He looked like Sylvia, but his forehead was beginning to break out.

"Max? Be back for dinner. Mama has the night off, and I made a casserole."

"Chess club at the library," he called. He turned and grinned at her. "And I'm not hungry—especially not for your cooking. Later."

She sighed. "Do all brothers become a pain at thirteen?"

"Sometimes it's sooner," Hannah said. "Is Daniel worried about a payback, thinking that if he rats out anyone, they'll come after him and his mother?"

"No way," Sylvia said.

"Why not?" Hannah said.

Sylvia stopped fiddling with her hair. "I thought you knew."

It hadn't been in the file. No one had mentioned it—not Daniel, not his mother. Hannah knew it was not an oversight. Sylvia said Daniel's uncle—his father's brother—was a Mala Sangre OG: an original gangster, an elder. She had heard the rumor around school and the streets: this uncle would not stand for any paybacks against Daniel, even if he ratted out someone from Mala Sangre. The war with the Fruit City Crips was a righteous rivalry, decades old. But innocent bystanders like Bennett and Daniel should not have been targeted. For their blunder, the shooters deserved to face the law. Everyone knew the uncle could make his threat stick, Sylvia said. But no information had shaken loose.

Daniel knew about the edict, Hannah thought. He must have known. He was safe, his mother was safe. Why would he keep silent? She was beginning to wonder if he had been telling the truth. Maybe he really saw nothing that night.

*   *   *

MALA Sangre had no clubhouse, no flag, and no precise uniform. But according to Sylvia, it had a headquarters: the northwest corner of Blailey Park, between the handball courts and the kiddie activity room. The police swept it occasionally, the last time right after the shooting, nearly a year ago. Hannah went there the next day at lunch hour, when the park did not wholly belong to the gang.

A guy in a knit cap, a yellow-and-black plaid shirt, and black jeans sat on a picnic table. He thoughtfully stroked

a tiny black beard nestled just below his lip. Three
younger kids huddled in a circle on the grass. Hannah sat
down at a table near the ball courts and pulled out a magazine and a sandwich. The group glanced at her once, then
went back to its wordless lounging.

Hannah looked up every minute or so. The group re-
arranged itself: three on the table with the bearded man.
Two on the grass. One left, two more came. The bearded
guy stayed, a king holding court, the sun around which
they revolved. A quartet of girls dawdled near the Sun
King for a time, pointing their toes into the grass and
pivoting their legs like dancers at the barre. Their hair
was streaked red, and they wore a matching shade of
bruise-purple lipstick. The girls seemed to sense Hannah
was watching them and turned precisely, a cold and thug-
gish corps de ballet, to stare at her. Hannah took some
leisurely bites of sandwich, then picked up the lunch bag
and magazine and adjourned to her car. No point in at-
tracting too much attention.

SHE came back the next day in late afternoon, armed with
a pair of binoculars, and parked on the other side of the
park, at a distance from the Sun King's court. He sat there
alone, smoking, surveying his little fiefdom. The lights
that dotted the park had begun to glow orange when a
courtier appeared.

He wore the knit cap pulled down to his eyebrows.
The denim shirt and baggy jeans—an imitation of prison
clothes—were huge on his little frame. A kid, Hannah
thought. A boy.

He feigned disinterest, kicking up dirt around the perimeter of the table. Finally, the Sun King jerked his chin
in a signal to approach. They walked away, down to the
handball court. Hannah picked up the binoculars and fo-
cused in on them in the fading light. The boy sidled closer
and kicked the dirt again. A few words passed. Then the

boy held his clenched hand over the man's palm and opened it. A wad of money? Hannah couldn't make it out. Whatever it was, the king pocketed it, nodded and lit a cigarette.

The boy started to walk away, then turned and said something. The king looked up. The boy awkwardly brought his elbows up. His hands were pointed down, thumbnails together, index fingers aimed away from each other. Then he tried another position, but hesitated, stopped. The Sun King shook his head and threw his cigarette away. He made the first sign, the M. And the second, the trickier letter, the S. The boy mimicked him haltingly, and the king curtly nodded approval. Then he shooed the boy away. He was coming straight at Hannah. She put the binoculars down and started her car.

The boy sauntered across the grass, smiling to himself. He took off his cap and scratched his forehead. Hannah felt her breath catch.

The boy stepped off the sidewalk, reached into a bush and pulled out a backpack. He shed the baggy clothes, and there, underneath them, were the Catholic schoolboy's white shirt, the corduroy pants. Hannah watched the transformation. Here was a boy who wanted in. He would do what was required. Sell the drugs. Learn the sign. Be down with Mala Sangre. Get in the brown Nova and take a drive. Do what you're told, and shut up.

He had complied, but he must have seemed nervous after that night, that drive. That dead cat was meant for him, not Sylvia.

*   *   *

IT was after eight when Berta led Hannah to Daniel's room. She knocked and then, with a sigh, opened the door. "He won't talk to you," she told Hannah.

He was lying on his bed, dime-sized headphones plugged into his ears. The volume was cranked so high that the surly, metallic music bled from them. Daniel silently sang along, mouth stretching for the high notes.

The walls around him were bare, stripped of posters that now stood rolled up, face out, stacked on their ends in a far corner. Michael Jordan's eyes stared sideways at her.

Daniel jerked when she touched his shoulder and yanked out the earphones.

"You could fucking knock," he shouted. "I've asked about a million times. I could have been jerking off in here, Mom."

"Sorry," Hannah said. "You jerk off to Rob Zombie?"

He slouched and reddened at the sound of her voice.

"Sorry. Thought you were . . ."

"It's no way to talk to your mother."

He nodded. "That's what she says. Every time I use the F word, a dollar goes into a jar. But it's her dollar, so . . ." He started to smile, to disarm her.

"Daniel, I know what happened," Hannah said. "You know it, too. Max Gonzalez was in that car." She watched his face. He gave away nothing. She could have been talking to Michael Jordan's poster. "Like you said, you never lied. You didn't recognize the shooter. You probably couldn't make out the sign Max threw—he does it pretty badly. But you recognized Max. He was the driver, wasn't he?"

Silence.

"I don't think he even realized it was you that night," Hannah said. "He probably found out when Sylvia did."

Daniel wet his lips. He started to speak, stopped. Finally, he croaked: "She was scared to death for me. Max was, too."

"Why didn't you tell her Max was involved?"

He shook his head. "Because she would go to the police. That's how she is—she'd do that, not think about what would happen after that. But I knew."

"What did you think would happen?"

"After they'd thrown away the key on Max, after he

maybe got killed in jail, she'd be stuck with me. A blind jerk who ratted her brother out."

Hannah felt a tick of anger. "You make all her decisions, Daniel. You decide how she'll feel. What's that about?"

Daniel started to put the earphones on. Hannah tugged them away.

"Listen. This is what you do: call her. She loves you, and she wants to help you. Keeping quiet about the drain Max is going down doesn't help anyone. You're punishing all the wrong people, Daniel."

He wet his lips again. "Mala Sangre will go after Sylvia and her parents."

"Your uncle won't let them."

He shook his head, a pretense of confusion. "I don't know what you're talking about."

"Now, that's a lie," she said. "Isn't it?"

He dropped his head.

"So make some calls, Daniel. Your uncle, and then Sylvia. Then call us. We can make this end."

He shook his head. "You don't understand. My mom will freak out when she hears I lied, that I protected someone in Mala Sangre, no matter what the reason. She's determined to keep my uncle's gang out of my life."

Hannah looked at the mine field of pellets under Daniel's shaved scalp. She put her hand on his, and guided his fingers over the lumps there, letting him read with her the damage that had been done to him.

"His gang's right here, Daniel. In your head, in your mind. Time to get it out."

* * *

THE trial for the three adult defendants took a week, and Daniel's time on the stand consumed less than an hour of that. He identified Max Gonzalez as the driver. And then Max, looking tiny and far younger than his thirteen years, sat in the witness box and identified the

shooter. Hannah knew the deal he'd cut after his fingerprints came back as match to those on the steering wheel:
he would serve a one-year term in another county's
juvenile hall, in protective custody. It wasn't certain that
even those precautions would keep him alive, but they
would help.

Max said the Sun King hadn't pulled the trigger, but
he had directed the operation while riding shotgun. Hannah watched a juror recoil at the phrase, so sickeningly
apt. The jury heard how Bennett died in a gutter, the life
seeping out of him. Palafox showed them the pictures of
Daniel after the shooting: bullfrog-swollen eyes. Bloodied
mouth. All because the Sun King had demanded a shotgun
sacrifice to consolidate his holdings: a block of little
houses in a poor Las Almas neighborhood.

*   *   *

D ANIEL and his mother left town even before the jurors
returned their three guilty verdicts. The Gonzalez
family disappeared immediately after Max's sentencing.
Daniel's OG uncle had juice, but the two families were
not going to rely on that. Hannah asked Palafox where
the families had gone, but he claimed ignorance.

"Fine," Hannah said. "Go ahead and lie to me."

"That's your reward," he said. "Good job, by the way.
We didn't see it in Max."

"He was never a suspect?"

Palafox shrugged. "He was living a double life out
there. Even got a certificate in the anti-gang class at
school. Laughing up his sleeve the whole time, probably.
Like some kind of mole in a Le Carré story."

"Or maybe he just didn't know which way to jump,"
Hannah said. "It can't be easy in a neighborhood like that,
when all the people you grew up with are choosing up
sides."

Palafox shook his head. "It doesn't matter what you
pick sometimes. Look at Bennett. And Daniel."

* * *

MONTHS later, when Hannah was studying for the bar exam, a wedding announcement turned up in her mailbox. There was no return address, no postmark—not even a stamp. The ceremony had been at St. Anthony's Church, according to the card, but there was no mention of a city, state, or country. That left Hannah free to imagine Sylvia and Daniel in a variety of locales, all of them places she liked: Eureka, among the redwoods. Taos, with the smell of piñon-wood smoke in the air. Cuernavaca's Borda Gardens, with Sylvia resting her hand lightly on Daniel's arm as they walked.

Of course, they could just as easily be in a crappy house in Rubidoux, a scant fifty minutes away, fighting over the choices they'd made. Even if she thought it was more likely, Hannah preferred not to dwell on that scenario. She saw Sylvia studying her nursing texts at night. She imagined Daniel learning to accept Sylvia's love, not mistaking it for pity. Even if he couldn't see her light, he could feel its warmth.

The day after the announcement came, she bought a little white cake from a bakery downtown and took it to Palafox's office. He read the cautiously worded announcement and smiled. They toasted the newlyweds with bitter, twice-heated county coffee and ate some of the cake. Then they went back to work.

CRIMINAL DOCKET:
THE DEFENDERS

The Triumph of Eve

Sarah Caudwell

When the divine Sarah burst upon the mystery scene with Thus Was Adonis Murdered, *she brought her unique voice to the legal mystery genre. Sadly, she died in late 1999, just as her long-awaited fourth book,* The Sybil in Her Grave, *was about to be released. Her acid wit, her malodorous pipe, her Whimsey will be greatly missed by both the legal and mystery communities.*

"WHEN I was a girl," said Eve, leaning back comfortably and sipping her brandy, "everyone assumed that I'd have to make my living from crime, but I was determined I wouldn't." She smiled; though she was, beyond question, no longer a girl, her dark eyes were still bright under arching eyebrows and the lines that the years had drawn on her features were of irony and skepticism. "So it was rather a disappointment when I began my career with a murder."

Although it was some years since Eve Lampeter had practiced as a barrister at 62 New Square, the older members of those Chambers still regarded her with sufficient affection, the younger with sufficient pride, for her elevation to senior judicial office to be thought a proper occasion for a Chambers dinner. As the habitual chronicler of events in New Square, I had been invited to be among the guests.

The dinner was held in the nearest restaurant to Lin-

coln's Inn to have what Basil Ptarmigan Q.C., the head
of Chambers, considered a more or less tolerable wine list.
During the meal we had conscientiously tested its merits:
by the time we reached the coffee and liqueurs the mood
of the gathering was relaxed and convivial. Basil had then
risen to make a graceful little speech, full of elegant compliments to the guest of honor, proposing the toast "To
women at the Bar."

"And to our progressing more rapidly in our profession," said Selena Jardine, "in the twenty-first century
than in the twentieth. Considering that it's nearly eighty
years since women were first admitted to the Bar, don't
you find it rather discouraging, Eve, that even now there
are so few women judges?"

"But you must remember," said Eve, "that judges are
usually appointed thirty or forty years after being called
to the Bar. And in the past forty years, things have
changed a great deal."

It was thus that she came to tell us about the murder—
which was, she added in extenuation, her first and only
crime.

"Ah yes," said Basil, "I remember about your murder,
Eve. You secured an acquittal, as I recall, before Mr. Justice Rattlestick—many seasoned criminal lawyers would
be proud to boast as much. A triumph, my dear Eve—not
merely for you personally, but, if I may so express it, for
the Chancery approach. We are not so ungracious, I hope,
as to ask you to sing for your supper, but I know we
should all like to hear about it."

Eve, at first demurring, yielded to universal persua-
sion.

"By the time I was come to the Bar," said Eve,
"women had already made some measure of progress—
there was nothing extraordinary in itself about a woman
being a barrister. Quite a number of women had been
called to the Bar since the end of the Second World
War and several had been very successful. They had all,

however, specialized in crime—not in commercial or property cases. Twenty years before, the accepted opinion had been that women couldn't be effective as advocates. The accepted opinion now was that they *could* be quite effective in those cases where they could appeal to the emotions of the jury—that is to say, in criminal cases. In civil litigation, on the other hand, where it was the judge who had to be persuaded, and what counted was clear, logical reasoning, they would of course be perfectly hopeless."

"Outrageous," said Selena, with warm indignation.

"Quite so, but still, as I say, a measure of progress. The trouble was, from my point of view, that I simply didn't want to practice at the criminal Bar. What I was interested in was the law of property—entails and contingent remainders and the rule against perpetuities. As far as I was concerned, criminal law hardly counted as law at all. So clearly the place for me was the Chancery Bar and my first step, after passing my exams, was to look for a Chancery pupillage.

"It was at that point that I began to get pitying smiles from everyone I asked for help or advice. In a profession, they said, not noted for radicalism, the Chancery Bar was the most conservative section—they used such expressions as 'reactionary' and even 'hidebound.' Very few Chancery barristers would be willing to take a woman as a pupil; even if I found a pupillage, I was most unlikely to obtain a tenancy afterward; and even if I did get a tenancy, I would never get any work—no solicitor would dare to instruct a woman in connection with a Chancery case. It was true that one or two women had somehow got tenancies in Chancery chambers; but they had, I was told, other sources of income—their professional earnings barely covered their Chambers expenses. If I wanted to make my living as a barrister, it would have to be at the criminal Bar.

"But I was an optimist at that age and rather obstinate,

so I went on looking for a Chancery pupillage. There was
no formal procedure for finding pupillage in those days—
one just asked anyone one could think of whether they
could help. In the end one of my tutors at Oxford gave
me an introduction to Christopher Dove, who was a senior
Junior at 62 New Square and the editor of the leading
textbook on easements of light. Christopher was quite old-
fashioned in many ways, but he didn't seem to mind at
all about me being a woman."

"That," said Basil, "was because he didn't notice. He
was often heard to speak of you as a nice young fellow,
very sound on the Settled Land Act."

"Basil," said Eve, "you exaggerate. Well, I enjoyed my
pupillage enormously. We were at the beginning of the
great boom in property values that characterized the 1960s
and some people, not always very scrupulous, had already
started buying up areas of land which they thought suit-
able for development. So there was a good deal of interesting litigation going on in the Chancery Division about
contracts for the sale of land and Christopher was getting
his fair share of it.

"I was short of money, of course, but I'd expected that.
Pupils weren't paid anything in those days—on the contrary, the pupil paid the pupil master a hundred guineas.
Apart from some teaching and editorial work, I had to
rely on the generosity of my parents to keep me from
starvation. Still, I wasn't unduly worried about my financial position—I thought that once I'd finished my first six
months of pupillage, and was entitled to accept instructions from solicitors to appear in court, I'd start to have
some fees coming in.

"When the great day came, however, it didn't appear
to be an occasion for which solicitors up and down the
country had been waiting with bated breath. The days
and weeks went by and not a single brief arrived with
my name on—not so much as a claim for possession of
a cowshed in Little Piddlecombe or an uncontested

winding-up on Monday morning in the Companies Court. After a month, I was feeling rather discouraged— when a friend in the Middle Temple rang up and said he was in difficulties on the following day and wondered if I could help him out, I wasn't in any mood to turn him down.

"He was junior counsel in a trial that was due to start at the Old Bailey and another of his cases had suddenly come up for hearing in the Court of Appeal—he wanted me to take over his brief at the Bailey. I didn't need, he said breezily, to know anything about the case—he was being led by Hector Pomfret, who was a very experienced criminal Silk and knew the case inside out—all I had to do was sit behind Pomfret and take a more or less legible note of the evidence. 'Money for old rope' was how my friend described it, and I have to admit that the brief fee was very attractive.

"By the time he got round to telling me that his client was charged with murder, I'd committed myself to doing it. So he sent the papers across to me and I spent the evening reading them.

"It wasn't even an interesting or glamorous sort of murder, just a common or garden bank raid that went rather horribly wrong—the senior cashier had tried to be heroic and one of the raiders had shot him. There were three men involved—the two who actually carried out the raid and the driver of the getaway car. From the descriptions given by witnesses, the police were pretty sure of the identity of the two raiders—a pair known in the circles in which they moved as Basher and Boozy. They both had impressive criminal records and usually worked together. Since the case was one of murder, the police search for them was fairly intensive and they were picked up only a few hours later. With them was a young motor mechanic by the name of Ronnie Baxter. On the assumption, of course, that he'd been the driver of the getaway car, he also was arrested, and like the other two charged with murder.

"Ronnie Baxter was my client. He had several convictions, though for minor offenses, and it seemed that he acted fairly regularly as a sort of errand boy for people engaged in more serious criminal activities. Still, he'd never been involved before in anything violent and I didn't get the impression that he was a dangerous criminal who deserved to be locked up for the rest of his life."

"It doesn't sound," said Selena, "as if the case against him was very strong."

"Well," said Eve, "it wouldn't have been, if it hadn't been for the alibi." She sighed and sipped her brandy. "Basher and Boozy, when questioned by the police, had very sensibly exercised their right to remain silent and left the Crown to prove its case. My client, on the other hand, had made a statement. He didn't know anything, he said, about the raid and hadn't seen Basher and Boozy until several hours after it happened. One or other of them had rung him up on the previous day and asked if he'd like to earn himself fifty pounds—when he said that he would, they'd arranged to meet.

"Before they could tell him, however, what it was that they wanted him to do, the police had arrived and arrested them all. Ronnie had no reason, he said, to think that it was anything illegal and he certainly didn't know that it had anything to do with a bank raid. Besides, he had an alibi—the raid had taken place in the middle of the afternoon and all that afternoon he'd been at home, in a house that he shared with his younger brother, Gary Baxter. His brother, he said, would confirm it." She sighed again.

"But he didn't?"

"Well, at first he confirmed Ronnie's story in every detail—even the police officers who interviewed him were quite impressed. And he seemed a respectable sort of character, not at all like Ronnie—no criminal record and a steady job working in an office for a well-known local businessman."

"Too good to be true?"

"I'm afraid so. A day or two later he'd spoken to his employer, a Mr. William Johnson, about the strain he was under on account of the charge against his brother. Mr. Johnson had tried to cheer him up by taking him out for a drink after work and Gary had admitted, after a couple of pints, that what was worrying him was the prospect of committing perjury. The truth was, he said, that Ronnie had gone out immediately after lunch, having specifically warned Gary to tell anyone who asked that he'd been at home all day.

"And Mr. Johnson, being an upright, law-abiding citizen, thought it his duty to report this conversation to the police. With evidence that Ronnie had tried to fabricate an alibi in advance for the time of the raid, the case against him was obviously a good deal stronger than it had looked at first.

"By a curious coincidence, I happened to know the place where the conversation between Gary and Johnson had occurred—or rather, as I had to keep reminding myself, was alleged to have occurred. It was a pub called the Golden Honeypot, quite close to where Gary and Ronnie lived, in a rather run-down area of north London. I wouldn't normally have had any occasion to be anywhere near there, but one of the cases I was working on with Christopher was about the sale of a house in the same area. Rather an interesting case," she added, her dark eyes lighting up with enthusiasm. "It eventually went to the Court of Appeal—you'll find it reported as *Bildora Ltd. v. Strange*. Our client claimed, you see, that Bildora Ltd. had tricked him into selling his house by—"

"Eve," said Selena, gently but firmly, "you were telling us about the murder."

"Ah yes. Well, a point had arisen in the Bildora case which I'd thought I might understand better if I actually saw the house. So one lunchtime I went and had a look at it, and afterward I stopped for a drink and a sandwich in the Golden Honeypot. It didn't seem likely, though, that my personal knowledge of the *locus in quo* would be of vital significance so far as Ronnie was concerned. Even if Mr. Johnson was lying—and I couldn't imagine why he should be—the last thing he'd be likely to lie about was the color of the wallpaper in the Golden Honeypot. Poor Ronnie—he was my very first client and there seemed to be nothing I could do to help his case. I went to bed, I remember, feeling rather despondent about it."

When she met Hector Pomfret in the robing room at the Old Bailey on the following morning, she had found her learned leader unsanguine about their prospects. Though Ronnie still adhered to his original story and appeared entirely bewildered by his brother's behavior, there could clearly now be no question of the defense calling Gary as a witness. The Crown, thought Pomfret, would also be reluctant to call him; but the evidence of Mr. Johnson would almost certainly be enough to persuade the jury that Ronnie, on the day of the bank raid, had been planning to engage in some serious criminal activity.

The best hope for the defense, said Pomfret—Eve understood him to mean the only hope—was to persuade the judge to rule Mr. Johnson's evidence inadmissible under the rule against hearsay; but the judge was Mr. Justice Rattlestick. Mr. Justice Rattlestick, so far as Pomfret was aware, had never in his judicial career made a ruling favorable to the defense when he could possibly avoid it; still, said Pomfret, evidently not wishing his junior to become discouraged, there was a first time for everything."

"A most unpleasant man, Rattlestick," said Basil Ptarmigan. "It was said that his chief disappointment in life was being appointed to the bench too late to have the chance of passing the death sentence on anyone."

"That," said Eve, "wouldn't at all surprise me—he struck me as soon as I saw him as that sort of man. He was good-looking, I suppose, though at that time of course he seemed to me to be quite old, but there was something repellent about him—something brutal and vicious about his mouth ... I remember thinking, when he first came into court, that he wasn't the kind of man one would care to be seen home by after a party."

The first day of the trial was occupied with the prosecution evidence about the bank raid, not in dispute so far as Ronnie Baxter was concerned: none of the witnesses claimed to be able to identify the driver of the getaway car. The morning of the second, following the announcement by counsel for the Crown that his next witness would be Mr. William Johnson, was devoted to legal argument, in the absence of the jury, as to the admissibility of Mr. Johnson's evidence.

"During which," said Eve, "Mr. Justice Rattlestick made not the slightest pretence of impartiality—he plainly regarded any barrister who defended a client on a criminal charge as party to a conspiracy to defeat the ends of justice. After the sheltered life I'd led in the Chancery Division, I could hardly believe that a judge could be so openly unpleasant. So it came as no surprise to anyone when he ruled against us and Mr. Johnson went into the witness box."

"And turned out, I suppose," said Selena with sympathetic pessimism, "to be the ideal witness?"

"Yes, from the point of view of the Crown. From ours, he was catastrophic. A sober, solid, sensible-looking man in his mid-forties, who'd built up a flourishing business from almost nothing and was now a pillar of the local community—active in the church and local politics and all that sort of thing. It was obvious that the jury would believe every word he said. And we had no basis for suggesting that they shouldn't—so far as we knew, there wasn't the slightest reason for him to be telling lies.

"If he was telling the truth, the only possibility consistent with our client's innocence seemed to be that Gary had been lying—not to the police, but when he talked to Mr. Johnson. Well, I knew that brothers don't always love each other as they should, but I found it difficult to imagine that Gary would have destroyed his brother's alibi out of pure malice.

"Mr. Johnson hadn't got where he was, he said, all by his own efforts—he wasn't ashamed to admit that from time to time he'd needed a helping hand. So he thought it was only right that he should offer a helping hand when he saw someone else who needed it. And one such person, it seemed, was Gary Baxter.

"Ronnie and Gary had been orphaned as quite small children, both their parents having died in an air raid during the Second World War, and they'd been brought up by their grandmother. Gary had still been only fourteen when she died and he'd just gone on living in the same house with no one but his brother to look after him or set him an example of how to behave. But in spite of this unpromising background Gary was trying hard to make something of himself and Mr. Johnson felt that he deserved help and encouragement. In the two years that Gary had been working for him, Mr. Johnson had always tried to make him feel that he could turn to his employer for advice if he had a problem, or even a modest loan if he ran short before payday. Which made it quite natural for him to confide in Mr. Johnson when his brother got into trouble.

"I began to wonder whether Gary could have any financial motive for wanting his brother out of the way. I'd assumed that the house they lived in was rented—people like Ronnie and Gary didn't usually own property in those days—but it now looked to me as if they might have inherited it from their grandmother. It occurred to me that it must be quite close to the one in the Bildora case and that the same developers might want to acquire it—if so, the sum involved could be quite substantial.

"During the luncheon adjournment, I asked our instructing solicitor whether he happened to know who owned the house. It turned out that it had indeed been part of the grandmother's estate and his firm were the executors of her will—that's how Ronnie came to instruct them when he found himself on a criminal charge. I asked him if I could see a copy of the will and he promised to have one sent down from his office.

"By the time it arrived we were back in court. I had to read it at the same time as taking a note of the evidence, but fortunately it was quite short and at first sight fairly straightforward—the two boys were to be allowed to go on living in the house and if either of them left the other one was to be allowed to go on living there. If and when they both left, it was to be sold and the proceeds were to be shared between them and half a dozen other beneficiaries."

"A simple, innocent criminal lawyer," said Selena, "would no doubt have taken these provisions at face value. But after six months' pupillage in New Square—"

"I could hardly fail to realize that their effect was to create a strict settlement within the meaning of the Settled Land Act. Which meant, of course, that if Ronnie ceased to live in the house Gary would be left as the person with the powers of a tenant for life—including the power of sale."

"And by virtue of section 106, if he sold the house in exercise of that power—"

"He'd be entitled to the income from the proceeds and the other beneficiaries wouldn't get a penny until he died. Which seemed to me to be such a thunderingly good motive for him to want Ronnie to be sent to prison that I felt like standing up and telling everyone about it straight away.

"Inexperienced as I was, however, I saw that this was unlikely to be the correct procedure. In fact, the more I thought about it, the more difficult it was to see how the the Settled Land Act point could be brought to the attention of the jury if Gary himself wasn't going to give evidence. I also began to think of objections which might be made to my theory. In particular, how would Gary have known the effect of the Settled Land Act on the provisions of his grandmother's will? It didn't seem likely that he spent his leisure hours reading textbooks on real property.

"I decided to mention the point to Pomfret after the four o'clock adjournment and leave it to him to work out whether it could be raised in the cross-examination of Mr. Johnson. Mr. Johnson was giving very detailed evidence about his conversation with Gary, which he seemed to remember practically word for word, so I didn't doubt that he'd still be in the witness-box the following morning.

"At half past three someone handed me a note addressed to Pomfret and I passed it to him. After reading it, he stood up and told Rattlestick that he was obliged to leave the court, being urgently required elsewhere in connection with other proceedings.

" 'Since your learned junior is still here to protect your client's interests,' said Rattlestick, with an unpleasantly sarcastic emphasis on the word *learned*, 'there can of course be no objection.'

"Five minutes later, counsel for the prosecution said that he had no further questions and sat down.

" 'Yes, Miss Lampeter?' said Rattlestick.

"I stood up and asked for an adjournment. I felt dizzy and slightly sick and my voice came out as not much more than a squeak, but I didn't seriously imagine that he'd refuse. My client was facing the gravest possible of charges and Johnson was the main witness against him: it was clear that the cross-examination should be conducted by leading counsel.

" 'Do you mean, Miss Lampeter,' said Rattlestick, 'that you are not competent to conduct the cross-examination?'

"I felt as if I were blushing all over. It was, of course, exactly what I meant, but not what I wanted to say. The press bench was full of crime reporters on the alert for some entertaining titbit and women barristers always make good copy, especially if they're young and quite attractive, and especially if they've done something silly—an admission by a woman barrister in open court that she was incompetent to conduct her case would have made their day. I took a deep breath and said that I could not claim to have the experience or eloquence of my learned leader.

" 'I didn't ask you that,' said Rattlestick. 'I asked if you were making the application on the ground that you were not competent to conduct the cross-examination of this witness?'

"He was looking at me with a sort of gloating enjoyment, like a tomcat playing with a plump little mouse. I was pretty green as a lawyer, but I had quite enough experience of life to recognize the expression—I saw that he was hoping that I would burst into tears. And unless I did, he wouldn't grant the adjournment.

"Well, I could easily have done it and perhaps I should have done—my duty, after all, was to my client, and it seemed to be the only way to make sure that his case was properly conducted. But I saw the reporters with their pencils hovering eagerly over their notebooks and I knew that if I did I'd never dare to go into court again and my career at the Bar would be over before it started. And I thought 'I'll be damned if I let the old bully do that to me.' So instead of bursting into tears, I gave him my best social smile, as if he'd made a rather poor joke at a cocktail party, and said that if he thought it convenient I would of course be happy to proceed with the cross-examination.

"I didn't entertain any hope of eliciting any answer from Mr. Johnson which might be at all helpful to our client's case—all I wanted was to keep him in the witness box until the four o'clock adjournment, so that he'd be available to be cross-examined by Pomfret on the following morning. I had a naïve confidence, in those days, in the ability of leading counsel to make bricks out of straw.

"I felt free, therefore, to put my questions in what I suppose one could call the Chancery style—that is to say, in a polite and friendly sort of way, without everlastingly suggesting that the witness was telling a tissue of lies. Mr. Johnson responded in the same spirit and we began to get along quite well.

"At this stage my personal knowledge of the Golden Honeypot began to come in rather useful. I was able to ask him in great detail about the surroundings in which the crucial conversation had taken place—where he and Gary had been sitting, whether the barman could overhear them, how loudly the jukebox had been playing and so on. He answered freely and at some length and I began to be quite optimistic about continuing in this vein until the adjournment.

" 'Miss Lampeter,' said Rattlestick, 'may I remind you that you are conducting a cross-examination, not making small talk at a ladies' coffee morning? Is the interior decoration scheme of the Golden Honeypot of any conceivable relevance to the case?'

"I said that I was trying to establish whether the witness would have heard clearly what Gary had said to him. But I didn't dare to ask any more questions on the same lines and it was still only quarter to four.

"I next tried asking the witness about Gary's relationship with Ronnie. From what Mr. Johnson had told us of the background, there were many things that the elder brother might have done to incur the resentment of the younger, and of which Gary might perhaps have complained to a sympathetic listener.

"'Miss Lampeter,' said Rattlestick, 'your client is charged with a more serious offense than stealing his brother's teddy bear. May I ask you again to confine yourself to questions having some relevance to the case?'

"There were still seven minutes to go to the adjournment and my mind was a complete blank, apart from my idea about the Settled Land Act. I asked whether Gary had ever said anything to Mr. Johnson about his financial circumstances and went on from there to ask whether he had said anything about the provisions of his grandmother's will.

"For some reason Mr. Johnson seemed rather flustered by the question—he said that he knew nothing about that and it wasn't for him to pry into what people left in their wills. I was puzzled by his reaction, but I didn't spend much time thinking about it. I saw, glancing at my watch, that it was only a minute or so to four o'clock and if I could think of some innocuous question which would see me through the remaining sixty seconds—

"'Miss Lampeter,' said Rattlestick, 'there is no need to be concerned about the time. I do not propose to adjourn until your cross-examination is complete.'"

"There was nothing I could do—it was pointless to prolong the agony. I did say, of course, that my learned friend Mr. Pomfret might have further questions to ask Mr. Johnson on the following morning and I assumed, therefore, that he would remain available.

"'No, Miss Lampeter,' said Rattlestick. 'The witness is plainly a very busy man who has come forward to assist the prosecution out of a sense of civic duty and has already sacrificed a considerable amount of time in order to give evidence. He should not be subjected to any further inconvenience. I should not be justified in requiring him to return here tomorrow or forbidding him to discuss the case with his friends and family. I don't know,' he went on, with a nauseating pretense of geniality, 'whether Mr. Johnson is a married man, but I dare say that if he is that would impose a considerable strain on him—isn't that so, Mr. Johnson?'

" 'Well, my lord,' said Mr. Johnson, 'I don't deny my Dora's going to be on at me tonight to tell her all about it.'

" 'Well, Miss Lampeter,' said Rattlestick, 'have you any further questions? Any further *relevant* questions?'

"I told him that I did have just one or two more, because, when Johnson mentioned that his wife's name was Dora, I'd suddenly remembered that *his* name was William. And it had occurred to me that when people are forming a private company, the kind where all the shares are owned by a husband and wife, they very often call it by a combination of their Christian names.

"So I asked him whether I was right in thinking that he was the principal shareholder in a company called Bildora Ltd. And when he said that he was, I knew why he wanted Ronnie to be sent to prison. After that it was all plain sailing, though I had a little difficulty in getting Rattlestick to understand the Settled Land Act point.

"Mr. Johnson's motives, from the point of view of the Chancery Bar, were perfectly straightforward and understandable: he needed the house for his development scheme and Ronnie didn't want to sell. If Gary had become the person with the power of sale, he would have had no choice: the loans that Johnson had made to tide him over until pay day amounted to a substantial sum— more than he had any hope of repaying. Gary had to do as he was told."

"A triumph indeed," said Selena, "both for you and for the Chancery approach. And I hope acknowledged as such by the press."

"Well, not exactly," said Eve. "As a matter of fact, they described it as a triumph of feminine intuition over masculine logic. Still, one can't have everything. Yes, thank you, Basil, I will have a little more brandy."

Decoys

Terry Devane

Terry Devane is the pseudonym of an award-winning author and attorney who lives in the Boston area. Mairead O'Clare is a new series character who makes her first appearance in a novel, Uncommon Justice, *in April 2001.*

"THERE are two reasons why people divorce," said Sheldon A. Gold, attorney-at-law. "One is that the bride expects her new husband to change, and he doesn't. The other is that the groom doesn't expect his new wife to change, and she does."

Mairead O'Clare, fresh from a discouraging experience as an associate at a large Boston law firm, stared at her new boss from the client chair across his desk. "When I signed on, Shel, you told me most of your practice was criminal defense."

Gold squirmed a little in his seat, the rumpled suit jacket scrunching at the collar against the cracked leather bustle of his chair. "And this case is no different, Mairead."

She didn't understand, but at least he'd pronounced her name correctly, "Muh-*raid*," unlike that horse's ass who headed litigation at Jaynes & Ward. "Wait a minute. I thought you said—"

"—divorce. I did." Gold reached for a manila folder, one of many on his cluttered desktop. "Only here, divorce was the motive for murder. Or at least, that's the prosecution's theory."

Mairead received the file from her boss's outstretched hand, noting that their secretary—Billie Sunday—had labeled the tab "Stanler, Harvey P.," followed by a red H, for "Homicide."

Mairead recalled the *Boston Herald* news coverage. "The police think he strangled his wife because of a prenuptial agreement, right?"

"Or because of its consequences. Harvey Stanler was fifty-eight when he married Jennifer Keats, age then twenty-four."

Jennifer. There'd been one at the orphanage when Mairead was growing up. Blond and blue-eyed, Jennifer had been adopted almost immediately, but not before making fun three times a day of Mairead's hemangioma, the purplish birthmarks covering both arms from fingernails to elbows.

Inside Mairead's head, Sister Bernadette's voice from the orphanage said, *Get over it, young lady*.

"You okay?" asked Sheldon Gold.

"Uh, sorry." Mairead refocused. "So, Harvey was smart enough to insist on a prenup."

"Or his lawyer was."

"And who was this lawyer?"

"Me," said Gold.

"Oh."

"It gets better." A sigh as he raked the fingers of one hand through his sandy hair. "The paragraph on lump-sum payment provided that in exchange for Jennifer renouncing all other claims, she'd get fifty thousand dollars if there was no divorce before two years from date of ceremony, but a hundred thousand if no divorce before year five."

"If no . . . 'divorce'?"

Gold shrugged. "So, I screwed up. Should have read no 'legal separation.' Then Harvey—"

"—would have been in charge of the calendar formula."

"Right." Another sigh. "But, as I phrased the provision, he wasn't, and even though divorce proceedings had begun, the formal court hearing wasn't going to happen before the fifth anniversary."

"And her family thinks her loving husband killed her."

"No. Jennifer Keats didn't *have* any family, at least so far as Harvey knows."

Mairead said, "Then it's the DA's office thinks he killed her?"

"At year four, eleven months, and seventeen days."

Thirteen to spare. "Good that our client left himself some margin for error."

"I don't think he did."

Mairead paused a moment, making sure she'd gotten Gold's drift. "You're saying Harvey's innocent?"

Her boss squirmed a little more. "I've known the man almost thirty years."

"Not what a judge would call responsive, Shel."

Gold looked out his eleventh-floor window, just a glance over his shoulder, really, toward the downslope of Beacon Hill. "I think he's been framed."

Mairead hadn't been working for Gold long, but she knew he had a private investigator named Pontifico "The Pope" Murizzi who'd work any case in which he—Murizzi—thought the accused wasn't the perpetrator. "So, the Pope's onboard, too?"

"No." Now squirming to the point of wriggling. "He met with Harvey, but our investigator doesn't share my view of him."

"Meaning, the Pope thinks he's guilty."

"Harvey doesn't come across well, first-impression-wise."

"Shel?"

"Yes?"

"That's not exactly a positive personality characteristic, capital-jury-wise."

One last sigh, deeper than the first two. "Meet with Harvey, Mairead?"

"Where is he?"

"Should take you only one guess," said Sheldon A. Gold.

*   *   *

"THIS is bullshit! The bitch is still nailing me from the grave."

Mairead O'Clare watched Harvey P. Stanler from her side of the attorney-client cubicle at the Nashua Street Jail. He had clotting hair the color of cream soda, thinning in the center of his head. Given the lines on the leathery face, Mairead voted for a dye job, no question. The man's craggy brow gave him a brutish look, almost like those prehumans in that flick *Quest for Fire*.

Oh, yeah, and one other thing. There was no screen or other divider between them, so she'd extended her hand to Stanler as the guard had brought him into the eight-by-eight room. After Mairead had introduced herself, Stanler had taken a look at the color of her hand and not extended his own.

You have to give Mr. Gold credit, young lady, said Sister Bernadette's voice. *He was right about his client's knack for first impressions.*

"Mr. Stanler—"

"I mean, Mairead, what the hell can the cops be thinking? I'm gonna kill Jen to save fifty thousand against rotting in jail while my daughter runs through almost three million?"

Mairead had read the file. "Your daughter, Wendy?"

"Right, right. She's thirty-one, and if the expression was 'wine, men, and song,' you'd have a pretty good idea of what she's like."

"Wendy's your daughter from a prior . . . ?"

"Marriage. I was born in the generation, we did the right thing. Not like you twenty-somethings."

Better and better. "Mr. Stanler—"

"Why do you think I had the vasectomy? I didn't want to knock up Jen, too. That'd be all I'd need at my age, playing father to a brat the age of my friends' grandkids."

Mairead resisted the temptation to comment on his comfort level in marrying a woman the age of his friends' children. "Mr. Gold wants me to find out—"

"Was Shel got me into this! Five years ago, he says to me, 'Harve, you're gonna marry a young one, be sure to protect yourself. That means a prenuptial agreement. And, if you're not firing blanks yet, an operation, too, because once there's a brat on the scene, the prenup isn't worth the paper it's printed on.' " Stanler raked the fingers of his right hand through his hair, so like Shel that Mairead nearly jumped in her chair. "So, I listen to my lawyer's advice, and here's where it lands me."

Cut to the chase, young lady. "If you didn't kill your wife, who did?"

"That's what . . ." Stanler suddenly seemed to run down. "Look, Mairead, I don't mean to be screaming at you, all right? You're just trying to do your job, and God knows I need somebody to help me. So, okay," he straightened a little in his chair, "I admit the marriage had gone sour—hell, we filed for divorce three months before Jen died. And I admit I told half-a-dozen people I'd like to strangle the little bitch, but that was just a figure of speech, you know? I mean, I had the prenup, and if I didn't get divorced soon enough to keep the fifty from being a hundred to her, so be it. Dave and I gross that much and more in a good month, high season."

"Dave Poitrast, your partner."

"In the import business, right. We been together ten years, and he's like the brother I never had, you know what I mean?"

Mairead's mind ranged back to the orphanage. *Boy, do I.*

Stanler said, "This thing's killing him, too."

"He feels for you."

"More than that. He's got to do the work of two men!"

The prosecution would pay us for the opportunity to cross-examine this ass in front of a jury. "Mr. Stanler, is there anybody else you can think of who might have killed your wife?"

"Just that shark of a divorce lawyer she hired, try and break Shel's prenup."

"That's Petra Lindsay?"

"Yeah. 'Petra,' she's got the eyes of something that eats what it kills." Then Harvey P. Stanler seemed to have a brainstorm. "Hey, since when did all you female 'esquires' get such funny names, anyway?"

*   *   *

"So, how's the new client?" said Billie Sunday.

Mairead O'Clare closed the door to their office suite behind her before replying to the middle-aged African-American woman sitting sidesaddle in the receptionist chair. "What can you do after writing *neanderthal* in all capital letters?"

Sunday went back to her old IBM Selectric III typewriter. "Underline it, then hang the sign around the man's neck."

Mairead nodded toward the middle-office door. "Shel in?"

"Uh-unh. You need to talk with him, he'll be back around four. He said."

Which meant, Don't count on it, honey.

"Billie, I'll be out interviewing witnesses."

Sunday's head and shoulders rose, her trademark silent laugh. "I won't be."

*   *   *

"**Y**OU'RE, like, my father's *lawyer*?" said Wendy Stanler around the rim of some kind of pink fizz drink
as she used a toothpick to drown a chunk of pineapple in
it.

Mairead didn't have to check her watch to know it
wasn't yet noontime. "Ms. Stanler—"

"As if. You can't be *that* much younger than I am, so
call me Wendy."

Great, thought Mairead, a Valley Girl who speaks in
italics. Stanler's streaked blond hair was cut in a ragged
shag; she wore a black tank top over black pedal-pushers
that were less sewn and more painted on. "I'm helping
Sheldon Gold with your father's defense."

Wendy Stanler sat on the leather sofa in what Mairead
guessed to be Harvey Stanler's den, given all the duck
decoys on the fireplace mantel and the two shotguns
crossed over it. Add the blood-red furniture and hunting-
camp Tartan carpet, and the room reeked of testosterone.

After answering the front door, daughter Stanler had
pulled down the earphones of a Walkman to her neck.
Given the volume of the retro-rock music Mairead could
hear from six feet away, it was a miracle Wendy had
registered the bell chimes at all. And, following the potential witness through the hallways, Mairead guessed that
this Stanler's butt bounced more in discos than on playing
fields.

Just outside the den, though, Wendy had stopped, even
shivered. "This is where it happened, you know?"

Mairead said, "I read the police report."

"Strangled, on her knees, probably. I was out at a club,
but she was just, like, a couple *feet* away from a phone."
Stanler had turned, her eyes not showing anything. "Bum-
mer, huh?"

Mairead had just nodded.

Now, in the den, Wendy drew her legs up on the
couch, knees nearly to her chin in the fetal position.
Which didn't prevent her from taking another slug of the

pink drink. "Okay, I'll bite. What *is* old Harve's defense?" She inclined her head toward the mantel. "That he would have shot the slut instead of strangling her?"

"He claims he didn't kill your stepmother, period."

A laugh, some of the liquid now fizzing out Wendy's nostrils. "More like my step*sister*."

She moved one hand to wipe away the drink trail, but slowly, languorously. Mairead was relieved the woman didn't lick her hand after she was finished.

Then Wendy said, "The little slut was only, like, *your* age."

"Did you resent your father marrying somebody so young?"

"Why, because it made *me* feel *old*?"

Touched a nerve there, young lady. "For any reason at all."

"Look—what was your name again?"

"Mairead."

"Well, look, Muh-*raid*, here's how the old man played his cards. Even before Mom died, he was mucho macho into hunting, shooting these poor little ducks from a camouflaged box at dawn on the Ipswich River, his decoys spread out on the cold water around him. But after she was . . . gone, Daddy *Dearest* also liked a warm bed and a hot chick in it. He'd even take the trophy bimbette of the moment to the 'Lodge'—what him and his best buds call the place where all the hunters hang. Harve and Dave used to pass them around."

Mairead felt her head canting to the side. "Your father and his partner used to . . . ?"

". . . share their chicks, like a swapshop." Wendy gestured with her glass, sloshing the drink over onto her fingers. "Those blotch thingies on your hands mean you don't have so many dates, I have to draw you a picture?"

Like father, like daughter. "Was Mr. Poitrast jealous that your father ended up with Jennifer?"

"*Jealous*? Now, that's *really* a laugher." This time

Wendy did lick her fingers for the liquid she'd spilled. "To Dave, it was more like shooting the poor ducks."

Mairead put that together. "Friendly competition."

Wendy puffed out her chest and squinched up her features. "A *manly* competition," she said in a deep voice. Then she relented. "Aw, shit. Did I hear old Harve say he was gonna 'strangle that little slut'? Sure. But did he really kill her?" A long drag on the pink drink, and some tears actually came into Wendy Stanler's eyes. "Like I really would have cared, you know?"

*   *   *

"I appreciate your seeing me on such short notice, Mr. Poitrast."

"Hey, for Harve? I mean, we aren't just partners, we're best friends."

Mairead O'Clare looked around the office. Orderly, with computers all over the place. The furnishings were classy and exotic, maybe the way all import companies looked. The view out the window, however, was just six feet of air well to a brick wall.

Poitrast motioned her toward an armchair while he sank into one behind his desk. Younger than Stanler by a decade, Poitrast seemed more athletic, despite a little paunch hanging over his belt. He also seemed like the personality guy, the one who made the rain by getting the deals that Stanler would execute.

Poitrast clasped both hands behind his head. "I am kind of under the gun, though, what with having to do Harve's stuff and my own, so I'd appreciate your getting to the point."

Anything for Harve, but . . . "Mr. Poitrast, I understand from the police file that Mr. Stanler left you here after receiving a phone call?"

"Yeah. From his wife—Jennifer."

"The night that Mrs. Stanler died, she called here?"

"Right."

"Did you answer the phone?"

Poitrast shook his head. "But I knew it was her. Harve used 'Jen'—his pet name for her—and that tone of voice."

"Tone?"

" 'Pissed off' would be a good description."

"Then what happened?"

"Harve blew out of here, and when I left maybe an hour later, his car was gone."

"Did he say anything to you before he left?"

"Afraid so."

"What?"

" 'I'm gonna strangle that bitch.' "

Consistency, young lady, is not always a virtue. "The Stanlers stayed in touch, despite the divorce?"

"Well, they weren't divorced yet, and while he wasn't supposed to call her—some kind of 'personal liberty' order, I think it was—she'd call him from their house."

Which had seemed odd to Mairead from the report. "Despite the prenuptial agreement, Mrs. Stanler was living in the house during the separation?"

"Another part of the agreement, actually. If they separated, she got to stay in one wing of the place."

Shel hadn't mentioned that, and Mairead had concentrated on the police and forensics information, not the prenup itself.

Poitrast said, "It's a pretty big house."

"I'm sorry?"

"Harve's place. It's plenty big enough for both of them—and Wendy, too—to live there without running into each other. While the divorce was chugging along, the arrangement saved Harve temporary alimony, and once the formal court hearing happened, Jennifer would be out of there with her lump sum."

"You're pretty familiar with the agreement, then?"

"Harve and I are partners. Hell, Ms. O'Clare, we went over that document line by line with a fine-toothed comb.

Missed a few things, account of we aren't lawyers. But I figured, Harve's gonna leap into the abyss, I'd help him out as much as I could."

Help him out. "You didn't exactly approve of the marriage?"

"Hey." Poitrast spread his hands like a priest at Mass. "My view's always been, why bother to contract for something you can pick up in a bar whenever the mood strikes?" Poitrast coughed. "Um, no offense."

"None taken," said Mairead.

Poitrast brought his hands back together on the desk. "Plus, if you are going to marry one, there sure as hell were better prospects."

"Better how?"

"Jennifer got it into her head that she was a great hostess for business meals, but the woman was a bigot, and it showed. Blacks, Hispanics, she even went off on a rant about AIDS in front of this gay client of ours, nearly cost us his business." A grim laugh. "Probably hated lesbians, too, though I can't recall she met any, you don't count Wendy."

"Harvey Stanler's daughter?"

"The one and only. Oh, Wendy always put up a good front, going to discos and dancing with guys. Even left with a few, if Harve was around to see it."

"She'd leave a club with a male so her father could witness it."

"That's right."

"Meaning, Mr. Stanler doesn't know about her orientation?"

"He thinks she's wild, but maybe not that wild."

"But you do."

Poitrast looked uncomfortable. "I tell you something, does it automatically get back to Harve?"

"Not automatically, but if it helps him . . ."

"I don't think it will, but I was in your shoes, Ms. O'Clare, I'd want to know about it." Poitrast frowned.

"We had a party, over at Harve's house. Just the close people, celebrate our tenth year of being in business together. Well, I go off to use the head, and as I'm coming back, Jennifer hits on me in the hallway."

"Mrs. Stanler, now?"

"Right. Makes kissy-face, even gropes me some. She says . . ." Poitrast frowned a little more. "She says, 'I should have stayed with the younger stud in the stable.' "

"In other words, you?"

"I 'dated' Jen for a while before she switched over to Harve."

Jen, his *partner's* "pet" name for her. "And what did you do?"

"Pushed her off, and she goes the opposite way, none too steady, either. Well, as I turn myself, I see Wendy, standing at the other end of the hallway, this smirk on her face. As I reach her, she says, 'Dave, it's too bad I like girls, otherwise *I* could go from you to Daddy and back again, too.' "

Jesus Mary, thought Mairead. *This is grosser than the soaps.* "She ever mention any of this to your partner?"

"Wendy now, or Jen?"

"Either."

"Not that I know of." Dave Poitrast checked his watch. "I'd think Harve would have said something to me, don't you?"

*   *   *

"M s. O'Clare, I have a pre-trial hearing in . . . twenty-seven minutes. I can give you no more than the first ten of those."

If Shel Gold had pegged Harvey Stanler just right, Harvey Stanler had done a pretty good job on Petra Lindsay. Mairead thought the woman's eyes projected that predator look Stanler had emphasized, but right now, Lindsay stood next to her desk piling papers into a tote briefcase. The divorce attorney was somewhere in her forties and not particularly attractive. However, from the quality of the furnishings, her practice was a step up the scale from even the import company Mairead had just left.

"Ms. O'Clare?"

"Yes?"

"You're down to nine minutes, forty-five seconds."

The phone bleated. Lindsay ignored it.

Mairead said, "Was your client in fear of her husband?"

"Rather a facetious question, given what he did to her."

The phone stopped in midring. "Any specifics before Jennifer died?"

Lindsay seemed not to see a paper she wanted to include. Turning to a file cabinet, she said over her shoulder, "My application for the personal liberty order is public record, so you can read it." Lindsay yanked a paper from the cabinet drawer. "But, basically, Harvey Stanler threatened to strangle her."

"Why?"

"I take it he didn't care for his wife anymore."

"Why?"

Lindsay looked over, showing her teeth in what Mairead couldn't really call a smile. "Like the Little Prince, who once he asks a question . . ." Lindsay went back to packing her bag. "Suffice it to say that Harvey believed Jennifer was using me to stall the divorce until the anniversary date that would have doubled the pot."

"Petra, I'm sorry to interrupt, but—"

She wheeled on the male voice. "What is it?"

A slim young man held a poker hand of pink message slips between trembling fingers. "That was your car-leasing agent. And you said you'd call the bank and the—"

"Not now. I'm in conference and nearly late for an important hearing."

"But they said—"

"Not now!"

The man backed off and away.

"Temp," said Petra Lindsay, fuming.

Mairead didn't nod. A polite temp who calls his boss for the day by her first name? *I don't think so, either, young lady.*

Lindsay stuffed another sheaf of papers into her tote-bag. "That going to do it, Ms. O'Clare?"

"You said my client thought yours was using you to stall until the money under the agreement doubled."

"Correct," she said in an impatient voice.

"And Mr. Stanler was upset about that."

" 'Enraged' might better capture his mood at our settlement conference. I told him that we would resolve the entire matter sooner for the enhanced payment per the agreement, but he felt that was—what were his exact . . . ? Ah, yes. Harvey felt that was 'piracy,' I suppose a bit of colorful jargon from his import business."

"So, if Mr. Stanler were just willing to pay the additional fifty thousand dollars quickly, he'd get his divorce without a trial being necessary."

"Without a contested trial, anyway." Mairead thought Lindsay's manner had softened just a bit. "Ms. O'Clare, I didn't draft their prenup. I didn't even represent Jennifer before the marriage. But if I could trade that timing glitch in the payment formula for Jennifer's life, I'd gladly forget my lawsuit."

"Your lawsuit?"

"The civil case I'll file once the prosecutor has established liability in the form of a criminal conviction. *The Estate of Jennifer Stanler v. Harvey Stanler*, for damages arising from his killing of her."

"You're Jennifer's—"

"Executor and sole beneficiary." Lindsay softened even more. "Jennifer really was afraid of your client, but she had no other family, so she named me in her new will, to be sure someone would have a reason to avenge her if anything . . . happened."

"And the hundred-thousand-dollar lump sum is your 'reason.' "

"Better than that, Ms. O'Clare." Now Petra Lindsay's eyes fairly glowed, as though she smelled blood in the water. "I'll be suing your client for breach of contract—the prenuptial agreement. By killing Jennifer, Harvey made it impossible for her to collect the lump sum. So, I'll be seeking every goddamned dime from Harvey Stanler and his business that his daughter and partner don't spend first."

*   *   *

"L ET me guess," said Sheldon Gold, swiveling a little in his bustle chair. "Dead ends, Mairead?"

"Or a series of threads that don't tie together." She stayed standing, pacing around the office as she spoke. "Jennifer Stanler was a bigoted bimbette, according to both Harvey Stanler's daughter and business partner, yet Harvey married her. His daughter's hiding her sexual orientation from her father, if the partner's to be believed, and the partner seems not to care much about who's 'dating' whom, if he and the daughter are to be believed. Jennifer's divorce attorney tried to cut an acceleration deal for the extra prenup money, but Harvey supposedly bridled at that as 'piracy.' "

"He would," said Gold, clearly bemused by the word.

"Well, I hope this makes you just as happy. The one thing everybody, including our client, agrees on is that Harvey threatened to strangle his wife. Loud and often."

Gold winced. "I'm picturing a parade of his closest circle, one at a time to the witness stand."

"And that's just the criminal trial. Once the jury comes back against Harvey Stanler, Petra Lindsay is also suing him civilly."

Mairead took a small amount of satisfaction in Shel's stricken reaction. "For what?" he said. "To bring a wrongful-death suit, she'd need a surviving family member as plaintiff, and Jennifer Stanler doesn't have any."

Mairead explained Lindsay's strategy to him.

Rubbing the side of his nose with an index finger, Gold said, "Clever. And the theory just might fly. You do any research on it?"

"When?" asked Mairead. "As I was walking up the stairs, your elevator being broken again?"

"You don't mind my saying it, Mairead, you should never rely on machinery."

"Well, you don't mind my saying it, I got an idea from our client's decoys."

Gold blinked. "His . . . ?"

"Decoys," she said. "The degenerate hunts little duckies with shotguns."

"And this gave you an idea?"

"Regarding how we might flush out the real killer."

Her boss came forward in his chair. "Tell me."

Mairead did.

Gold nodded slowly, then more emphatically. "If the Pope will go for it, I like your ploy."

"Any chance you might have the elevator fixed before I have to traipse down eleven flights to see him?"

"Mairead, feel light on your feet. I think you're about to learn that chicanery is much more reliable than machinery."

"Shel?"

"Yes?"

"What the hell does *chicanery* mean?"

*   *   *

As Mairead O'Clare stepped onto the narrow dock running out toward Pontifico Murizzi's boat, she could see him, sitting in shorts and a T-shirt on the back deck. The boat itself was over forty feet long, blue and white with a small top level that sported a steering wheel and two high-backed, padded bar stools that Mairead had heard the Pope call "captain's chairs."

Just one more thing about him I don't understand. Doesn't a boat have only *one* captain?

Murizzi called out to her first. "Want to go for a ride?"

Mairead got close enough to answer without feeling she was shouting. "Just a proposition."

The Pope stood up, and Mairead "appreciated" him again. A shade under six feet, muscles subtle and ropy, even though he was as old as his boat was long. Murizzi had black, curly hair, a lot on his head, and just the right amount on his arms and legs. His face, though, looked rugged and a little hard, what Mairead believed twenty years on the Boston police force—nine of them in Homicide—would do to you.

The Pope gave her a hand as she stepped on the ribbed, rubber strip affixed to the gunwale and then down onto the deck—which was more like a patio, what with folding lawn chairs and a small table for drinks.

Murizzi said, "You want a beer while you proposition me?"

No smile, not even a smarmy undertone to his words. "Sure."

He went downstairs—what she'd also heard him call "below." Mairead was barely seated when the Pope came back with two clear mugs of some amber ale.

"Sam Adams Summer Brew," said Murizzi, handing her one as he settled back into his chair. A couple of gulls screamed and wheeled in the air, a third in the water trying to lift off with some unimaginably ucky prize.

The Pope leaned forward toward Mairead's beer and clunked—the mugs were plastic, so they couldn't exactly "clink"—before saying, "So?"

"Harvey Stanler."

"The obnoxious asshole who strangled his wife."

"Allegedly."

"I met him, Mairead."

"And didn't believe him."

"Right."

She took a slug of the ale. Smooth, with some kind of spice flavor. "I met him, too. And some other people."

Murizzi sipped at his, then rested it on the table. "And you feel different."

"Uh-huh, and here's why."

The Pope listened, taking only one additional sip when Mairead was almost done.

As she finished her story and slugged some more of her ale, Murizzi said, "So, you want me to work the case."

"Not exactly."

Mairead was glad he waited for her to say something more, but even more glad when the Pope spoke first.

"What exactly?" he said.

She told him, and Mairead O'Clare was gladdest of all when Pontifico Murizzi began to grin.

* * *

". . . AND you're like, *what*?" said Wendy Stanler.

The Pope, sitting in the den of the Stanler house, tried to answer her as elaborately as he could. "I'm Jennifer's brother, Bob Keats. I saw something on our local news, and I came up immediately."

"From where?"

"New York City."

"Jennifer wasn't *from* New York."

"No, but that's where I decided to settle after leaving home."

Murizzi watched the young woman try to process the news.

"Well, like, what do you want from *me*?"

"Just to introduce myself," he said.

"Why?"

"Because I think we'll be seeing a lot of each other, what with your father's murder trial and my civil suit."

"*Civil* suit?"

"Against your father, for the wrongful death of my dear

sister." The Pope swung his head around the room. "Just think, all this will soon be mine."

*   *   *

" . . . AND you're her long-lost . . . ?"

"Brother," said Pontifico Murizzi, watching the expression on Dave Poitrast's face as Harvey Stanler's partner half-stood from behind his desk in the nice import office. "But I haven't really been lost. It's just that Jennifer and I didn't stay in very close contact after she married."

Poitrast's expression went from surprised to skeptical. "And why was that?"

"Well, I'm afraid she was somewhat ashamed of me."

"Ashamed?"

"Of my . . . orientation, Mr. Poitrast. I'm gay, you see, and that gave Jennifer a lot of problems."

"Tell me about it."

"I'd rather tell you my hopes for a rational settlement."

From skeptical to shocked. "Settlement of what?"

"My wrongful-death case against Mr. Stanler." The Pope looked longingly around the office. "And a good chunk of change will, I assume, have to come out of this fine business you two seem to have built."

*   *   *

" . . . WHICH may be your version, Mr. 'Keats,' but Jennifer never mentioned any 'brother.' "

"And I've already told you why that might be," said Murizzi, settling a little deeper into the chair in front of Petra Lindsay's impressive desk. "I'm sorry my sister didn't come clean with you. However, that's hardly—"

"Just what is it you want?"

"Ah, a lawyer who can get to the point. Pity I'm retaining other counsel."

"For what?"

"To represent me, of course. In the wrongful-death suit I'll be bringing against Harvey Stanler. But as the executor of her estate—at least for the moment—you probably should know how to reach me, eh?"

And for the third time that morning, the Pope gave someone he'd just met the number of a room at a rundown motel just outside downtown Boston.

* * *

WHAT a dump, thought Jennifer Stanler's killer, surveying the motel that night from the driver's side window. Just two strips of rooms perpendicular to a rundown avenue, half a dozen vehicles parked in various slots outside the twenty or so doors and windows. Not exactly the Ritz, but not much chance of any "on-site security" interfering, either.

Leaving the car across the street, the killer waited for a break in traffic, then walked briskly, the trench coat flapping against shins, the baseball cap pulled firmly down around ears, the templates of the sunglasses pressing into cartilage.

But, with luck, for only a few minutes more.

In the motel's parking lot now, the killer slowed down, just another traveler unlucky enough to reserve a crummy room sight unseen. Watching the numbers on the doors, counting down to the one Bob Keats had mentioned earlier that day.

109 . . . 108 . . . 107!

A quick look around. Nobody in sight, parking lot or sidewalk.

Before trying the door, the killer peeked into the room through the window, the drapes not fully drawn. A figure lay on the bed, facing away with sheets and blanket pulled up near a chin. Black, curly hair rested on the pillow.

Jennifer's brother, asleep.

The killer's right hand went into the trench coat's front pocket, coming out with a revolver, four-inch barrel. No need to try the door or even to knock. Just six bullets through the glass and into the figure on the bed.

The killer leveled the muzzle, then squeezed off the first round, shattering the window of room 107 and making the killer's ears ring. Five more shots followed, the figure in bed shuddering a little from each. As the person in the trench coat turned triumphantly away, however, the flat of a hand slashed down on the right wrist, causing the killer to drop the revolver while crying out and sinking down in pain.

From her knees now, Petra Lindsay looked up at Pontifico Murizzi, Mairead O'Clare coming out the door to room 108 behind him.

Lindsay virtually barked her words. "You didn't have to break my goddamned arm!"

*　　*　　*

"So who picked out the wig for the mannequin in the bed?" said Sheldon Gold, standing in his office suite's reception area.

Mairead raised her hand, the Pope grinning from the other reception chair as he had on his boat.

Billie Sunday stopped typing a form at her desk, swiveling her head to glance at Murizzi. "I know five reasons *I'd* kill you, but why'd the lawyer-woman want you dead?"

Mairead spoke first. "It seems Petra Lindsay had financial problems, big-time. I got a sense of that when I visited her office, her supposed 'temp' interrupting her with urgent calls from her car-leasing company and bank. But I had my doubts about Stanler's daughter and partner as well, so we kind of 'created' a brother for Jennifer."

Gold said, "A decoy who could upset everybody's apple cart, lure the real killer into showing herself."

Sunday looked to Mairead. "Then it was this Lindsay who did the strangling?"

The Pope broke in. "At the motel, she was ticked off

enough about her arm to blame Jennifer Keats for the whole thing. Seems the two of them talked about killing Harvey Stanler in his own house, make it look like a burglary gone violent. Which meant Jennifer would inherit a lot more than her prenup lump sum. But then Lindsay got to thinking."

Mairead said, "Why split the money with Jennifer, when with her divorce client dead, Lindsay could bring a clever lawsuit and end up with all three million of Harvey Stanler's net worth?"

Murizzi nodded. "And eliminate an unreliable co-conspirator at the same time."

Billie Sunday shook her head. "Lindsay kills her own client instead of the husband and loses the only witness against her if anybody tumbled to the crime."

Sheldon Gold said, "Two birds with one stone."

Which again reminded Mairead O'Clare of the wooden ducks on Harvey Stanler's mantel, but she decided enough had been said about decoys.

A Well-Respected Man

Margaret Coel

Margaret Coel writes the Wind River series of mystery novels, featuring Arapaho attorney Vicky Holden and Jesuit priest John O'Malley. The books have been nominated for many awards, including the Willa Cather Award for Best Novel of the West. Her short stories with the same characters have appeared in several anthologies.

THE jangling noise grew louder, like a siren closing in from a far distance. Vicky Holden groped for the alarm clock on the nightstand and pressed the button. The noise continued. Struggling upright in the darkness, one elbow cradled in the pillow, she reached for the phone on the far side of the clock.

"Vicky, that you?" A man's voice, the words rushed and breathless. "Oh, man, I thought you wasn't there. They got me locked up in jail."

"Who is this?" Vicky said. She heard the sleepiness in her own voice. The luminous numbers on the clock showed 5:22.

"Leland Iron Wolf." Another rush of words. "You gotta get me outta here."

An image flashed into Vicky's mind: lanky frame, about six feet tall; cowboy hat pulled forward, shading the dark, steady eyes that took in the world on its own terms, thick black braids hanging down the front of a western shirt. Leland was about twenty-five years old, the only grandson of Elton Iron Wolf, one of the Arapaho elders. The old man had raised the boy after his parents were killed in an accident. Vicky had never heard of Leland in any kind of trouble.

"What happened?" she asked, fully awake now.

Words tumbled over the line: the police on the Wind River Reservation arrested him an hour ago. He was still sleeping, and there they were, outside pounding on the front door. They turned him over to the sheriff, and next thing he knew, he was in the county jail.

Leland hesitated. Vicky heard the sound of incomprehension in the short, quick breaths at the other end of the line. Finally: "They think I shot the boss. Killed him. *Nokooho.*"

Crazy indeed, Vicky thought. Killers did crazy things, but Leland Iron Wolf . . . He was not a killer.

"Who was shot?" she asked.

"Jess Miller. My boss over at the Miller ranch. I hired out there a couple months ago."

Vicky knew the place—a spread that ran into the foothills west of Lander. The same spread that Jess Miller's father and grandfather had worked. The family was well respected in the area. Over the years, they had occasionally hired an Arapaho ranch hand.

"What happened?" She was out of bed now, phone tucked under her chin as she switched on the light and began rifling through her clothes in the closet.

"How the hell do I know?" Impatience and desperation mingled in Leland's voice. "I rode in from doctoring calves and picked up my pay at the office in the barn. The boss was alive and kickin', his same old mean self when I left."

"What time was that?" Vicky persisted.

"About seven, almost dark. You gotta get me outta here, Vicky." The words sounded like a long wail.

Vicky understood. For an Arapaho accustomed to herding cattle on open ranges, warrior blood coursing through his veins, there was nothing worse than to be locked behind bars. It was death itself.

"I'm on my way." She tossed the jacket and skirt of her navy blue suit onto the bed. Then an ivory silk blouse. "Don't say anything until I get there—understand?"

"Hurry," Leland said.

Vicky pushed the disconnect button, then tapped in the numbers of the sheriff's office and asked for Mark Albert, the detective most likely handling the case. He picked up the phone on the first ring.

"This is Vicky Holden," she told him. "I'm representing Leland Iron Wolf."

"Figured you'd be the one calling." Sounds of rustling paper came over the line.

Vicky ignored the implication that only an Arapaho lawyer would take an Arapaho's case. She said, "What do you have?"

"Evidence that Leland Iron Wolf murdered one of the county's prominent citizens."

"Have you questioned him?"

"We Mirandized him, counselor, and he said he was gonna call a lawyer." The words were laced with sarcasm.

Vicky drew in a long breath, struggling to keep her temper in check. "Give me the details."

"Donna Miller, that's the wife, found Jess's body in the barn last evening about eight o'clock. Shot in the chest, right in the heart, to be precise. Shotgun that killed him was dropped outside the barn."

Vicky said, "Leland left the ranch at seven."

"Mrs. Miller says otherwise." Vicky flinched at the peremptory tone. Mark Albert was a tough adversary. "The missus was in the kitchen around eight o'clock. Looked out the window and saw Leland going into the barn. Couple minutes later she heard a gunshot and ran outside. That's when she found her husband."

Vicky could feel the knot tightening in her stomach.

His same mean old self, Leland had called his boss. She said, "What's the motive, Mark?"

"Oldest motive in the world. Cash." A little burst of laughter sounded over the line. "Jess Miller paid Leland in cash every Friday evening. Wife says Indian ranch hands always preferred cash to checks . . ." The unspoken idea hung in the quiet like a heavy weight: local bars prefer cash. "Besides," the detective hurried on, "that's probably the way of Jess's daddy, and his daddy before him. Old families have their own ways of doing things. Point is, the cashbox is gone."

"A lot of people must have known about the cash," Vicky said.

Mark Albert didn't say anything for a moment. Then: "There's something else. We got some good prints off the shotgun. They look like Leland's. We'll have confirmation in a few hours."

Vicky stared out the bedroom window at the dawn glowing red and gold in the eastern sky. Prints. Motive. Opportunity. Mark Albert had them all, but that didn't mean Leland Iron Wolf was guilty.

"When's the initial hearing?" she heard herself asking.

"Monday, one o'clock, county court."

"I want to talk to Leland right away."

"You know where to find him."

*   *   *

THE metal security door slammed behind her as Vicky followed the blue-uniformed guard down the concrete hallway. A mixture of television noise, rap music, and ringing phones floated from the cell block at the far end of the hallway. Odors of detergent and stale coffee permeated the air. The guard unclipped a ring of keys from his belt, unlocked a metal door, and shoved it open. Vicky stepped into a small, windowless room. "Wait here," the guard ordered, closing the door.

Vicky dropped her briefcase on the table that took up

most of the room. She shivered in the chill penetrating
the pale-green concrete walls. Leland had been locked up
how many hours now—two? three? He would be going
crazy.

The door swung open. Leland stood in the doorway,
eyes darting over the windowless walls, arms at his sides,
hands clenched hard into fists. He had on a bright orange
jumpsuit that looked a couple of sizes too large for his
wiry frame. His black hair, shiny under the fluorescent
ceiling light, was parted in the middle and caught in two
braids that dropped down the front of the orange jumpsuit.
He started into the room, shuffling, halting, glancing back.

Vicky held her breath, afraid he would turn around and
hurl himself against the closed door. "Tell me what you
know about Miller's death." She kept her voice calm, an
effort to hold the young man in the present. She sat down
and extracted a legal pad and pen from the briefcase.

Leland sank into the chair across from her. He was
quiet a long moment, calling on something inside of him.
Finally, he said, "Somebody shot him is all I know."

"He was alive when you left the ranch?"

Leland's head reared back. The ceiling light glinted in
the dark eyes. "You don't believe me?"

"I had to ask." Silence hung between them a moment.
"Where did you go?"

Leland shifted in the chair and shot a glance at the
closed door. "Just drove around."

"Drove around?"

"I had some thinkin' to do."

Vicky waited. After a moment, Leland said, "I got the
chance to manage a big spread down in Colorado. They
need a real good, experienced cowboy, so a buddy of
mine workin' there give the owner my name. I gotta decide if I'm gonna leave . . ." He exhaled a long, shuddering breath. "Grandfather don't have nobody but me, and
he don't have much money, you know. If I go down to
Colorado, it's gonna be real hard on him."

Vicky swallowed back the lump rising in her throat. Leland had just confirmed the motive. With several thousand dollars, Elton Iron Wolf could get along for a while and Leland could move away. She pushed on: "Did you stop anywhere?"

The young man was shaking his head. "I think best when I'm just movin', you know." A glance at the walls looming around them. "I drove up to Dubois and back. Got home about ten."

Vicky made a note on the pad. *Dubois. No alibi.* She looked up. "Look, Leland." She was searching for the words to soften the blow. "I'm going to level with you. Mrs. Miller says she saw you going into the barn just before her husband was killed. The detective says your fingerprints are probably on the shotgun."

A mixture of surprise and disbelief came into the young man's face. "My prints are all over that shotgun. I took it out a couple days ago after some coyotes been killin' the calves."

"Who knew you used the gun?" Vicky persisted.

"The boss's kid, Buddy. He rode out with me. Got a real kick outta watching me pick off a coyote. Helps out on the ranch when school's out. Pretty good cowboy for fifteen years old."

"Any other ranch hands?"

Leland gave his head a quick shake. "That's it. Me and the boss and sometimes the kid. We pretty much took care of things. Boss didn't like a lotta people around, pokin' into his business was the way he put it. Him and his wife and those two kids, they liked their privacy."

"Two kids?"

"Boy's got a sister, Julie. She's thirteen. Real pretty little thing. See 'em comin' down the road together after the school bus let 'em off. Just the two of 'em, like they was each other's best friend. Good kids. Real quiet like their dad."

"You said Jess Miller was mean."

Leland nodded. "Yeah, he could be mean all right, if he didn't like the job you was doin'. About the only time he had much to say was if he wanted to lay you out. Rest the time, he kept to hisself. Tended his own business."

Vicky could feel the jitters in her stomach: prominent rancher who minded his own business, close family, Indian ranch hand with fingerprints all over the murder weapon and a motive to help himself to the cashbox. Selecting the words carefully, she said, "You may have to stay in jail a while, Leland. Just until I can get to the bottom of this."

Leland blinked hard. "What're you gonna do?"

"You'll have to trust me," she said with as much confidence as she could muster.

*   *   *

THE sounds of organ music resounded through the church as Vicky slipped into the back pew. Ranchers in cowboy shirts and blue jeans and businessmen filled the other pews. There were only a few women. Vicky recognized some of the mourners: the mayor, the chamber of commerce president, the owner of the steakhouse on Main Street, all friends of Jess Miller. She wondered if the murderer was among them. What had she expected to find by coming here? She was grasping, grasping for some way to clear Leland.

At the hearing, the county attorney had trotted out what he called "a preponderance of evidence," and she had been left to argue that there was some other explanation. "I look forward to hearing it," the judge had said. Then he'd denied bail and remanded Leland to the county jail.

Vicky exhaled a long breath and turned her attention to the Miller family in the front pew: the small woman dressed in black, a black lace veil draping her head, the thin-shouldered boy with sandy hair, the dark-haired girl throwing nervous glances from side to side.

The organ music stopped abruptly, leaving only the

hushed sounds of whispering and shifting in the pews. A minister in a white robe mounted the pulpit, eyes trained on the family below. He cleared his throat into the microphone and began a flat, perfunctory talk: fine man in our community, cut down in his prime, loving wife and children, devastated by death. The heavens cried out for justice.

After the service concluded, Vicky kept her place, watching the mourners file past the family, nodding, shaking hands. Suddenly the boy wrenched himself sideways, and Vicky noticed the gray-haired woman approaching him. She bent over the pew, trying to get his attention, but he kept his head averted, as if the woman were not there. She moved tentatively toward the girl, then the mother. Both kept their heads down, and finally the woman moved away. She reached into a large black bag and pulled out a white handkerchief, which she dabbed at her eyes as she exited through a side door.

Vicky hurried out the front entrance and made her way around the side of the church to the parking lot. The woman was about to lower herself into a brown sedan. "Excuse me," Vicky called, walking over.

The woman swung around, surprise and fear mingling in her expression. She pulled the car door toward her, as if to put a shield between herself and the outside world.

"I didn't mean to startle you," Vicky said. "You must be a friend of the family."

The woman shot a nervous glance at the businessmen and cowboys filing toward the rows of cars and trucks in the lot. "I would say that family has few real friends," she said. "I came for the children." Slowly she reached a hand around the door. "Elizabeth Shubert. Lander High counselor."

"Vicky Holden." The other woman's hand was as smooth and cool as a sheet of paper. "I represent Leland Iron Wolf."

"I thought that might be the case." Elizabeth Shubert

gave her head a slow shake. "I don't believe Leland is capable of murder."

"You know him?" Vicky heard the surprise in her voice.

"I knew him when he was at the high school. A fine boy."

"Mrs. Shubert . . ."

"Miss," the woman interrupted.

"Would you be willing to talk to me?"

The woman sank into the front seat and peered through the windshield. A line of vehicles waited to turn into the street. The hearse that had been parked in front of the church was pulling away. A black limousine followed, three heads bobbing in the backseat. "I shouldn't be talking to you," she said after a moment. "I must get back to school."

Vicky gripped the edge of the door to keep it from shutting. "Miss Shubert, Leland faces a first-degree murder charge. He's innocent." She hesitated. All she had was an instinct that this woman knew something. She plunged on: "Is there anything you can tell me, anything at all, that might help him?"

Elizabeth Shubert was quiet. She reached up and tucked a strand of gray hair into place, her eyes fixed on some point beyond the windshield. "Come to my house at four-thirty." She gave the address. "White house on the corner. You can't miss it."

*   *   *

VICKY leaned into the bell next to the blue-painted door. From inside came a muffled sound, like the tingling of a xylophone, followed by hurried footsteps. The door flung open. Elizabeth Shubert stood back in the shadow of the front hallway, allowing her gaze to roam up and down the street. "Come in, come in," she said, a hushed tone.

When they were seated in the living room, Vicky said,

"I couldn't help but notice the way the family reacted as you extended your condolences."

Elizabeth Shubert picked up the flower-printed teapot on the table between them and poured the steaming brown liquid into two china cups. Handing a cup and saucer to Vicky, she said, "I'm sure they must blame me for . . . well, for what happened."

"For Jess Miller's murder?"

"Oh, no." The woman sat up straighter. One hand flew to her throat and unadorned fingers began crinkling the collar of her white blouse. "For what happened before. You see, I was worried about Buddy and Julie. Whenever there's a precipitous drop in grades and a change in personality, well, naturally, you wish to inquire as to the reason."

Vicky shifted forward. She held the other woman's gaze. "When did this occur?"

"Well, it's not as if they were brilliant students, you understand." Elizabeth Shubert made a little clicking noise with her tongue. "Average, I would say. But they were going along as usual until recently. Several teachers reported they were both flunking classes."

"What about the personality change?"

"Well, not so much the boy." The woman rested her eyes on a corner of the living room for a moment. "Buddy's always been a loner. Tends to his own business. Perhaps he seemed a little more withdrawn and morose lately, but, frankly, I attributed that to the poor report. The change was in Julie. Such a quiet, nice girl until . . ."

Vicky waited, one hand wrapped around the china cup in her lap.

"It's hard to explain," the woman went on. "Julie became very outgoing, I would say. Yes, very aggressive and pushy. You could hear her shouting in the halls. She was distracting in class, giggling and cutting up and generally making a nuisance of herself. She was sent to my office four times in the last two weeks. Well, I thought it was just an adolescent phase." The woman leaned forward and set her cup and saucer on the table. The china made a little rattling noise. "It was more than that."

"How so?"

"The way she flaunted herself. Deliberately provocative, I would say. The tightest, shortest skirts, the lowest-cut tops, that sort of thing." The woman looked away again, then brought her gaze back. "Believe me, girls can be very brazen these days, but this was not like Julie Miller. It was as if suddenly she had become someone else."

Vicky set her own cup and saucer on the table. "What did you do?"

"I'm not certain I did the right thing." The woman spoke slowly, remembering. "I called Mr. and Mrs. Miller last week and asked for a meeting. I was terribly concerned about the children, you see."

"Yes, of course. What did the parents say?"

"The parents? Well, Mrs. Miller said nothing. She remained silent through the entire meeting. She just sat there, never taking her eyes from her husband. He did all the talking. He was very upset. Accused me of violating their privacy. Said he would tend to his own children. If they were having problems, he would straighten them out, and I should stay out of their business. And that's not all." Elizabeth Shubert looked away again, pulling the memory out of a shadowed corner. "He threatened to bring a lawsuit against me."

"A lawsuit!" Vicky felt a jolt of surprise. "On what possible grounds? That you were concerned about his children?"

"That I had defamed his family." The woman gave a little shudder. "It was ridiculous, of course. But I don't mind telling you, it frightened me. I don't want any trouble with the school district. You see, I'm due to retire next year, and I'm a woman of modest means." She glanced around the living room: the worn sofa and chairs, the faded doilies on the armrests, the gold carpet crisscrossed with gray pathways. "Mr. Miller was a well-respected man, and he was very angry. Unfortunately, he must have thought Buddy had told me something because . . ."

She stopped. Her hands were clasped now into a tight ball in her lap. "Oh, dear." A tremor had come into her voice. "I shouldn't be telling you this. It's exactly what Mr. Miller warned me against. I have no proof of anything." She gripped the armrests and started to lift herself out of the chair, a motion of dismissal.

"Please, Elizabeth." Vicky moved to the edge of her own chair. "What happened to Buddy after the meeting?"

The woman sat back into the cushions. A muscle twitched along the rim of her jawline. Finally, she said: "Mr. Miller punished the boy."

"You mean, he beat him?" A coldness rippled along Vicky's spine. In her mind, she saw the widow and mother, head lowered under a black lace veil. A silent woman. Had she finally had enough? Had she finally decided to protect her children?

"I have no proof," Elizabeth Shubert was saying. "But the boy was absent for two days after the meeting. When he came back, he had a note from his mother saying he'd been home with a cold. But I didn't believe it, not for a minute."

"Did you report this to social services?"

Elizabeth Shubert was rubbing her hands together now. "I took the steps I believed necessary. I called Buddy into my office. I told him of my suspicions. He said his father was a fine man, that I shouldn't say bad things about him, that his father would sue me for defaming the family. He used almost the same words his father had used, and I remember thinking, *This poor boy has been brainwashed.* But I had no proof. Nothing. Nothing." The woman shook her head; moisture pooled at the corners of her eyes. "Oh, I know I should have reported my suspicions, but what good would it have done? Jess Miller was an upstanding citizen from a very old family. No one would have believed me."

Vicky didn't say anything. She was wondering if Donna Miller had reached the same conclusion: no one could stop her husband.

The woman was crying softly now. "Excuse me," she said, half stumbling to her feet. She disappeared through an alcove. In a moment she was back, blowing her nose into a white handkerchief.

Vicky got to her feet. "You must tell the sheriff what you've told me," she said.

"Oh, I did." An aggrieved note came into the woman's voice. "I called the sheriff the minute I heard about the murder. Not that it did any good." She gave a little shiver.

"What do you mean?"

"I'm sure Mrs. Miller and the children denied everything. They probably said I was a meddling old lady. That's why they rebuffed me today at the church."

"What if . . ." Vicky began, slowly giving voice to the shadowy idea at the back of her mind, "Donna Miller shot her husband to protect her children."

Elizabeth Shubert nodded. "That thought has been tormenting me."

*   *   *

OUTSIDE, Vicky sat behind the wheel of her Bronco trying to arrange the pieces into a picture that made sense: a well-respected man, a perfect family with a cancer eating at its heart, a mother who knew when Leland Iron Wolf would pick up his pay and who must have known he had recently used the shotgun. She could have waited until Leland drove off, then gone to the barn, shot her husband—in the heart, Albert had said. She wore gloves, so Leland's prints were the only prints on the gun. After she had hidden the cashbox, she had called the police. But who would believe it? Certainly not Mark Albert.

Vicky slammed one fist against the edge of the steering

wheel. Leland Iron Wolf was about to spend the rest of his life in prison for a murder he didn't commit. He trusted her, and she had come up with nothing. Nothing but a sense of what had happened, a vague and unprovable theory. She rammed the key into the ignition. The engine growled into life, and she pulled into the street, turned right, and headed west. She intended to pay a condolence call on the grieving family.

*   *   *

VICKY drove under the wooden arch with the letter M carved in the center. She passed the cars and trucks parked in front of the red-brick ranch house and stopped in the driveway that ran from the house to the barn. As she let herself out, she glanced about, then made her way to the front door.

"What do you want?" Donna Miller stood in the doorway, a small woman with sloped shoulders and sunken chest. She looked at Vicky out of red-rimmed eyes, the most notable feature in a narrow, plain face. Her hair was streaked with gray and brushed to one side, as if it had simply been put out of the way. She was still in the black dress she had worn to the church earlier. A hum of voices came from inside the house.

"I'd like to talk to you," Vicky said. She had already told the woman that she represented Leland Iron Wolf.

"I have nothing to say to you. I have guests." Donna Miller glanced over one shoulder at the knots of people floating past the entry. Vicky glimpsed Buddy and Julie standing together in the shadows near the staircase.

"I've spoken to Elizabeth Shubert," Vicky persisted.

"Elizabeth Shu . . ." The thin lips tightened on the name. "That woman has no right to . . ." Suddenly she moved backward. "Come in." As Vicky stepped inside, the woman nodded toward the door on the other side of the staircase. "We'll talk in there," she said. The boy and girl had disappeared.

The room was small, with a desk against one wall and two upholstered chairs pushed against the opposite wall. Thick, gauzy curtains at the window gave the air a grayish cast. Donna Miller closed the door and sank back against it. "I know the ugly rumors that woman has spread. The sheriff's looked into them and found them completely false."

"Mrs. Miller," Vicky began, struggling against the sense of hopelessness rising inside her. What did she expect? That this woman would incriminate herself? She pushed on: "Leland Iron Wolf has been charged with a murder we both know he did not commit."

"I don't know what you're talking about." There was a rigid calmness to the woman. She stared at Vicky out of gray, blank eyes. "The sheriff has conducted a thorough investigation. He has arrested my husband's murderer."

"What kind of man was your husband?" Vicky asked, taking a different tack.

The woman blinked, as if she were trying to register the meaning of the question. "He was a very fine man. Ask anyone in the area. He was well respected." She tilted her head toward the closed door and the muffled sound of conversations coming from the main part of the house.

"What about your children?"

"My children? They're very well adjusted, ask anyone." Another tilt of the head toward the door. "They were fortunate to grow up on the ranch. They're very close. They never needed other friends. They had each other."

"How did your husband treat them?"

"What right do you have to ask these questions?" Donna Miller said, a shrillness in the tone that seemed to surprise her. She straightened herself against the door. "He was wonderful to the children, of course. He protected them. He protected all of us in our kingdom." One hand fluttered into the room. "He always called the ranch our kingdom where we could do things our own way." A waviness had come into her voice, a hint of tears. "We could live the way we wanted, with no outsiders telling us what we could do."

Vicky waited for the woman to go on, but Donna Miller had sunk into silence. At any moment, Vicky knew, the woman would tell her to leave. She took a chance: "He abused the children, didn't he? He beat your son. And your daughter?" Vicky caught her breath, a sharp lump in her chest. *Such a nice quiet girl. A complete change in personality.* "What did he do to your daughter, Mrs. Miller?"

"That woman has no right to speak such filth."

"You decided it had to end," Vicky said. "You wanted to protect your children."

"No!" The word came like a cry of agony from a lonely, faraway place. "Go away. Go away and leave us alone."

Suddenly the door swung open against the woman. She stumbled, off balance, and Vicky grabbed her elbow, steadying her. Buddy stood in the doorway, a tall, gangly boy with light hair flopping over his forehead. Behind him was Julie in a tight, black dress with a neckline that dipped into the cleft of round, firm breasts. The boy reached back, grabbed his sister's hand and pulled her into the room. Then, he closed the door.

Turning to his mother, he said, "What's going on? I seen this lady talking to Miss Shubert in the church parking lot. Is she a cop?"

The mother shook her head. "This is Leland's lawyer. She's just getting ready to leave. You and Julie go on out and talk to people."

"Don't you worry, Mother. I'll take care of this. I'll protect you now, just like I told ya." The boy stepped forward, shielding both women. His eyes fixed on Vicky's. "That Indian killed my father and he's gonna get what's comin' to him. You best be goin' now."

Vicky stared at the boy, the narrowed shoulders pulled square, the chin jutting forward in shaky confidence. She had it all wrong. It wasn't Donna Miller who had killed her husband, it was the son. Not until afterward, after the terrible deed had been done and Jess Miller lay dying in the barn office, did his wife summon the courage to protect her child. And now, Vicky realized, her only hope was that Buddy would insist upon protecting his mother.

"I know what happened, Buddy," she said, choosing the words carefully, threading a pathway for him to follow to a logical conclusion. "Your mother killed your father, didn't she?"

A little cry of anguish came from the woman. Vicky pushed on: "She said she saw Leland going to the barn, but that's a lie. It was dark at eight o'clock, and there are no lights between the house and barn. The sheriff is putting it all together. He's talked to Miss Shubert."

The woman was sobbing now, and Julie had dropped her face into both hands. Moisture seeped through the girl's slim fingers. The boy turned toward them. "Don't worry," he said again, a tremor in his voice. "I'll take care of you."

Slowly he turned back. He pushed back the hank of hair that had fallen forward. A vein pulsated in the center of his forehead. "Me, I could take it, 'cause I'm a man," he said. "But he was always hitting Mom, see, and she's just a little lady. Then he started . . ."

He hesitated. His eyes went blank, as if he could no longer take in the reality. "He started hurting Julie, see. And no sheriff or social worker was gonna come out here and tell Jess Miller to stop. Nobody's gonna tell Jess Miller what he can do in his kingdom. That's what he always said. So I took the shotgun that ranch hand had shot off, and I put a stop to it."

Vicky felt a sharp pang of relief and with it, something else—a hot rush of anger that burned at her cheeks and constricted her throat. "All of you were willing to send an innocent man to jail for the rest of his life," she said, the words choked with rage. She backed to the desk and picked up the phone. "I'm going to call the sheriff's office."

She punched in the numbers. From somewhere in the house came the muffled voices of mourners, the clap of a door shutting. She listened to the electronic buzz of the phone ringing on Mark Albert's desk, her eyes on the family huddled together, shoulders touching, hands entwined. Everything seemed suffused with sadness.

"Detective Albert." The voice boomed into her ear, jarring her back to herself.

"One moment," she said, barely controlling the tremble in her voice. She cupped one hand over the mouthpiece and, looking beyond the boy and girl, children yet, she caught the woman's eyes. "Mrs. Miller," she said, "you'll want to call a lawyer for your son."

Victim by Consent

Nora DeLoach

The author of seven Mama mysteries, Florida native DeLoach now lives in Decatur, Georgia. Several of her titles have been offered as featured alternates by the Mystery Guild. She is working on her ninth Mama book; Mama Pursues Murderous Shadows *is her latest release.* Mama Cracks a Mask of Innocence *will be released Spring 2001.*

WHEN Johnny Galvin was arrested, he lived 435 miles from Atlanta where I was brooding over the absence of both my boyfriend and my parents. Cliff Roberts, the guy I'd been dating for the past few years, was in Phoenix at a seminar. My parents were in Boston attending a reunion of my father's Air Force buddies.

Spring in Atlanta is an artist that lightly paints the city with lush leafy canopies of dogwoods, vivacious pink, red and white azaleas, fragrant magnolia blooms, fiery crepe myrtle trees, and purple plum trees. Then she dusts everything with tons of yellow pollen.

With watery eyes and running nose I drove to Lenox Square Mall, Perimeter Mall, Cumberland Mall, and both South and North Lake Malls. When I'd finally decided to go back to my den of an apartment, I'd put extra weight on my charge cards.

That was Saturday and Sunday.

Now it was Monday morning. I was planted in my

office thinking that I'd never visited Massachusetts or Arizona when my intercom went off; it startled me. I picked up the phone to hear my boss's voice summon me to his office.

Sidney Jacoby is a prominent defense attorney in Atlanta. My name is Simone Covington. I've been one of Sidney's paralegals for almost five years.

If you've read the exploits in my Mama mystery series, a series in which I've chronicled my mother's use of her sleuthing intuition, you know that my boss and I enjoy an excellent working relationship. Today I learned that Sidney also shared a good working relationship with his housekeeper. Rita Galvin was seated in a chair opposite him.

I'd met Rita on several occasions when Sidney had invited me to his home for dinner parties. "Simone," he said to me after I'd said hello to her, "Rita's boy is in trouble and he needs a defense lawyer."

I was confused.

Sidney leaned back in his chair. "You know I'm in the middle of the Weber trial and I can't break away—I want you to take care of this matter for me."

I smiled nervously at the housekeeper. "If Rita's son needs a defense attorney, I don't think I'm the person to help him."

"Simone," he said, totally ignoring my protest, "I've told Rita that you will go with her tomorrow morning to Orlando and she appreciates your efforts. Gale is getting plane tickets, a rental car, and hotel reservations for you as I speak."

"What do you want me to do?" I asked, still a little perplexed. I knew Sidney had confidence in my abilities; he'd demonstrated it time and again with the kind of investigative responsibilities he'd delegated to me. But this was a stretch. Rita's son was obviously in serious trouble. Otherwise, why would he need the services of a defense lawyer?

"Talk to Johnny," Rita Galvin said to me, a musical Caribbean lilt to her voice that denoted her exotic West Indian heritage. "My child is scared—he's not accustomed to being put in jail like a common criminal."

Sidney looked at Rita reassuringly. "Johnny has been arrested for the murder of his wife—get his side of the story!"

"After that, what?" I asked, still puzzled.

"Call me," he said, his tone making it clear that he was satisfied with his instructions and he didn't anticipate any more questions or objections.

I stood and walked out of Sidney's office. Sidney nodded and Rita followed me. She was short, not five feet tall, with a bronze complexion that had red undertones. "My dear," Rita told me in a somber voice, "Johnny is a temperate man, one who often makes rash statements now and again but he would never go beyond the words that rush from his mouth!"

We were standing in the office reception area, waiting for Sidney's secretary to finalize travel arrangements.

I tried to look as if I believed the woman. Truth was, I'd heard more than one killer be described as not being capable of taking another's life. And my boyfriend is a divorce lawyer. Everything that I'd learned from listening to Cliff's experiences with clients confirms that a man who wouldn't normally consider taking another human life can, under certain circumstances, find reasons to kill his wife.

*   *   *

BY seven o'clock the next morning I had given my assignment considerable thought. "I can do this!" I told myself while looking into my bathroom mirror. With my confidence intact, I was determined to get information that Sidney could use.

*   *   *

"TELL me something about your son and his wife," I asked Rita once we were aboard Delta 1715 flight en route to Orlando.

"Johnny is the youngest of my seven children," Rita told me. "My oldest daughter, Phoebe, also lives in Orlando. Phoebe and I met Johnny's young lady and we were pleased. Chloe was cheerful, full of life, and simply crazy about my son. She treated Johnny as if he was something to eat and my son thrived on the attention."

"Do you know how Johnny and Chloe got along after their wedding?" I asked.

"No, I don't. But Phoebe swears that things were okay between husband and wife until six months ago. She told me that she now remembers Johnny saying to her around that time that Chloe was beginning to scare him."

My eyebrow rose. "What did he mean?"

Rita shook her head. "Phoebe had no idea until this horrible thing happened. Johnny only mentioned his fear that once and Phoebe never followed him up on it."

By three o'clock the plane had landed, I'd picked up the rental car and we were turning off John Young Parkway onto 33rd Street. We were headed for the Orlando Correctional Center. My youngest brother, Will, lives in this town. I'd visited enough to know how to get around the place.

After being checked in at the center, we waited until a prison official brought Johnny into a room that separated us by a plate glass window. Johnny picked up the telephone, and his mother picked up the phone on our side. They exchanged a greeting, then Rita explained my role. Johnny nodded his understanding. I reached for the phone in his mother's hand.

"What happened?" I asked the tall lanky young man whose features clearly identified him as Rita's son.

Johnny's first words cut straight through to the core of his dilemma. "The first year and a half after we got married, things were fine between me and Chloe," he told me, his face agitated, his voice pinched. "Then my wife developed a fixation on herself. She began to interpret everything that happened as if it was a personal affront to her. She grew dark, very, very angry, and suspicious. She began to complain that things on her job were wrong, that people were talking down to her. It escalated to people were plotting against her, then I was cheating on her. The last night I stayed in the apartment I woke to find Chloe standing over me with a knife mumbling something about how she had to cut my heart out of my chest. I swear, the only thing Chloe didn't find fault with was her precious cat, T. C."

"Sounds like your wife might have suffered from some kind of mental disorder. Did it ever occur to you to get her medical help?"

Johnny jaw dropped, his eyes grew wide. "There was no way I could get that woman to a doctor," he said defensively. "Chloe turned mean as a rattlesnake. She was difficult, defiant, distrustful . . . I couldn't do anything to help her!"

Rita Galvin touched the glass partition that separated her from Johnny. The pain in her eyes told me she yearned to touch her son.

Johnny looked into Rita's eyes. When he spoke again, his voice had moderated as if he was aware that his agitation was having a negative effect on his mother. "I left Chloe and moved in with Phoebe. For a while, things were fine. Then last Friday night Chloe called her mother and told her that she was scared that I was going to kill her."

He hesitated. "My mother-in-law, Blanche, is strange. I didn't meet her until after Chloe and I were married. Anyway, Blanche took Chloe seriously. She called my sister and prophesied fire and brimstone against me. Phoebe suggested I try to get to the bottom of what Chloe was talking about so I phoned Chloe."

Again he hesitated as he struggled to control his composure.

I waited.

He took a deep breath, then continued. "When I talked to Chloe, she told me that if she died, I'd get the chair for it. She slammed the phone down in my ear. That's why I went over there. I wanted to try to talk some sense into her.

"I knocked first. Chloe didn't come to the door. I remembered I still had my key, so I used it to get into the apartment. Chloe was in the living room, sitting on the sofa. She was naked from her waist up with only a small throw pillow in her lap. T. C. was curled up in the corner. I took one step toward her. Before I reached the sofa, Chloe pulled out this gun from underneath the pillow and shot herself between her breasts. T. C. screeched, then ran under the chair. The next thing I knew, the police was there!"

"Did you touch the gun?"

He nodded. "The cops said it was in my hand when they got to the apartment but I don't remember picking it up. You see, when I went to the apartment I was mad. I mean I was ready to throw down with Chloe, knock her upside the head if necessary. I wanted her to stop trying to make me out to be some kind of monster. I wasn't prepared for her to shoot herself, nor did I expect the look on her face when she pulled the trigger. The only time I'd seen that kind of an expression was in a psycho movie—her eyes held an excitement, almost an ecstasy.

"A few minutes after the police arrived, Blanche showed up. She started baptizing me with words of condemnation again. Then she told the cops that Chloe had called her to say that I was headed for the apartment, raging like a bull. Blanche even pulled a letter from her bosom and gave it to the cops. Chloe had written it a few weeks earlier—best as I can remember, it said something like I'd slipped into the apartment in the middle of the night and tried to kill her. All of it was a lie, but the police took me in for questioning. Nothing I told the cops made a difference but I swear I didn't do it," he pleaded. "I was satisfied just not having to live with that crazy woman!"

I had to admit, the evidence seemed overwhelming. The police walking in and finding Johnny holding the gun, the letter of fear written by his wife, and Chloe's phone call to Blanche were enough for an arrest.

I promised Johnny that I'd get back to him. I took Rita to her daughter's house and then registered into the Wyndham Hotel on International Drive. After I'd eaten in the hotel's restaurant, I called Sidney and reported exactly what Johnny Galvin had told me.

"Dorothy Williams, a defense lawyer in Orlando, is the granddaughter of an old friend," Sidney told me when I'd finished the story.

"I've hired her to assist you. She can only give you a few days so cut to the chase."

I couldn't help but wonder what was there to chase. If the evidence was correct, Johnny had killed his wife; that was all to it.

"Dorothy will call you the first thing tomorrow morning," Sidney continued, breaking my chain of thought. "She'll help you post bail, get the police report, and talk to Chloe's mother. Once that you've done that, call me again."

*   *   *

ON Wednesday morning, Dorothy and I hooked up at my hotel. She was a tall, thin blonde who impressed me as being a solid lawyer with enthusiasm for her work. Our first order of business was to post bail for Johnny, put him in a taxi, and send him home to Rita and Phoebe.

Then we headed to the records division of the police department. This city police force is a far cry from the small town of Otis, South Carolina, where my mother's baking mesmerized the sheriff and his deputy so that she can get any information she wants. A uniformed officer told us that we couldn't get a copy of the official police report until the next morning.

Dorothy found a phone and called Blanche Sears, Chloe's mother, to see if it was okay for us to pay her a visit. When she hung up the phone, she gave me a thumbs-up signal.

Mrs. Sears lived in Peppermill, a subdivision off Orange Blossom Trail. I remembered my brother telling me that these homes, only four miles south of the Florida Mall, were less than twelve years old. It was one of many subdivisions that had sprung up as Disney expanded and brought jobs and people to central Florida.

The house we drove up to was stucco in adobe brown. The yard was neat, but the only shrubbery was two cedars on each side of the garage. It was a contrast to Atlanta's flora and to the surrounding yards, which were landscaped with an assortment of tropical flowers.

Blanche Sears was six feet tall; her body was big, although not muscular. Her complexion was the color of French's mustard, her hair long and black. She had a strong nose with wide nostrils. Her eyes were large, like the cartoon character Betty Boop. They were also heavy with black pencil and mascara. Wrapped around her legs was the biggest gray and black cat I'd ever seen. I remembered that Johnny had mentioned Chloe's cat, T. C. I couldn't help but conclude that Blanche had taken over the care of the feline.

Blanche didn't say anything but stepped back inside the house and motioned us to enter. The smell of the house reminded me of a shop in Underground Atlanta that sells incense and candles. The first room was the living room. The furniture was old; perhaps a few pieces could be considered antique. The white walls were bare, making the furniture the focus of the room.

Blanche motioned us to follow her. We walked into

the family room. Dorothy and I sat at opposite ends of a long, stiff, uncomfortable sofa. When our hostess sat in an overstuffed armchair facing us, the cat jumped into her lap and she began stroking it.

The walls in this room were covered with photographs of the same person. I assumed it was her daughter, Chloe. If so, she had pictures of Chloe as a baby, as a toddler, at school. There was a long low bookshelf with more pictures of Chloe.

Blanche Sears's chin tilted up a quarter of an inch.

"I'm sorry about your daughter—" I started to say in what I considered my most sympathetic voice.

She cut me off. "How can you sit there and look me in the face and say such a thing? You who have come to this city to see that my daughter's killer goes free," she said, her voice low, without emotions.

Now folks, let me tell you, I'm usually quick on the reply. But I wasn't expecting this; the contradiction in this woman's vindictive words and her rational manner was enough to throw anybody off.

Dorothy came to my rescue. "We're not interested in freeing a killer," she said, her voice masterfully skillful. "We're trying to make sure that all the facts are known so that justice can be served."

I looked over at Dorothy then cautiously spoke again. "I understand that your daughter was in fear of her husband for some time."

The flatness of Blanche's tone with her poignant words hit me again like poisonous fangs. "Fear stalks to strike a confused prey!"

Dorothy and I exchanged glances again. I shifted in my seat. I was beginning to feel like a child in school who was trying to get her teacher's approval. I didn't like this woman. For the sake of getting insight to report back to Sidney, I had to try to keep my manner professional and ignore her. "I understand that your daughter's marriage was happy until about six months ago. Do you have any idea what went wrong between Chloe and Johnny?"

This time, she shook her head slightly, but nothing in her manner changed. "Time carries deceitful seeds on the wind to settle in fertile soil that blossom into destruction."

"I understand," I said. "But am I correct in assuming that you didn't approve of Chloe's marriage?"

"Marriage is the union of two souls. There are certain souls that should never be together. *My daughter should have known that!*"

By now, I was ready to throw down and give this philosophical woman a jab that would push her mind in the direction my questions were headed. Instead of saying what I wanted to, I continued, "Perhaps you can tell me in your own words what went wrong between Chloe and Johnny."

Blanche's words poured with a steady beat. "You have come here to seek information from me to use in a court of law to free the killer of my daughter. If you don't forget your mission, you will share his guilt, his depth of degradation. Your death will be full of pain, your blood will drop to the streets. You and Johnny Galvin will simmer in hell together, boiling in the oil of torment for all eternity. If you are wise, you will listen to me. Leave this place, rid yourself of any involvement with this man, allow justice to proceed, permit Johnny Galvin to join all the other demented souls in eternal condemnation with all unfit dogs."

"Okay," I said, when she took a breath, "why did your daughter kill herself?"

Blanche Sears's countenance immediately changed—I had scored by saying something that pushed her into a reaction. The woman's eyes took me by the throat and held there until I understood that she wasn't about to dignify my question with a response.

I backed off, acknowledging that she was right. The question was evidence that I was losing my cool, something that I knew better than to do. I apologized, then asked what I considered a less offensive question. "What would be the reason Johnny would want to kill Chloe?"

As quickly as Blanche had reacted, she regained her posture. Once again, her eyes glazed without emotion. "There is a thin line between love and hate," she muttered. "Its threshold can be easily crossed."

That's it! I thought. This interview wasn't going anywhere. The situation was becoming too stressful. Mrs. Sears was getting to me and I didn't want her to know it. I shot a look at Dorothy. She caught the hint. When she stood up, I was already on my feet.

"We appreciate your taking the time to talk to us," Dorothy said.

"Are those pictures of Chloe?" I asked.

Blanche Sears nodded. My eyes moved from her face to the hands that stroked the cat; it had a slight tremor. For the first time since I'd met the woman, I felt she was grieving her daughter's death despite her seeming self-control. I took a deep breath, turned and followed Dorothy to the front door. We exited without saying a word.

"I'm not usually skittish, but Blanche Sears was a bit too off center for my taste," I said to Dorothy, once we were in the car and headed toward the Orange Blossom Trail entrance of the subdivision.

Dorothy patted my hand, as if she sympathized with how Blanche Sears had gotten to me.

"I wish my mother were here to get a read on her," I told her. "Mama would know exactly what Blanche Sears was trying to pull on me."

"Mrs. Sears was trying to get into your head," Dorothy told me.

"Are you putting me on?"

"I've seen Mrs. Sears's mind control tactics before. You noticed that every time she spoke, her voice was even, almost rhythmic. It's the tone used by people who are expert in mind control."

"That was spooky but it was her answers that pricked my nerves . . . she spoke in riddles."

"She was trying to muddle your thinking. Let me share with you one of my clients' experiences. Now grant you, this may be an extreme case, but my client, I'll call her Irma, is a reasonably intelligent woman. Irma met a stranger on the street. She told me that the stranger had an oddness about her, but Irma swears that the oddness held a certain attraction. They talked. Irma said she remembered being impressed with the depth of their conversation. She enjoyed it so much, she was happy when the woman invited her to have lunch. After only a few hours, Irma was persuaded to go to her bank and withdraw all of her savings to give to this stranger."

"Sounds like your client was hypnotized," I muttered.

"Irma was opened to suggestions," Dorothy responded. "But a psychologist friend told me that the information Irma assimilated was influenced by something that she had earlier experienced. She had learned that her minister had deceived his congregation; something that this odd but intriguing stranger said instilled a measure of confidence in my client. Irma's thinking and behavior was changed because at that particular time she needed to trust."

"I don't know how Blanche Sears expected to influence my thinking, but the only thing she got out of her tactics was to give me a headache and to make sure I tell Sidney that I didn't like her!"

We laughed. I swung by the hotel, where I dropped Dorothy to get her car. Then I headed for a drugstore. The truth was my headache was the result of the pungent odor of Blanche's home and her cryptic responses. The whole experience called for a dose of Maximum Strength Excedrin.

Once I was medicated, I headed for Johnny and Chloe's apartment; I wanted to get a take on the neighborhood since I knew that my report of the scene of the

crime should include the external layout as well. I parked
across from the apartment where I couldn't help but notice
a fight between a man and woman. Their facial expressions, loud voices, and swinging hands told me that they
were dealing with some serious issues. The woman kept
moving her wedding ring up and down her finger, then
she took it off and flung it to the ground. The man threw
up his hands as if he was frustrated then walked away.
The woman yelled a few obscene words, turned, and
walked in the opposite direction.

Chloe and Johnny's marriage wasn't the only one in
discontent, I thought, about the same time I noticed the
sky. It had grown dark and sheet lightning flashed on the
horizon. I decided to grab a bite to eat, go to my room
and indulge in a long hot bath. The meeting with Chloe's
mother made me feel soiled. It took me all of forty-five
minutes to feel clean again.

*   *   *

THE next morning the heavens had broken open with
downpours of torrential rain, accompanied by sharp
lightning and loud, rolling thunder. Dorothy called early
and told me not to bother getting dressed. She wasn't
comfortable letting me drive in this weather since many
of the city's streets were flooded. She'd brave the weather,
go to the police department, pick up the material, and drop
the reports at my hotel room.

Grateful, I called room service and ordered breakfast,
then got my pencils and yellow pad ready to go through
every piece of the reported evidence with a fine-toothed
comb.

PHOTOS of the crime scene were included in the package
that Dorothy delivered. She also had a piece of news—
one of her sources inside the prosecutor's office told her
that the lawyer assigned to the case planned to build it on

the fact that the autopsy report didn't find any gunpowder on Chloe's hand. If Chloe had committed suicide as Johnny insisted, gunpowder should have been on the hand that held the gun.

With this in mind, I studied the pictures and read the coroner's report meticulously. I knew that Sidney wanted details, specifics.

The first thing I did was to note the crime scene from the police photos:

1. Small brown throw pillow
2. Saturday-night special handgun
3. Pool of blood coming from underneath Chloe's torso
4. Position of Chloe's crumpled body
5. A gray and black cat
6. A blue box, the size of a small match box, on the table
7. A gold wedding band next to the blue box

Well, I said to myself, since I'm an acting lawyer I might as well put on Sidney's hat and pretend that I'm trying this case. How could I take what's before me and defend my client?

The exercise started in the morning and ended around midnight. I was exhausted. The only break I'd had was when room service delivered the food I'd ordered. Tomorrow morning, I decided, I'll call Dorothy and get her to take me to the hospital where Chloe's body had been taken. The admission report would be the last piece of documentation I'd get before calling Sidney to give him another report.

* * *

AT nine o'clock the next morning I treated Dorothy to breakfast. Next we visited the Orlando Regional Medical Center. At noon I had Chloe's hospital admission report with evidence Sidney could use in court to plant reasonable doubt that Johnny had shot Chloe.

I thanked Dorothy for her assistance. Our good-bye was short; she was due in court at two p.m. and she had to complete a legal memorandum to be presented to a judge first thing Monday morning.

I gathered everything I had pulled together, called Rita and Johnny, and assured them that things were going to be fine.

Now I felt justified in giving some attention to my social life. I'd already talked to my brother Will to let him know that I was in town. We'd decided that if I finished my business early, we'd have some fun time at Disney's Pleasure Island. I told him that I had sewn things up and that I was ready to party!

                    *   *   *

O N Monday morning, Sidney and I met to go over the evidence I'd collected. Everything was spread out on a table in front of the large window in the office's conference room. I started by highlighting that the police report stated that bags were put on Chloe's hands at the scene of the crime.

"What bothered me was seeing T. C. in the crime scene pictures," I confessed. "I couldn't help but wonder how carefully the evidence had been preserved if a cat was allowed to meander around the room during the process. Could it be that the police were so convinced that Johnny had shot his wife that they allowed the crime scene to be compromised? Then I remembered Chloe's wedding ring on the table next to the sofa. Was it possible that Chloe took her wedding ring off as a symbol of this final break in her marriage, a break that would end up in her death and her husband's execution?

"Since Dorothy had learned that the prosecutor's case hinged on the absence of gunpowder on Chloe's hands, I asked myself, why would the gunpowder not be there if

Johnny was telling the truth? Maybe the police report was incorrect, maybe they didn't preserve all of the evidence. I decided to get the hospital admission report. And that's when I found the bombshell! The nurse at the Orlando Regional Medical Center who received the body noted that *she* had bagged Chloe's hands at the hospital. They weren't bagged at the apartment as reported by the police.

"So," I said to Sidney as if I were standing in front of a jury summing up my argument, "Chloe Galvin's hands were not bagged at the house as reported by the police. While the medics were strapping her body on the gurney, putting her in the ambulance, and taking her into the hospital, her hands got bumped around, and the gunpowder could have been rubbed off. Thus, the absence of the powder doesn't prove that Chloe Galvin didn't kill herself as reported by her husband!"

Sidney grinned, clearly pleased. "Simone, you're brilliant. A defense lawyer can blow a prosecutor's case out the window with proof of contamination of evidence."

I was pleased. "Tell Rita that the way I see what happened was that Chloe was a victim by consent," I said to my boss.

Sidney's eyebrow rose.

"If I were writing this story about a case my mother had worked on," I said, thinking that even though I hadn't been invited to Arizona or Massachusetts, my week had been full of excitement, "I'd entitle it 'Mama Challenges a Victim by Consent.' "

Now it was Sidney who looked puzzled.

"Blanche was livid when Chloe married Johnny, something that Chloe must have expected since she didn't introduce Johnny to Blanche until after they were married.

"Blanche Sears is into mind control. It's my theory that she had a measure of success in influencing her daughter's thinking in the past. So she started injecting negative thoughts into her Chloe's mind. The problem, however, was that Chloe loved Johnny. The poor woman had to wrestle with her own emotions while assimilating the distortions Blanche fed her. When Johnny left and moved in with his sister, the pressure became too great for Chloe to handle. She decided she didn't want to live without Johnny, but, because of her mother's repeated negative insinuations, she couldn't ask him to return home. The stress broke through her psychological skin. That is when she devised the plot to kill herself and have Johnny executed for it. This may not have been the intent of Blanche's manipulation but it was the result of it. The medical examiner's report states that there were no controlled substances in Chloe's blood, but I'm curious about that blue pillbox next to the wedding ring. There may be evidence that Chloe suffered from an emotional disorder. If so and she had stopped taking her medication, her mother's suggestions could have had such an effect, don't you think?"

Sidney shrugged. "We'll dig further, if necessary. But in my experience, once the DA finds that the police compromised the evidence, they'll rethink their case." He pushed his intercom and called his secretary. "Gale," he said, "see that Simone gets a thousand-dollar bonus for her work on the case of *Johnny Galvin v. the State of Florida.*"

When the thought of my forthcoming charge card statements flashed across my mind, I smiled.

The Only Good Judge

Carolyn Wheat

Creator of Cass Jameson, Brooklyn defense lawyer, Wheat is also a writer of award-winning short stories, many of which are available in a collection from Crippen and Landru (Tales Out of School). She conducts writing workshops and is currently turning her talents to nonfiction in the form of magazine articles and travel writing.

WHAT do you say to a naked judge?

I said yes. Averting my eyes from the too, too solid judicial flesh.

I mean, the steam room is a place for relaxation, a place where you close your eyes and inhale the scent of eucalyptus and let go the frustrations of the day—most of which were caused by judges in the first place, so the last thing you want to do while taking a *schvitz* is accept a case on appeal, for God's sake, but there was the Dragon Lady, looking not a whit less authoritative for the absence of black robes, or indeed, the absence of any other clothing including a towel.

She'd been a formidable opponent as a trial judge, and we at the defense bar breathed a sigh of relief when she went upstairs to the appellate bench. The Dragon Lady was one of the great plea-coercers of her time; she could strike fear and terror into the hearts of the most hardened criminals and have them begging for that seventeen-to-life she'd offered only yesterday.

Yes, I said she "offered." I know, you think it's the district attorney who makes plea offers while the judge sits passively on the bench. You think judges are neutral parties with no stake in the outcome, no interest in whether the defendant pleads out or goes to trial.

You've been watching too much *Law & Order*. The Dragon Lady made Jack McCoy look like a soft-on-crime liberal. She routinely rejected plea bargains on the ground that the DA wasn't being tough enough. She demanded and got a bureau chief in her courtroom to justify any reduction in the maximum sentence.

So what was she doing asking me, as a personal favor, to handle a case on appeal? I almost fell off the steam room bench. I was limp as a noodle well past *al dente*, and I'd been hoping to slide out the door without having to acknowledge the presence of my naked nemesis parked on the opposite bench like a leather-tanned Buddha. It seemed the health club equivalent of subway manners: you don't notice them, they won't notice you, and the city functions on the lubrication of mutual indifference.

But she broke the invisible wall between us. She named my name and asked a favor, and I was so nonplussed I said yes and I said "Your Honor" and three other women in the steam room shot me startled open-eyed glances as if to say, who are you to shatter our illusion of invisibility? If you two know one another and talk to one another, then you must be able to see us in all our nakedness and that Changes Everything in this steam room.

They left, abruptly and without finishing the sweating process that was beginning to reduce me to dehydrated delirium. I murmured something and groped my way to the door. I left the Dragon Lady, who'd been there twice as long as I had, yet showed no signs of needing a respite; like a giant iguana, she sat in heavy-lidded torpor, basking in the glow of the coals in the corner of the room. She lifted a wooden ladle and poured water on the hot rocks to raise more steam.

I stumbled to the shower and put it on cold, visualizing myself rolling in Swedish snow, pure and cold and crystalline.

The frigid water shocked me into realizing what I'd just done.

A favor for the Dragon Lady.

Since when did she solicit representation for convicted felons?

Four days later, she was dead.

My old Legal Aid buddy Pat Flaherty told me, in his characteristic way. He always said the only good judge was a dead judge, so when he greeted me in Part 32 with the words, "The Dragon Lady just became a good judge," I knew what he meant.

"Wow. I was talking to her the other day." I shook my head and lowered my voice to a whisper. "Heart attack?"

A sense of mortality swept over me. The woman had looked healthy enough in a reptilian way. I'd noticed her sagging breasts and compared them to my own, which, while no longer as perky as they'd once been, didn't actually reach my navel.

But give me ten years.

"No," Flaherty said, an uneasy grin crossing his freckled face. "She was killed by a burglar."

"Shot?"

"Yeah. Died instantly, they said on the radio."

"Jesus." At a loss for words—and believe it or not, considering how much I'd resented the old boot when she was alive, annoyed at Flaherty for making light of the murder.

Good judge. It's one thing to say that about a ninety-year-old pill who dies in his sleep, but a woman like the DL, cut down in what would be considered the prime of her life if she were a man and her tits didn't sag—that verged on the obscene.

The big question among the Brooklyn defense bar: should we or should we not go to the funeral?

We'd all hated her. We'd all admired her, in a way. I loved the fact that she used to wear a Wonder Woman T-shirt under her black robe. She was tough and smart and sarcastic and powerful and she'd been all that when I was still in high school.

But she'd also been one hell of an asset to the prosecution, a judge who thought her duty was to fill as many jail cells as possible and to move her calendar with a speed that gave short shrift to due process of law.

In the end, I opted to skip the actual funeral, held in accordance with Jewish custom the day after the medical examiner released the body, but I slipped into the back row of Part 49 for the courthouse memorial service two weeks later.

What the hell, I was in the building anyway.

I was in the building to meet Darnell Patterson, the client she'd stuck me with. It had taken me two weeks to get him down from Dannemora, where he was serving twenty years for selling crack.

Twenty years. The mind boggled, especially since he wasn't really convicted of the actual sale, just possession of a sale-weight quantity, meaning that someone in the DA's office thought the amount he had in his pocket was too much to be for his personal use. Since he'd been convicted before, he was nailed as a three-time loser and given a persistent felony jacket.

"It's like they punishing me for thinking ahead," he said in a plaintive voice. "I mean, I ain't no dealer. I don't be selling no shit, on account if I do, the dudes on the corner gonna bust my head wide open. I just like to buy a goodly amount so's I don't have to go out there in the street and buy no more anytime soon. I likes a hefty stash;

I likes to save a little for a rainy day, you hear what I'm saying?"

"Yeah," I said. "You're the industrious ant and all the other users are grasshoppers. The law rewards the grasshoppers because they bought a two-day supply, whereas you, the frugal one, stocked up."

"You got that right," he said with a broad smile. "I think you and me's gonna get along fine, counselor. You just tell that to the pelican court and they'll knock down my sentence."

It was conservative economics applied to narcotics addiction. Maybe I could get an affidavit from Alan Greenspan on the economic consequences of punishing people for saving instead of spending. I could hear my argument before the appellate court:

"Your Honors, all my client did was to invest in commodities. He wanted a hedge against inflation, so he bought in quantity, not for resale, but to insure himself against higher prices and to minimize the number of street buys he had to make, thus reducing his chances of being caught. Punishing him with additional time for his prudence is like punishing someone for saving instead of running up bills and declaring bankruptcy."

The more I thought about it, the more I liked it. The appellate judges—"pelicans" in defendantese—had heard it all. They were unlikely to buy the "mandatory sentences suck" argument and they had no interest in hearing the drug laws attacked as draconian, and they sure as hell didn't give a damn about my client's lousy childhood. Supply-side economics had the advantage of novelty.

When I walked out of the ninth-floor pens, I still had no idea why I'd been asked to take Darnell's case. The sentence was a travesty, of course, far outweighing whatever harm to society this man had done, but what was new or unusual about that? And why had the Dragon Lady, of all people, taken such an interest in a low-level crack case?

With her dead, I'd probably never know.

I had no inkling of a connection between the case and her untimely death.

It took the second murder for the connection to become apparent.

The deceased was a district attorney we called the Terminator; that quality of mercy that droppeth as a gentle rain from heaven was completely absent from his makeup. So once again, there were few tears shed among us defense types, and, in truth, a lot of really bad jokes made the rounds, considering how Paul French died.

He fell out a window in the tall office building behind Borough Hall, the same building that housed the Brooklyn DA's office, but not the actual floor the trial bureau was on. Which, in retrospect, should have told us something. What was he doing there? Had he fallen, or was he pushed? And had the Dragon Lady really died at the hands of a clumsy burglar who picked her house at random, or was somebody out to eliminate the harshest prosecutors and judges in the borough of Brooklyn?

His own office called it suicide. Word went around that he was upset when someone else was promoted to bureau chief over him.

Bullshit, was what I thought. I knew Paul French, tried cases against him and was proud to say we were even— three wins for him, three for me, which in the prosecution-stacked arithmetic of the criminal courts put me way ahead as far as lawyering was concerned. And I knew that while he might have enjoyed cracking the whip for a while as bureau chief, it was the courtroom he loved. It was beating the opponent, rubbing her nose in his victory, tussling in front of the judge and selling his case to the jury that got his heart started in the morning. He might have gotten pissed off if someone else got a job he thought should have been his, but no way would that have pushed him out a tenth-story window.

The suicide story was bogus, a fact that was confirmed

for me when two cops rang the bell of my Court Street office and said they wanted to discuss Paul French. I invited them in, poured them coffee—Estate Java, wasted on cops used to drinking crankcase oil at the stationhouse—and congratulated them on not buying the cover story. The man was murdered; the only question was which of the fifty thousand or so defendants he'd sent up the river could legitimately take the credit.

The larger and older of the cops opened his notebook and said, "You represented a Jorge Aguilar in September of 1995, is that right, counselor?"

It took a minute to translate his fractured pronunciation. It took another minute to recall the case; 1995 might as well have been twenty years ago, I'd represented so many other clients in so many other cases.

"Jorge, yeah," I said, conjuring up a vision of a cocky, swaggering kid in gang colors who'd boasted he could "do twenty years standing on his head." Despite his complete lack of remorse and absence of redeeming qualities, I'd felt sorry for him. In twenty years, he'd be broken and almost docile, still illiterate and unemployable, and he'd probably commit another crime within a year just so he could get back to his nice, safe prison. He could do twenty years, all right. He just couldn't do anything else.

It took all of thirty seconds for me to disabuse them of the notion that Jorge's case killed Paul French. "Look," I pointed out, "the whole family rejoiced when the kid went upstate. It meant they could keep a television set for more than a week. And he was no gang leader; the real gang-bangers barely tolerated him. So I don't think—"

"What about Richie Toricelli, then?" The older cop leaned forward in my visitor's chair and I had the feeling he was getting to the real point of his interrogation.

"Now we're talking. Toricelli I could see killing Paul French. I'm not sure I see him pushing anyone out a window, though. I'd have expected Richie to use his sawed-off shotgun instead. He liked to see people bleed."

The younger cop gave me one of those "how can you defend those people" looks.

"I was appointed," I said in reply to the unspoken criticism. Which was no answer at all. I wouldn't have been appointed if I hadn't put myself on a list of available attorneys, and I wouldn't have done that if I hadn't been committed with every fiber of my being to criminal defense work.

I'd long since stopped asking myself why I did it. I did it, and I did it the best way I knew how, and I let others work up a philosophy of the job.

Some cases were easier to justify than others. Richie Toricelli's was one of the tough ones.

And if you thought he was a dead loss to society, you ought to meet his mother.

"Tell you the truth," I said, only half-kidding, "I'd sure like to know where Rose Toricelli was when French took his dive."

"She was in the drunk tank over on Gold Street," the younger cop said, a look of grim amusement on his brown face. "Nice alibi, only about fifty people and ten pieces of official paperwork put her there."

"Pretty convenient," I said, hearing the echo of the Church Lady in my head.

"Counselor, you know something you're not telling us?"

I dropped my eyes. A slight blush crept into my cheeks. I hated admitting this.

"I changed my phone number after Richie went in," I said. "For a year, I lived in fear that Rose Toricelli would find some way to get to me. She didn't just blame Paul French for Richie's conviction, she blamed me too."

The older cop cut me a look. Skeptical Irish blue eyes under bushy white eyebrows over a red-tinged nose. I got the message: *You're gonna do a man's job, you need a man's balls. Afraid of an old lady doesn't cut it.*

It pissed me off. This guy didn't know Richie's ma.

"You look at her, you see a pathetic old woman who thinks her scurvy son is some kind of saint; I look at her and I see someone who wants me dead and who could very easily convince herself that shooting me is the best way to tell the world her boy is innocent."

"Did she ever make threats? And did you report any of this?"

"Only in the courthouse the day they took Richie away. And, no," I said, anger creeping into my voice, "I didn't report it. I know what cops think about defense lawyers who get threats. You think we ask for it. And I didn't want to look like a wimp who couldn't handle a little old lady with a grudge."

What really chilled me weren't Rose Toricelli's threats to do damage to the sentencing judge, to Paul French, to me—that was standard stuff in the criminal courts. What really had my blood frozen were the words she said to her son as they shuffled him, cuffed and stunned like a cow on his way to becoming beefsteak:

"You show them, Richie. You show them you're innocent. It would serve them right if you hung yourself in there."

For a year after that, I waited for the news that Richie's body had been discovered hanging from the bars. Doing what Mamma wanted, like he always did.

But as far as I knew, he was still alive, still serving his time, which gave him an iron-bar-clad alibi for French's death, so why were the cops even bringing it up?

The question nagged at me even after the cops left. I turned to my computer, supplementing the information I pulled up with a few phone calls and discovered something very interesting indeed.

Once upon a time, Richie Toricelli's cellmate had been Hector Dominguez.

You remember the case. It made all the papers and even gave birth to a joke or two on Letterman. Funny guy, that Hector.

He'd kidnapped his son, claiming the boy's mother was making him sick. A devout believer in Santeria, he accused his ex of working roots, casting spells, that sapped the boy's strength. He said God told him to save his little boy from a mother who had turned witch.

You can imagine how well that went over in the Dragon Lady's courtroom. She gaveled him quiet, had him bound and gagged because he wouldn't stop screaming at his sobbing wife. He hurled curses and threats throughout the trial, bringing down the wrath of his gods on the heads of everyone connected to the proceeding.

The day he was to be sentenced, they found the doll in his cell. Carved out of soap, it wore a crude robe of black nylon and sported a doll's wig the exact shade of the Dragon Lady's pageboy. Out of its heart, a hypodermic syringe protruded like a dagger.

Like I said, a lot of criminal defendants threaten the judge who sends them upstate, but a voodoo doll was unique, even in the annals of Brooklyn justice. The *Post* put it on the front page; the *News* thundered editorially about laxness in the Brooklyn House of Detention; *Newsday* did a very clever cartoon I'd taped to my office bulletin board; and the *Times* ignored the whole thing because it didn't happen in Bosnia.

I really wasn't in the courtroom when Dominguez was sentenced because I wanted to see the show. Unlike the two rows of reporters and most of the other lawyers present that day, I had business before the court. But I had to admit a certain curiosity about how the Dragon Lady was going to handle this one.

The lawyer asked her to recuse herself, saying she could hardly be objective under the circumstances. I could have told him to save his breath; the DL was never, under any circumstances, going to admit she couldn't do her job. She dismissed out of hand the notion that she'd taken the voodoo doll personally; it would play no part, she announced in ringing tones, in her sentencing.

Hector Dominguez was oddly compelling when he began to address the court. His English was so poor that an interpreter stood next to him in case he lapsed into his Dominican Spanish, but Hector waved away the help, determined to reach the judge in her own language.

"You Honor, I know it looking bad against me," he said in his halting way. "I just want to say I love my son with my whole heart. *Mi corazon* is hurt when my son get sick. I want her to stop making him sick. Please, You Honor, don't let that woman hurt my boy. He so little, he so pale, he so sick all the time and it all her fault, You Honor, all her doing with her spells and her evil ways."

The child's mother dabbed at her eyes with a tissue, shaking her head mournfully.

The DL gave Dominguez two years more than the District Attorney's office asked for, which was already two years more than the probation report recommended.

This, she insisted, had nothing to do with the doll, but was the appropriate sentence for a man who tried to convince a child that his loving mother was a witch.

Dominguez's last words to the DL consisted of a curse to the effect that she should someday know the pain he felt now, the pain of losing a child to evil.

The papers all commented on the irony of a man like Hector calling someone else evil. And Letterman milked his audience for laughs by holding up a voodoo doll in the image of a certain Washington lady.

But three years later, when the boy's mother was charged with attempted murder and the court shrinks talked about Munchausen's syndrome by proxy, the attitudes changed a bit. Now Hector was seen, not as a nut case who thought his wife was possessed, but as a father trying to protect his son and interpreting events he couldn't understand in the only context he knew, that of his spirit-based religion.

He was up for parole, and it was granted without much ado. He was free—but his little boy, six years old by now, lay in a coma, irreparably brain-damaged as a result of his mother's twisted ministrations.

By not listening to him, by treating him like a criminal instead of a concerned father, the Dragon Lady had prevented authorities from looking closely at the mother's conduct.

He had shared a jail cell with Richie Toricelli. That had to mean something—but what?

The theory hit me with the full force of a brainstorm: defendants on a train. Patricia Highsmith by way of Alfred Hitchcock.

What if Ma Toricelli, instead of killing the prosecutor who sent her precious Richie upstate, shot the Dragon Lady—who had no connection whatsoever to her or her son? And what if Dominguez, who had no reason to want Paul French dead, returned the favor by pushing French out the window? Each has an alibi for the murder they had a motive to commit, and no apparent reason to kill the person they actually murdered.

The more I thought about it, the more I liked it. I liked it so much I actually asked a cop for a favor. Which was how I ended up sifting through DD5s in the Eight-Four precinct as the winter sun turned the overcast clouds a dull pewter.

I learned nothing that hadn't been reported in the papers, and I was ready to pack it in, ready to admit that even if Ma Toricelli had done the deed, she'd covered her tracks pretty well, when one item caught my attention.

The neighbor across the street had seen a Jehovah's Witness ringing doorbells about twenty minutes prior to the crime. He knew the woman was a Witness because she carried a copy of the *Watchtower* in front of her like a shield.

This was a common enough sight in Brooklyn Heights, where the Witnesses owned a good bit of prime real estate, except for one little thing.

Jehovah's Witnesses traveled in pairs. Always.

One Jehovah's Witness just wasn't possible.

My heart pounded as I read the brief description of the bogus Witness: female, middle-aged, gray hair, gray coat, stout boots. Five feet nothing.

Ma Toricelli to a T.

I wasn't as lucky with the second set of detectives. I was told in no uncertain terms that nothing I had to say would get me a peek at the Paul French reports, so I left the precinct without any evidence that Hector Dominguez could have been in the municipal building when French took his dive.

Still, the idea had promise. I had no problem picturing Rose Toricelli firing a gun point-blank into the judge's midsection and I was equally convinced that in return for the Dragon Lady's death, Hector Dominguez would have pushed five district attorneys out a window. But proving it was another matter.

I pondered these truths as I trudged down Court Street toward home. The sidewalks wore a new coat of powder, temporarily brightening the slush of melting gray snow. Dusk had arrived with winter suddenness, and only the snow-fogged streetlights lit the way. I was picking my way carefully in spite of well-treaded snow boots, my attention fixed on the depth of the chill puddle at the corner of Court and Atlantic Avenue, when the first shot zipped past my ear.

I didn't know it was a shot until the guy in the cigar store yelled at me to get down.

Get down where?

Get down why?

I honestly didn't hear it.

I couldn't even say it sounded like a car backfiring or a firecracker. And I didn't hear the second shot either, although this one I felt.

A sting, like a wasp or a hornet, and blood coursing down my cheek. A burning sensation and a really strong need to use a bathroom. I was ankle-deep in very cold

water and couldn't decide whether to keep making my
way across the street or run to the shelter of the cigar
store. While I considered my options, a black SUV
swerved around the corner, straight into the icy puddle,
drenching me in dirty, frigid water.

That did it. I turned quickly, wrenching my knee, and
hoisted myself onto the curb. I slid at once back into the
puddle, landing hard on my backside. A couple of teen-
agers stopped to laugh, and I suppose it would have been
funny if I hadn't been scared out of my mind. Limping
and holding my bleeding cheek, I slipped and slid on my
way to the amber-lighted cigar store on the corner.

Tobacco-hater that I am, I'd never been inside the cigar
emporium before. The scent was overwhelming, but so
was the warmth from the space heater on the floor.

The counterman met me at the door, a solicitous expression on his moon face. He was short, with a big bris-
tling mustache and two chins. He reeked of cigar smoke,
but I didn't mind at all when he put an arm around me
and led me into the sanctuary of his store. He seated me
on a folding chair and offered the only comfort he possessed. "Want a cigarillo, lady? On the house."

I started to laugh, but the laughter ended in tears of
frustration and relief.

I was alive.

I was bleeding.

I'd been shot at.

The cops were on their way, the cigar man told me,
and then he proudly added that he'd seen the shooter's
car and had written down the license plate.

The cops, predictably enough, talked drive-by shooting
and surmised that a gang member might have been walking nearby when the shots rang out. Since my attention
was fully absorbed in not falling into the puddle, King
Kong could have been behind me on the street and I
wouldn't have noticed.

The second theory was the Atlantic Avenue hotbed-ofterrorism garbage that gets dragged out whenever anything happens on that ethnically charged thoroughfare. Just because Arab spice stores and Middle Eastern restaurants front the street, everything from a trash fire to littering gets blamed either on Arab extremists or anti-Arab extremists.

I have to admit, I was slow. Even I didn't think the shooting had anything to do with my visit to the Eight-Four precinct.

That didn't happen until the next day, when I learned that the car whose license plate the cigar man wrote down belonged to one Marcus Mitchell.

Marcus Mitchell had been royally screwed by Paul French in one of those monster drug prosecutions where everyone turned state's evidence except the lowest-level dealers. People who'd made millions cut deals that had the little guys serving major time for minor felonies, and Mitchell was a guy who had nothing with which to deal.

My own client gave up the guys above him and walked away with a bullet—that's one year and not even a year upstate, a year at Riker's, which meant his family could visit him and—let's be honest here—he could still run a good bit of his drug business from his cell. I know, that sucks, but French was only too happy to get the goods on the higher-ups and made the deal with open eyes. All I did was say yes.

All Marcus Mitchell did was keep his mouth shut, and he did that not out of stubbornness but out of sheer ignorance. He'd been the poor sap caught with a nice big bag of heroin, but the only thing he knew was that a guy named Willie handed it to him at the corner of Fulton and Franklin and told him not to come back until it was all sold.

For this, he got twenty to life. Released after three years on a technicality, but by that time his wife had left him, he'd lost his job, and his parents had died in shame. He had plenty of reason to want Paul French dead.

But why had he taken a potshot at me?

I had taken the day off work, called in shot. It was in the papers, so the judges bought it and told me to take all the time I needed to recuperate, then put my cases over a week. I sipped Tanzanian Peaberry while I felt the blood ooze into the gauze bandage on my cheek and reconsidered my theory.

It was still sound, except for two little things.

One: there were three, not two, defendants on a train.

Two: Ma Toricelli's chosen victim wasn't Paul French—it was the defense lawyer she blamed for her son's conviction. Me.

It went like this:

Ma Toricelli kills the Dragon Lady for Hector Dominguez.

Dominguez kills Paul French for Marcus Mitchell.

Marcus Mitchell tries to kill me for Ma Toricelli.

This time the cops listened. This time they questioned everyone in the building where Paul French died and found several witnesses who described Hector Dominguez to a T. Add that to the description of the bogus Witness, squeeze all three defendants until someone cracked, and the whole house of cards would tumble down.

I went to the arraignment. I was the victim, so I had a right to be there, and besides, I wanted to see firsthand the people who'd tried to end my life in an icy puddle.

When the time came for Ma Toricelli to plead for bail, she thrust her chin forward and said, "She was supposed to be my boy's lawyer, but all she did was look down on him. She never did her job, Your Honor, not from the first day. She thought Richie was trash and she didn't care what happened to him."

I opened my mouth to respond, then realized it made no difference what I said. Even if I'd been the worst lawyer in the world, that didn't give Rose Toricelli the right to order my death. And I'd done a good job for Richie, a better job than the little sociopath deserved.

Perhaps my mental choice of words was what caught my attention.

If I really thought Richie was a sociopath, had I done my best for him? Or had I slacked off, let the prosecution get away with things I'd have fought harder if I'd truly believed my client innocent? It was a hard question. There were cases I'd handled better, but I honestly didn't see Richie getting off if Johnnie Cochran had been his lawyer. Still, my cellside manner could have been improved; I could have at least gone through the motions enough to convince Richie's mother that I was doing my best.

*   *   *

T HE letter came in due course, as we say in the trade. It was enclosed in a manila envelope with the name of a prominent Brooklyn law firm embossed in the left corner. I had no clue what was inside; I had no business pending with the firm and no reason to expect correspondence from them. I slit the thing open with my elegant black Frank Lloyd Wright letter opener, the one my dad gave me for Christmas two years ago.

Another letter with my name handwritten on the front, no address, no stamp, fell into my hands.

This one's return address was the Appellate Division, Second Department.

It was a message from beyond the grave.

Ms. Jameson:
I'm sure you have had reason to wonder why I asked you in particular to handle the case of Darnell Patterson on remand from this court.

Let us just say that I have had reason to regret the current fashion for mandatory minimum sentences and maximum jail time for defendants who commit nonviolent offenses. While I am not one to condone lawbreaking, I firmly believe in distinctions between those who are truly dangerous to society and those who are merely inconvenient.

Mr. Patterson would appear to fall into the latter category. I trust you will agree with me on this point and use your best efforts on his behalf.

You and I, Ms. Jameson, have seldom seen eye to eye, but those traits of yours that I most deplore, your tendency toward overzealousness and your refusal to "go through the motions" on even the most hopeless case, will prove to be just what Mr. Patterson needs in a lawyer.

I expect you will wonder what brought about my change of heart with respect to low-level narcotics cases.

I also expect you to live with your curiosity and make no effort to trace my change of heart to its roots. Suffice to say that it is a private family matter and therefore is nobody's business but my own.

Once again, I thank you for your attention to this matter.

There was no signature. The Dragon Lady had died before she could scrawl her name in her characteristic bold hand.

The compliments brought a traitorous tear to my eyes—especially since the words weren't true.

Mostly true. I was well-known in the Brooklyn court system as a fighter who didn't give up easily, who didn't back down in the face of threats from prosecutors or judges. The DL had been right to rely on me.

But Richie Toricelli hadn't been. I'd been so disgusted by his crimes, so turned off by his attitude, that I'd given less than my best to his defense. Ma Toricelli, for all her craziness, had a point. I'd phoned it in, done a half-baked job of presenting his alibi witnesses, given the jurors little reason to believe his story over that of the prosecution.

The irony was huge. The DL, of all people, sending me compliments on my fighting spirit while Ma Toricelli planned to kill me for rolling over and playing dead on her son's case. Me bailing on Richie and the Dragon Lady getting religion over a three-time loser who hoarded drugs like a squirrel saving up for winter.

The image of Hector Dominguez's voodoo doll swam before my eyes—the weapon protruding from its soap heart wasn't a knife, but a hypodermic. "May you lose a child to evil," he'd cursed, and perhaps she had. Perhaps reaching out to help Darnell Patterson was a way of atoning for that child. Perhaps she'd finally seen that justice needed a dose of mercy, like a drop of bitters in a cocktail.

I sat like a stone while the letter fluttered to the hard-wood floor of my office.

Pat Flaherty had been right after all.

The Dragon Lady *had* become a good judge.

THE VIEW FROM THE BENCH

Mixed Blessings

Margaret Maron

The first book in the acclaimed Deborah Knott series, Boot-
legger's Daughter, *captured all four major mystery awards,
an unprecedented—and unmatched—sweep for a single
novel. The books have continued to live up to that promise,
as Judge Knott wrestles with her conscience on and off the
bench. Margaret is a past president of Sisters in Crime and
a past director on the national board of Mystery Writers of
America. Like Sarah Caudwell, she is a proud recipient of the
legendary Whimsey Award.*

THE first time I saw it was two years ago. I was driving
back from Broward's Rock, an upscale resort island
down near the South Carolina–Georgia border. Not a
place I could normally afford to vacation in, but my friend
Annie owns a bookstore there and had invited me for a
long weekend. As the daughter of an ex-bootlegger and
someone who grew up sweating through my share of the
farmwork, I'm always interested in seeing how the other
half live and play.

Anyhow, I had left the island and was heading west
on a little two-lane road. Fortunately, the sun had already
set, but there was still a blazing gold-and-red afterglow in
the western sky. A few miles before I reached I-95, a
reddish light appeared on the right shoulder up ahead. It
was as if a ragged patch of glowing sky had dropped onto
the roadside and was bobbing along eastward. The car
ahead of me slowed to a crawl and I tapped my brakes,
too, to warn the car behind.

To my bemusement, it was a full-sized plastic cross, illuminated from within so that it gleamed bright red in the twilight. In the brief moment it took me to drive past, I only had time to note that it rode on the back of a sturdily built man with dark hair and ragged beard and a determined look on his face.

A large lighted plastic cross was not the oddest sight I'd ever seen along southern roads—after all, this *is* the Bible Belt—but it tickled me to picture him lugging it onto the ferry to Broward's Rock. The tiny town at the ferry landing is open to anyone, but what about the gated communities that take up most of the island? Would the guards at those gatehouses turn him back or look the other way as he passed? And if he made it through, what would all those wealthy vacationing golfers from up north or the Midwest make of him?

I made a mental note to call Annie when I got home and ask, but like so many of my mental notes, it faded before I reached the North Carolina line where Pancho's South of the Border, the ultimate in tacky rest stops, gave me a whole new set of absurdities to contemplate.

*   *   *

THE next time I saw that cross was in the last place I could have imagined: my own church, the First Baptist Church of Dobbs.

Our minister, the Reverend Carlyle Yelvington, is a thoughtful, dignified intellectual, as befits the pastor of the oldest and wealthiest Baptist church in Colleton County. He entreats his congregation to lead a moral life by gentle appeals to logic and ethics. Charismatic techniques horrify him and he would never get down and mud-wrestle someone into salvation, but he's smart enough to know that a good rousing fire-and-brimstone sermon can act like a bracing spring tonic for the Baptist soul. Accordingly, he has a carefully screened roster of more dynamic preachers whom he invites to come and witness to us five or six times a year when he has to be away.

Unfortunately, the more dynamic preacher he'd invited this Sunday was himself called away at the last minute, and instead of consulting with Mr. Yelvington's secretary, he took it upon himself to send a substitute of his own choosing, which is how we wound up with Brother Reuben in the pulpit shouting out a message of damnation and redemption, "Yea, even to those amongst you to whom much has been given without you giving back to the Lord who's blessed you with so many worldly goods, who's set you on such a high horse that you think you got in the saddle all by yourself."

In ringing tones, Brother Reuben explained how, only last week, a man of God had appeared in the doorway of his poor little mission down in Fayetteville, laboring under a heavy burden, "a burden put on him by the Lord Jesus Christ himself, a burden to go out into the highways and byways and preach the word of God. Well, my friends, that's what he's done all week down there in Fayetteville and when I got the call Thursday night to come here this morning, I knew that the Lord had laid a blessing on you and that He wanted Brother Buck to come on up here to Dobbs, to bring his burden into this fine and stately house of worship and preach His word right here."

With that, he turned to the double doors that led back to classrooms and robing room and church offices and shouted, "Brother Buck, in the name of our Lord Jesus Christ, come forth!"

The doors swung open and there was that same bright red cross that I'd first seen in South Carolina, riding on the shoulders of the same dark-bearded man. I now saw that he was older than my brief impression, probably late forties or early fifties. He wore a blue T-shirt imprinted with the words "I am a soldier of the Cross," and his face and muscular arms were deeply tanned. I also saw that the cross was ten feet tall and constructed of bright red

Plexiglas, crimson as the blood of Christ. Two little hard-rubber wheels, the kind you see on push mowers, were mounted on an axle through the base of the cross to make it easier to carry, but the thing still must have weighed a ton. When Brother Buck mounted the dais and stood beside Brother Reuben, it towered another four feet above their heads.

Wilma Carter, Mr. Yelvington's elderly secretary, sat in appalled silence in the pew ahead of mine, but my friend Portland Brewer was cracking up beside me.

"Friends," said Brother Reuben, "this is Brother Buck Collins and he's got a message you should open your hearts and hear. Tell 'em, Brother Buck!"

Buck Collins's testimony began with a certain predictability: the dissipated youth, the drugs, the gambling, the drunken nights of wenching and whoring.

Okay, every word might have been true, but over the years I've noticed that reformed sinners tend to—well, not lie exactly, but more like "enhance" the darkness of their sinfulness in order to dramatize the extent of their reformation and redemption.

Anyhow, five years ago, in the depth of his degradation, his sister persuaded him to go to church with her one Sunday morning. The preacher seemed to speak directly to his heart.

"And I went out of that house with my soul on fire, tormented by the flames of hell. That very same night, friends, our Savior appeared to me in a dream, saying 'Go out into the highways and hedges, and compel them to come in, that my house may be filled.' Well, friends, two days later, I set out on my journey with nothing but a backpack and my new faith in the Lord, who promised to provide my daily needs. Even the poorest man is rich when the Lord looks after him."

However, he'd no sooner set out, than he met an evangelist carrying a small cross of two poles lashed together. "As soon as I saw it, I knew immediately that Jesus wanted me to bear His cross, too, so I went back home and got this one built."

("A classic case of penance envy," Portland whispered in my ear.)

He had been on the road ever since, traveling from church to church, mission to mission, spreading the word of redemption and salvation to all he met along the highways and back roads.

"Amen, Jesus!" said Brother Reuben when the testimony ended. "And now I'm gonna ask the choir to lead us in singing 'The Old Rugged Cross.' "

The choir, which had planned a joyous Purcell anthem, had to scramble for their hymnals and that lugubrious dirge.

*   *   *

TWO mornings later, I saw the cross yet again. It was leaning sideways on its base and crosspiece in the hallway outside Major Dwight Bryant's door. Dwight and I have known each other since I was in diapers and he was a lanky kid in and out of our house like one of my eleven older brothers. Since I'm a district court judge now and he's second in command under Sheriff Bowman "Bo" Poole with offices here in the Colleton County Courthouse, we still see each other almost every day, and I often take my lunchbag down to his office while he eats a sandwich at his desk.

Today's was an enormous BLT made with tomatoes from my daddy's garden that I'd brought him the day before. I love BLT's, too, but I'm not six-three, which is why I was eating peach yogurt.

"Don't tell me Brother Buck's in jail here," I said, settling into the chair across from him.

"Change the subject," he told me.

"Why?" I asked indignantly. And then it dawned on me.

"Don't you read your calendar?" he teased.

Well, I do, of course—mostly to see if any of my friends or neighbors are going to be standing in front of me, which happens more often than I'd really like. But my eyes had slid right over the name of Buck Collins, who would be the subject of a probable cause hearing this afternoon. So quite properly, Dwight and I couldn't talk about it, even though I was dying of curiosity.

* * *

WHEN his name was called, Buck Collins walked down from the jury box where the jailer had seated all his prisoners. Like the rest of them, Collins was dressed in an orange polyester jumpsuit. He took his place behind the defendants' table and I asked if he was represented by an attorney.

"No, ma'am," he answered softly.

I explained his right to one should he so desire and how the state would pay the costs if he couldn't afford it. When he shook his head again, I asked him to sign the waiver in front of him that would affirm his decision and to hand it to my clerk.

As he started to write, a man stood up three rows back and said, "Your Honor, can I hire him a lawyer?"

I could have gaveled him out of order, but I like to allow a little leeway, especially since I recognized Brother Reuben and what were probably several of the Makely mission regulars seated in the same row as the stranger.

"Your name, sir?" I asked, motioning him forward.

"Jack Marcom, ma'am. From Brunswick, Georgia."

He was neatly dressed in pressed chinos and blue plaid shirt with a button-down collar. A pair of wire-rimmed sunglasses dangled from his shirt pocket. He held a blue canvas porkpie hat in his hands and the top of his head was nearly bald, making his long face look even longer. Mid-forties, I'd say. A couple of years younger than Buck Collins, but not quite as muscular.

"What's your relationship to Mr. Collins?" I asked, motioning him forward.

"He's my wife's brother and I can get a lawyer for him if—"

"No," said Collins, who had stood stolidly till then, not looking around when Marcom spoke. "I hold myself accountable and I don't want a lawyer, so let's just get this over with. Please, ma'am?"

"We will," I said. "But you're accused of a serious crime and I'd advise you to consider Mr. Marcom's offer."

"C'mon, Buck," his brother-in-law entreated. "Let me do this."

Collins finished signing the paper, gave it to my clerk and returned to the defendants' table, all without acknowledging the other man's presence.

"Can't I get him one anyhow?" Marcom asked me.

"No!" said Collins.

"Be seated, Mr. Marcom," I said. "Mr. Collins is the only one who can make that decision and if he chooses not to be represented, that's his right. Go ahead, Mr. Nance."

"This is a misdemeanor possession of stolen property, Your Honor," said Chester Nance, the ADA who was prosecuting today's calendar. "Also misdemeanor breaking and entering. Call Officer Walker to the stand."

The Dobbs police officer took the stand, was sworn in and stated his name and rank.

"Describe to the court what you observed last night around ten-fifteen," said Chester Nance.

In careful pedantic legalese, Officer Walker described how he was patrolling the town last night when he saw a man walking alone on the sidewalk outside First Baptist. Since downtown still rolls up the sidewalks at nine o'clock on a Monday night (my words, not Walker's), a pedestrian was unusual enough that he kept the man in sight in his rearview mirror.

"Then I saw him turn into the walk that goes around to the offices at the rear of the church. I drove around the corner, parked my cruiser, and came up through those bushes back there. I heard what sounded like breaking glass and arrived just in time to see the defendant reach through the door window, unlock the door from inside and turn the knob."

"And what did you do at that point?" asked Nance.

"I identified myself and placed him under arrest. Upon being searched, it was discovered that he had four credit cards which we ascertain to belong to four members of the church choir."

Nance held up a plastic bag with the multicolored cards, which he wished to place in evidence.

I took the bag and could read the names through the plastic. All were prominent, well-to-do women. I myself have never seen the point of having more than one credit card, but these women probably had stacks and wouldn't have noticed one missing card for days if Collins hadn't been caught. They were trusting souls to leave their purses in the robing room where anyone could get at them. Still, the only one I've ever seen carry a pocketbook with her choir robe is Miss Nora McBride, an elderly spinster who has an estimated worth of three million dollars and a soprano voice that soars like an angel.

I handed the bag back to Chester Nance, who said, "No further questions, Your Honor."

I looked at the defendant. This close, I could see the flecks of gray in his beard and hair, the weathering of his skin. His eyes met mine, then dropped, as if in shame.

"Do you have any questions for this witness?" I asked him.

"No, ma'am. I just want to plead guilty and start serving my time."

I excused the witness. "Any priors, Mr. Nance?"

"Not in the state of North Carolina," said the ADA.

"At least, not under this name. We haven't heard back from Georgia yet, and I have a feeling we're gonna find he's done this before."

At that point, Brother Reuben stood and raised his hand, "Ma'am? Judge? Can I speak on Brother Buck's behalf?"

"Very well. Step forward."

The preacher came up to the bar railing and said, "Judge, I know it looks bad, but this is a good man sitting here. Weren't you in that church Sunday morning?"

I nodded.

"I thought I remembered you," he said happily. "Well, if you were there, then you musta seen the goodness in his face, the sincerity in his voice—"

"But not the credit cards in his pocket," jibed Chester Nance.

"Now, I don't know how the devil managed to tempt Brother Buck," said Brother Reuben slipping deeper into earnestness, "but I do believe God told him it was wrong and I do believe God sent him there last night to put back that which he had stolen."

I looked at Collins. "Is that the way it happened?"

He nodded. "But I don't expect you to believe me and it doesn't really matter because I wasn't thinking straight. I see that now. I was trying to get away from this sin without paying the price."

Something about his mock-meek humility goaded me. "Tell me something," I said. "Just how many times have you done this before?"

"Done what?"

"Used men like Brother Reuben here to take you into affluent churches where you can find opportunity to steal? If there were some way to trace back on you, would we find a trail of missing credit cards or other items?"

He tried to meet my eyes and failed miserably. I might have wanted to give Collins the maximum sentence then and there, but the reality was that whether he got any jail time would depend on whether he had any prior convictions.

"Will two days give you enough time to hear from Georgia?" I asked Nance.

He nodded.

"Then bring him back in two days and I'll hear his plea and set the sentence."

"Could we post a bond for him?" asked Brother Reuben.

I looked at Nance, who shrugged. "I've got no problem with that."

"Very well," I said. "Bond is set at five hundred dollars. See the clerk downstairs."

*   *   *

BUCK Collins was the last case on my docket and I signed a couple of forms for my clerk, looked over the calendar for tomorrow, read through some pending files, then called it a day.

As I came down the steps at the rear of the courthouse on my way to the parking lot, I found Collins's brother-in-law loading the Plexiglas cross into the back of a ten-year-old white Chevy pickup. With sunglasses covering the lines around his eyes and that blue canvas hat covering his bald spot, he looked ten years younger than he had in court. Lettering on the truck door let me know that Jack Marcom was the owner of Marcom's Cabinet Shop in Brunswick, Georgia—Cabinets and Bookcases Our Specialty. Not all that prosperous, if you could judge by the age of the truck. I noted that his only jewelry was a cheap wristwatch and a plain gold wedding band. The men who were helping him tie the cross down had the pasty faces of recovering alcoholics.

In front of the truck was a shabby old Buick station wagon with two more men leaning against it, probably waiting for Brother Reuben to finish up with the bail bondsman and paperwork that would get Collins released from jail.

Marcom recognized me even though I was no longer wearing my black robe and he tipped his hat. "I want to thank you, ma'am, for letting Buck out on bail. It'd near 'bout kill my wife to hear her brother had to stay in jail."

"Is she up here with you?" I asked.

"No, ma'am. I was coming up to Florence, South Carolina, this weekend to see about some walnut trees that blew down during that last hurricane. Good walnut's hard to come by. And Bonnie, that's my wife, Buck's sister? Anyhow, Bonnie said long as I was this far north, how 'bout I come on up and check on him. Make sure he's okay. She worries about him out on the road, so whenever I get the chance, I bring him some fresh clothes, new shoes, some of Bonnie's homemade fudge. She was hoping now that winter's coming on, maybe he's walked far enough north, that maybe I could swing him around, get him to walk south for a change."

"How did you know where to find him?"

"Oh, he called Friday morning. Calls collect most times. He's the only family Bonnie's got. Besides me and the kids, of course. She told him to call her every week even if he didn't have the money and he's pretty good about it."

Marcom's matter-of-factness took me aback. As a child of a cynical culture, I was both amused and offended by Brother Buck Collins's wacky zeal. But clearly Jack Marcom saw him as the much-loved brother of his much-loved wife and took his ministry very seriously.

I walked over to get a closer look at the bright red cross. "You know, I saw Mr. Collins a couple of years ago when I was in South Carolina," I said. "It was almost dark, but the cross was all lit up. Does it still have a light inside?"

"Here, let me show you," he said, with almost proprietary pride.

He tugged at a section just beneath the crossbar and it popped right off. I saw that it had been held in place by strip magnets glued to the inner surface and to the plastic section itself. Inside was a small lightbulb wired to some flashlight batteries. A slotted section just below that held a thick packet of the inspirational leaflets and Bible tracts that Brother Buck had distributed at our church on Sunday. I suppose since the cross was hollow, he could have used it as a rolling suitcase except that clothes would have blocked the light. As it was, the light couldn't reach the very bottom of the cross because of the section that housed the wheels. That's why it had seemed to float on Collins's shoulders and off the ground when I first saw it in the twilight.

Now that I was up close, I marveled at the workmanship that went into that cross. Instead of just butting the pieces together so that the raw edges were exposed, someone had carefully beveled all the edges so that the joints were almost invisible.

"Before he went on the road," I said, "was Brother Buck a cabinetmaker, too?"

Marcom gave a rueful laugh and shoved his blue hat to the back of his head. "Buck's a good man, Judge. Out here doing good for the Lord as the Lord leads him, but you give him any kind of a power tool and you're just asking for trouble."

"So you're really the one who built this?"

"Well, we all have to use the talents we have where we can, don't you think? Bonnie, she said it was the least we could do to help his mission. And it's been real educational, some of the places he's been, the people he's met. Why, Jimmy Carter stopped along the road one time and talked and prayed with him for over an hour. Can you imagine that? A president of the whole United States? And when Buck came through Pinehurst a couple of months ago, some millionaire let us stay in his guesthouse right on the golf course." Awe and modest pride were in his voice. "Treated us like we were just as good as anybody else, which is what the Bible tells us, of course, but some people—"

I didn't get to hear the rest of his story because I saw Brother Reuben and Buck Collins push open the courthouse door and start down the steps toward us. Talking to Jack Marcom about the cross was one thing; socializing with someone I'd soon be passing judgment on was quite another. As I moved away, I asked Marcom if he'd be in court on Friday.

He nodded. "With a lawyer, if Buck'll let me."

*   *   *

I stopped by Aunt Zell's to pick up a pair of slacks she'd hemmed for me. She and Uncle Ash were on their way out to supper and they invited me to join them, but I wanted to get home before dark and work on the perennial flower border I'd planted beside my new porch. The weeds were about to take it.

As I drove out of Dobbs, I was not surprised to come upon that cross again. Highway 48 leads not only to my house, but on to Fayetteville as well. What did surprise me was that the cross was now lashed to the top of Brother Reuben's battered old station wagon and Buck Collins was in the front seat. Trailing along behind was Jack Marcom in his pickup, accompanied by a couple of the mission derelicts. Why wasn't Collins riding with him?

*   *   *

ON Thursday morning, while signing some forms for ADA Chester Nance, I asked if the state of Georgia had come through with anything on Buck Collins.

"Nope. South Carolina says they detained him briefly

on a misdemeanor theft, but had to turn him loose for lack of evidence."

"That wouldn't have been at Broward's Rock, by any chance, would it?" I asked.

"Nope," said Chester. "Charleston."

I knew it would be a major and thoroughly unlikely coincidence and it was certainly a hair or two out of line as presiding judge. Nevertheless, at lunchtime, I called my friend Annie and caught her at her bookstore. She remembered Buck Collins and his red Plexiglas cross perfectly.

"That's when Laurel's diamond earrings went missing from the choir room."

Annie's mother-in-law is a true eccentric who's prone to sudden enthusiasm, but I'd never heard that singing in a church choir was one of them.

"Oh, yes," Annie said grimly. "Two contraltos were out that morning and Laurel insisted on filling in for both of them. At the last minute, she decided that diamonds didn't go with her robe and she just pulled them off and put them in her purse and never once thought that the purse might not be safe there."

"Was Brother Buck in the choir room?"

"Yes, and we'd already had opening prayer and the first hymn before he joined the services. Laurel didn't notice her earrings were missing till we were on our way to Sunday brunch. We raced right back to the church and searched it thoroughly, but no luck. They weren't insured, either. That's when she noticed one of her credit cards was missing. We called some of the other choir members and they had missing credit cards, too."

The upshot was, Annie told me, that her husband, Max, rounded up their local police chief and took a speedboat across the channel. "When they got off the ferry, Max and the chief were waiting for them."

"Them?"

"His brother was with him that morning. I think he'd

brought Buck Collins some new shoes. The old ones were worn out."

"So did they find anything?"

"Not a thing. The earrings were a matched pair of flawless diamonds, one carat each, but small enough to be hidden somewhere maybe, but what with the credit cards, too . . ." Her voice trailed off uncertainly. "Collins insisted that they do a strip search on both of them and the chief complied. He even checked to see that the heels of their shoes weren't hollowed out. And Max searched the cross himself. Did you know it's hollow and has a light inside?"

I told her I did.

"You know, Deborah, our church gets a lot of summer visitors and I didn't like wondering if one of them was the thief, but Buck Collins struck me as a very sincere man. I'd hate to think I was such a bad judge of character. And speaking of summer visitors, when are you coming back to see us? Laurel's talking about taking the LSATs and applying to law school."

I laughed and told her to wish her mother-in-law good luck for me.

But after I hung up, I had to shake my head at Annie's trusting nature. She always thought the best of everyone. Buck Collins might have radiated innocence and sincerity to her; to me, he just looked guilty and ashamed.

And well he should. I'm always a little cynical about reformed sinners who parade their redemption so publicly. Bragging that the Lord provided for all his daily needs.

Right.

With a little help from whatever his sticky fingers could pick up. Even if they were fenced for only ten percent of their actual value, two carats of flawless diamonds would pay for a lot of flashlight batteries. They would print a lot of Bible tracts. No to mention a few religious T-shirts.

I thought of his sister down there in Brunswick. Another trusting soul, who helped the Lord provide, sending him shoes and homemade fudge. Least he could have done was give her a little credit.

Fudge? Shoes? Buck Collins had been on the road five years, he said. That added up to a whole bunch of shoes. And probably warm jackets for the winter, not to mention underwear and jeans. Of course, the missions he stayed at could have provided some of his clothing, but I was willing to bet that every time he called home (and called collect, let us not forget), sister Bonnie was in his ear with "What do you need?" and "What can I send you?" then sending her patient and loving husband out five or six times a year to find him.

It was a wonder the poor man had time to keep his business going. And not going too well if I could judge by his old truck, his simple clothes, and the fact that his only jewelry was a cheap wristwatch and a plain gold band.

So maybe Buck Collins was right. The Lord had indeed provided by providing him with a devoted sister and generous brother-in-law.

But here in Colleton County was where this Buck stopped, I thought grimly. If Chester Nance didn't turn up any prior convictions by tomorrow morning—and one count of littering was all it would take—then the most I could do would be to hit him with a hefty fine and put him on probation with some community service thrown in. My only consolation was that this conviction would show up the next time things went missing from a church robing room.

I sat in court that afternoon dispensing justice. Or trying to. The B+ student on his second marijuana possession. The two migrant laborers who'd tried to knife each other but now claimed to be the best of friends. The relentless woman who kept calling her neighbor at three in the morning just because his dog barked a little. ("A little?" the woman screamed. "A *little?* Let me tell you—")

And all through it, like a refrain—shoes and fudge, fudge and shoes. I found myself thinking about love and wondering if it went both ways.

At the break, I sent a note to Chester Nance, asking him to make sure the cross was in my courtroom the next morning.

*   *   *

So there it was, a fourth—and I hoped final—time. My bailiff propped it in the jury box, which was pretty appropriate. Brother Reuben and Jack Marcom were there once again to lend moral support as Buck Collins took his place at the defendant's table. Today's T-shirt was dark green with a scattering of flowers and the words "Consider the lilies of the field."

"You haven't changed your mind about an attorney?" I asked, when Chester Nance finished reporting that he could find no prior convictions of any misdemeanor or felony on Collins.

"No, ma'am."

"Mr. Collins," I said, "you are not under oath, but it's my job to ascertain the truth and I hope you will give it."

He looked at me warily.

"Did you take those credit cards?"

"I do plead guilty, Your Honor."

"That's not what I asked, Mr. Collins. Did you personally take those cards out of their purses Sunday morning?"

"It was a temptation too strong to resist. I *am* guilty."

I had to admire his wiliness. In another time, another place, he might have made a great trial lawyer.

"Yes or no, Mr. Collins. Did you take those cards?"

"Yes!" he said, almost exploding. "Yes, I took them, okay? There's a place I know that buys credit cards if you can get them there within twelve hours."

"Which you were prepared to do?"

"Yes, ma'am."

"And this isn't really the first time, either, is it? You took a pair of diamond earrings down in South Carolina, didn't you?"

"They searched me," he said. Behind the neatly trimmed beard, his face blazed red with embarrassment. "They didn't find them."

"Because you'd hidden them in the cross?" I asked.

"They looked there, too."

"Did they look in the secret compartment?"

He gaped at me. "How do you know about that?"

I directed the bailiff to bring the cross to him.

"It's in the wheel housing, isn't it?" I said. "You want to show me?"

With a sigh, Collins pulled off the magnetized strip of red plastic that allowed access to the wheel axle. Then he pulled at the inner plate that appeared to separate the housing from the hollow interior so that the leaflets couldn't fall down into the wheels and jam them. Instead the real separator, a rectangle of white plastic that didn't match the rest, was another four inches higher up, forming a neat little cubby hole plenty big enough to hold earrings or credit cards or maybe even a small kitchen sink.

"This is where I hid them," said Collins.

"You built it specifically to have a place to stash stolen goods?" I asked.

"Yes, ma'am."

"Oh, shoot, Buck!" said Jack Marcom on the front row behind him. "I already told her you barely know which way's up on a circular saw. She knows you didn't build that."

"You be quiet, Jack!" He whirled around and shook his finger in his brother-in-law's face. "You just be quiet, you hear?"

He turned back to me. "I said I was guilty. What more do you need?"

"The truth, Mr. Collins. And in your case, the truth will set you free. As Mr. Marcom says, I have heard about your incompetence with tools. And this place that buys credit cards if you get them there within twelve hours? Carrying a cross, you could barely get out of Colleton County in twelve hours.

"You call home every Friday and tell your sister where you are and what you'll be doing. And if it's hanging out in someone's guesthouse by the eighth green or preaching to the well-to-do, then your brother-in-law shows up with fresh clothes, new shoes or food, doesn't he?"

"Bonnie and Jack, they believe in what I'm doing," said Collins.

"Did you ever think how expensive it must get for them?" I asked. "All those collect calls? How many children do your sister and Mr. Marcom have?"

He sighed. "Four."

I looked over at Marcom. "Four children to feed and clothe on top of helping your wife's brother, Mr. Marcom. When did you add that little box over the wheel housing and when did Mr. Collins finally stumble on it? Monday? Did he catch you retrieving those credit cards he tried to return that night?"

"He didn't know anything about it," Collins said stubbornly. "I had somebody in Charleston fix it for me."

Jack Marcom stood up, twisting his hat in his hands. "Your Honor—"

"You be quiet, Jack!" Collins roared. Then his voice softened. "You think about Bonnie and those little children depending on you and you just be quiet, you hear me?"

Marcom sat back down and Collins faced me resolutely.

*   *   *

"So what did you do?" Dwight asked me as we waited for the microwave popcorn to finish before sticking a video of *Stage Door* in my VCR.

(The ending's a little too schmaltzy for both of us, but we like seeing Lucille Ball before she became Lucy, and watching Katharine Hepburn come to terms with "the calla lilies are in bloom again" is always fun.)

"What *could* I do?" I said. "Without any priors, the law only allows a fine and community service."

I tore open the popcorn bag. The buttery aroma immediately filled the kitchen.

"But what about his brother-in-law? He might've been stealing from the rich to give to the poor, but he was still a thief and you let him off?"

"*I* didn't let him off," I said, nettled. "Collins let him off by swearing he did it all by himself. My only consolation is that if there's a next time and something goes missing, this is going to show up on his record."

"*If* there's a next time?" Dwight asked cynically.

"If," I said firmly. "I have a feeling Brother Buck had his eyes opened this week and that he really is going to trust the Lord to provide from now on, instead of his sister and brother-in-law."

"A fully reformed, reformed sinner," Dwight teased. "And all because of you."

I was still uncomfortable with the whole situation—punishing the technically innocent while the technically guilty went free? And yet, there was a certain rough justice at work here, though I never would have admitted it. And Brother Buck and Jack Marcom had each received a lesson in sacrificial love. All the same . . .

"This isn't the way it should have turned out," I mourned.

Dwight patted my shoulder. "Well, now, you don't

know that, Deborah. The Bible does say that the Lord works in mysterious ways."

"Maybe," I said. "I just wish He wouldn't do it in my courtroom."

SINS OF THE BROTHER
BY
MIKE STEWART

"Chillingly believable."

—*The Washington Post*

"*Slick, intelligent.*"

—*Publishers Weekly*

0-425-17887-0
$5.99/$8.99